MW01227243

ISBN: 979-8-9890666-8-1

Dedication

To my family

To my mother who instilled in me the love of writing from a young age and saved everything I ever wrote.

To my father who instilled in me a love of reading as we shared novels growing up.

To my daughter Samantha who read my initial drafts and provided insightful comments.

To my daughter Delaney who encouraged me along the way and was always there to act as my sounding board.

To my bonus daughter Courtney who shares my love of writing and provided encouragement and support.

To my bonus son Taz who has consistently encouraged me to be a bestseller author so the whole family can retire.

And finally, to my wife Misty whose love and support made all of this happen. She would lovingly look over at me relaxing on the couch after a long day in the office and ask, "*Are you done with the book yet? Why aren't you in the den writing?*

Acknowledgments

Thank you to my sister Kerri Hagerty for her insight into the procedures and techniques of police investigations.

Thank you to Robin Mackey of Robin Mackey photography studio in Copan, Ok for the wonderful book cover, website, and author photos.

Thank you to Leslie Liautaud for your mentorship as you helped me edit and market my book hoping to be as successful as you. Check out her book *Black Bear Lake*. One of my favorites.

Thank you to Bill Raskin for your advice as I navigated the publishing world. Check out his book *Cardiac Gap*. Fantastic.

Thank you to Rob Hill for his insight into the gruesome of world of investigation of crimes against children. We need more warriors like you.

Thank you to Karen Diehl for being a marketing genius and helping this dinosaur navigate the world of social media.

Thank you to the amazing team at Roosevelt Publishing that have shown extreme patience with all my novice questions about editing, marketing, and my nemesis, social media.

And finally thank you to all my proofreaders who suffered through earlier drafts of my work providing comments and suggestions, without which, this project would never have happened.

Thank you all.

Chapters

"Daisy, Daisy!" she screamed desperately. *"Somebody please help me!"*

"What is it? What is wrong?"

"My dog. I don't know. My Daisy. She is sick. Oh God, I... I think she is dying," Angela cried out in anguish.

"She looks very ill. Quick, we need to get her to an emergency vet. Here, let me grab her, my car is right over there, let's go." He said this in a frantic voice to match the emotions of thc girl as he lifted Daisy into the backseat of his awaiting vehicle.

The plan was unfolding perfectly. All of Angela's life, she had been warned about strangers, told about the evils of the world, and constantly reminded to be aware of her surroundings. Yet, all those lessons were forgotten as she watched the life slowly drain from her best friend. After the man laid Daisy gently in the backseat, without hesitation, Angela readily jumped into the vehicle to console her suffering companion.

CHAPTER 1: THE MISSION

Bamako, Mali

Dane could smell the rain in the air from his balcony as the sun began to recede from the sky and once again provide the cover of darkness for the next round of horrors. That darkness was the forces of evil pitting brother against brother, tribe against tribe, and religion against every designated non-believer. What started as a simple insurrection in the north turned into a country-wide civil war. The Tuareg movement for independence was hijacked by Islamic extremists for their own benefit. They left a wave of destruction across the north, even going so far as to demolish many famous religious and cultural structures in the renowned city of Timbuktu. Bugs Bunny won't be going there anytime soon and of course, that only left the rest of the country with one reasonable and sane option. War.

During the war, the military forces lazily remained in the capital city and, surprisingly, initiated a coup against a President who was about to leave office in less than a month. One month, Dane thought, shaking his head in disbelief. All this bloodshed over one month seemed senseless. As the north of the country fell apart, they decided to bring chaos to the south as well, causing more turmoil.

Dane, along with his second-in-command, Tyler Johnson, and a few thousand other foreigners, found themselves stuck right in the middle of the unfolding violence. Throughout the day, there were periodic bursts of violence, but the bulk of the ordinance was exchanged after dusk. Thankfully most civilians were safe, locked away in the respective embassies, but not him and Tyler. They were left exposed and vulnerable.

The Malian military Special Forces, loyal to the former president, were scattered and horrifically outnumbered. They had been the most lethal forces available in the country and of course had been expended first on the battlefields of the north in the previous months fighting the Tuaregs and their Al Qaeda allies. Once the Special Forces were weakened and no longer posed a significant threat, the conventional military leaders, who had stayed safe in the south, struck the final blow and seized control of the country. With their superior numbers and control over crucial communication channels, the television station, radio station, and the airport, they established dominion over Mali. They showed no mercy as they relentlessly hunted down the remaining Special Forces soldiers and anyone else who opposed them.

Pure and utter chaos ruled. The soldiers had very little discipline to begin with and shed any semblance of those traits once it was apparent that the impoverished souls of the country were powerless to stop them. The soldiers stripped their uniforms, adopting sunglasses, scarves and a variety of colorful shirts as they prowled the streets. I

Heavily intoxicated, they fired at anything that moved. Occasionally they were able to form some semblance of a checkpoint where they would rob, rape, and quite often murder with impunity.

Amid this lawlessness, Dane and Tyler moved throughout the city, providing aid when needed to stranded Americans and allies due to the armored vehicles they had at their disposal. These vehicles, riddled with bullet holes from daily encounters with the local forces, bore witness to the dangers they faced daily.

He and Tyler had only been in country for two months when the hostilities broke out. Their mission was to select and train an elite force that would be capable of defending the country against the slow, steady wave of terrorists that found a new safe haven in the impoverished countries of Africa after losing the stronghold they once held in the middle east. The soldiers they were training would confront the lawlessness exacerbated by the collapse of Libya, which led to a free flow of weapons onto the black market and into the hands of al-Qaeda in the Islamic Maghreb or AQIM. This infamous terrorist group had set their eyes upon the Algerian Government and fragile countries throughout northern and western Africa, becoming a pestilence across the great northern deserts sweeping into the urban centers causing destruction and mayhem. The was their day job. The two men were working to gain access to the northern portion of the country. They were tasked with taking one of the major players in AQIM off the board.

Dane often reflected on those tense first weeks when the city of Bamako awoke to a fresh new reality.

On the first day, he had risen earlier than planned due to the relentless crowing of a feral rooster that seemed to stalk their compound relentlessly. Despite all his efforts, that demon bellowed its morning shrill at the first glimmer of sunlight regardless of the plans of men. Dane didn't bother to even set an alarm at this point. He had tried everything short of shooting the beast from his balcony window. That might be a little extreme. He even attempted to buy the rooster from its owners, but they probably sensed his devious intentions and refused to sell it.

As per routine, after a quick trip to the bathroom, Dane threw on a pair of gym shorts and headed downstairs to the first-floor kitchen. The two men shared a two-story townhouse several miles from the embassy, towards the northern edge of the city. The top floor consisted of two bedrooms with private bathrooms, an office, a decent-sized storage room, and a large covered front deck that had been converted into a make-shift gym. It was a good space, but it required constant cleaning due to all the dust and particles in the air. The first floor had a fairly large kitchen and an enormous living room. There was another bedroom for guests, along with an additional bathroom. The laundry facilities were actually outside of the main house.

Their compound was completely walled with a vehicle and passenger entrance manned at all times by two locally provided guards. Locally mandated was more accurate and Dane had to pay their salaries each month. However, they were decent guys and always good for a laugh. They also proved very helpful once the city exploded into chaos since they traveled the streets daily, lived in the communities, and spoke by radio with hundreds of other guards throughout the city. They followed troop movements and disturbances with military precision and often advised Dane and Tyler on hotspots to avoid when they ventured out. There was a small pool at the entrance to the home. He had been shocked to find that it was an embassy requirement that all residences have some sort of pool. The reasoning had been that in the event there was a disturbance in the country and fresh water was not available, the embassy personnel would have something they could boil or purify. That prediction came true when the borders were closed during the insurrection and chemicals to treat the city's water supply were denied entrance.

Lastly there was a small shed at the rear of the house that served as a laundry/office for the guards. It was also a perk for them to be able to use the laundry machines since they did not have those sorts of luxuries in their own homes.

For once, the automatic coffee timer engaged as advertised and actually had sweet nectar waiting for him. Dane poured a large mug and proceeded to the second floor for the next step in the morning process. That was a morning smoke on the balcony, which facilitated the best-known opportunity for a weather prediction. Will there be a light sandstorm today or a heavy one? Dane knew smoking was an unhealthy habit, but it was better than breathing the air in this city. He would quit when he returned stateside.

The city seemed constantly shrouded in a haze from the extreme heat and humidity, and the sands from the desert were constantly trying to retake the urban center. It seemed like the sand was trying to swallow this place whole. He proceeded down the hallway just as Tyler was cracking his door. He exchanged the typical morning grunt with his partner, neither man interested in any banter without several cups of coffee. Tyler was heading towards the stairs for a similar routine. However, instead of coffee, he would be grabbing some odd colored energy powder for his shaker cup before hitting the gym. Dane needed to wake up first before attempting any physical activity while Tyler just seemed to pop out of bed and hit the weights. He turned from Tyler, lit his cigarette, and opened the door to the balcony.

CRACK! ...CRACK! CRACK! CRACK!

As the bullets struck the doorframe above his head, Dane reacted swiftly, sacrificing his cup of coffee as he immediately dropped to the ground for safety. Tyler followed suit, seeking shelter in the doorway of his room. Several more bullets could be heard smacking the sides of the house as some sort of running gun battle ensued in the streets below. It was eerie since it was generally quiet outside during the morning hours, yet the weapon fire came out of nowhere. The streets were not congested with traffic in this part of the city. Closer to the main downtown area the streets were overrun with vehicles of every shape and description along with the annoying motorbikes that apparently knew no rules of the road.

These motos as they were called, drove every which way to include between columns of traffic, up on sidewalks, and often in the wrong direction. But today, it was silent outside except for the gunfire. Crawling on his stomach, Dane made his way back into the house toward his battle gear and weapons. It seemed that his protective gear in his room was a hundred miles away.

"Hey," yelled Tyler. *"What the hell are you doing Coop?"*

He shrugged. Tyler was pointing at him as he crawled past the doorway where he laid prone.

"No smoking in the house!"

What started as a regular groundhog sort of day ended in chaos and the first sign of the turmoil to come began during the holiest of morning routines, that first cup of coffee to kick start the day. Dane couldn't help but chuckle as his friend and battle buddy still found time for humor in that situation. They had vastly different backgrounds, and their paths through the Army, finally landing at the unit, had been as different as the men themselves, but they still retained that military humor that demanded making fun of one another no matter what the circumstances. Dane had grown up on the east coast. He had a typical suburban upbringing that eventually found him at the University of Boston. It was there that he met his wife, Jenny, and the two seemed destined to take on the world together. That was at least what Dane's parents had thought before he joined the Army right out of college as an enlisted soldier, much to their dismay. Dane had chosen the path of the Rangers in the service, and he and his bride soon found themselves in Savannah, Georgia. He would complete nine years with the Rangers, deploying several times, fathering two children, and eventually attending selection for the unit.

Tyler, on the other hand, had grown up on the streets of Detroit and joined the Army right out of high school. He was sent to the eighty-second airborne at Fort Bragg, North Carolina, where he would spend the next three years taking online courses and training whenever possible to attain his true goal and earn the coveted green beret of the Special Forces. But here is where the similarities ended. Tyler was very outgoing, in contrast to Dane's more conservative demeanor. Tyler spent most of his waking hours either in the gym or shooting the shit in the team room. All flash, Dane used to tease Tyler, who would respond by asking if he had any pulse whatsoever, and of course, they always kept up the rivalry between the Rangers and Special Forces, poking fun at one another for each organization's perceived faults. Most civilians imagine Special Operations as one big group of soldiers, when in fact it is composed of many units from all the branches of service. The SEALs pick on the Air Force Para Jumpers, the Rangers pick on the Special Forces, and the highest tiered elements pick on all of them. It is always in good fun and with respect.

"Man, you Rangers are all uptight and dress-right-dress," joked Tyler. *"Your spiffy uniforms and shiny weapons don't help*

you blend into the environment and truly understand your enemies."

"While you Special Forces guys are growing your beards, gelling your hair, and donning your cool indigenous clothes talking about how you are blending in and learning about your enemy," Dane responded, *"the Rangers just killed all of them."*

Over the next several weeks, there wasn't much cause for humor. Tragically, most of the soldiers that Dane and Tyler had been training were murdered. There were rumors of mass grave sites on the northern outskirts of the city but the State Department turned a blind eye and denied the request for the two men to investigate. They wanted to ignore the whole violent affair, peacefully negotiate with the new regime, and return to a democracy. It was a little late for that.

The diplomatic officials were not your typical political appointees. Most grew up in the system, starting off as Peace Corp volunteers, which was referred to among the soldiers as dirty-feet. From there, they were posted in several other outreach organizations, USAID, etc., and then finally in senior state department positions. They were true believers, and although he and Tyler were cynical when it came to their causes, they did admire their devotion and dedication. Many of the officials, however, loathed the presence of any military personnel. These men were instructed to keep a low profile, forbidden from showing the slightest sign of military equipment, and even issued orders that prohibited each man from carrying a side-arm. That order went completely ignored.

There was no way Dane and Tyler were not going to have at least some protection against the dangers of Mali.

They sat in their house with warm cups of coffee in their makeshift TOC, Tactical Operations Center. It was a simple room with tables and chairs, but the reinforced doors, windows, and safes for classified storage gave them some semblance of security. Tonight's operation was too sensitive to run out of an embassy. Military forces prowled the streets and watched key establishments where they believed anti-government activities would take place. All Western embassies were on that list, and tonight's mission was too important to take that chance. Democratic forces had clearly lost, but if they could spirit some of the key players out of the country, perhaps those players could one day re-group and renew the former democratic state. Then those forces could get them close to their target in the north. They were playing the long game.

The mission was to pick up their key leader in the anti-terrorism force and get him and his family across the border into Burkina Faso. Oumer had been in hiding for several weeks after his home was raided and torched to the ground. Dane and Tyler kept the plan simple. Tyler would arrive at the rendezvous site an hour earlier and provide overwatch. He would observe Oumer's approach to ensure he wasn't followed. Once clear, he would contact Dane, who had been taking his own precautions, and would arrive after the completion of his surveillance detection route. Once the pickup was complete, Tyler would drive ahead and ensure the route to the border was clear for

Dane and the company. Staying several miles back, Dane would have ample time to change course if Tyler radioed back a warning.

The execution was flawless. Dane easily picked up his passengers and could see the sign of relief on Oumer and his wife's faces. Their baby girl was sound asleep in her mother's arms. The border was only a few miles away. The turn-off point, to avoid any checkpoints, is even closer. Things were going too well.

"We got a problem Dane," the radio chirped in the rear vehicle.

"What is it Tyler?"

"I have soldiers at a checkpoint sitting right at the turn-off we were planning on taking instead of the actual border." Tyler responded. *"There isn't an earlier place for you to detour."*

"Shit," exclaimed Dane. *"Go to the contingency plan. Stay safe."*

Both men knew what that meant. The plan was for Tyler to act as a rabbit to distract government forces if they intervened. Even though the military had control of the government, they did not have enough soldiers to police the city, let alone the whole country. The head of the coup was more interested in solidifying his power in certain places throughout the city to help him maintain power. The radio and television station offices were heavily guarded, so only his approved messages were broadcasted. The airport was another key piece of terrain for him to control what and who came in and out of the country. And lastly, he kept a large force at his military headquarters in the city's heart. He had hunted down and killed most of the military forces loyal to the former president, but he wasn't taking any chances. Because of this military posture, Dane and Tyler knew that any force they encountered in the countryside would be small without nearby reinforcements.

The soldiers were also often leader-less, so if they were told not to let anyone get by them, they would follow that simple order without fail. This contingency was also based on two points; one logical and one emotional. The logical answer was that even though Dane and Tyler could easily ambush and kill the soldiers, those deaths would draw more attention to this particular crossing and possibly cause stricter curfew enforcement in the future throughout the entire area, including parts outside the city proper. The second and emotional aspect was that these soldiers were just following orders. Dane and Tyler had no particular beef with them. Their leaders were the ones making the disastrous decisions so, why should the common soldier suffer if they could avoid it?

Their prediction of the soldiers' strict adherence to orders was exactly what happened. Tyler blew past the checkpoint, trusting in the vehicle's armor, as the soldiers fired wildly and then mounted their vehicle for pursuit while leaving the turn-off free and clear for Dane.

The plan never survives first contact, hence the contingency option. He just had to trust that Tyler would lose the soldiers and arrive safely at the link-up point. He turned off his headlights as he rounded the last corner and pulled off the main road to begin the last three-mile trek to the border. Both men had scouted this route months ago as part of an escape and evasion route if they ever needed to leave the country quickly or evacuate personnel covertly. This was certainly one of those times. The route was barely a road, and it was difficult to navigate without lights, but Dane did not want to advertise their presence. When he finally pulled into the rendezvous point safely across the border, everyone in the vehicle breathed a sigh of relief.

After thirty agonizing minutes, Tyler finally arrived to meet up with Dane on the other side of the border. There were a few new bullet holes in his Toyota 4 Runner, but nothing the armor couldn't handle.

"What the hell did you do to my vehicle?" Dane asked with a smirk.

"You are worried about the vehicle? How about worrying about if I am okay," Tyler responded.

Both men laughed and began to transloading gear from Dane's pickup truck into the 4Runner. The plan was for Oumer and his family to take the truck Dane had acquired from an asset, while the two soldiers would return to Mali in the 4Runner. They made sure that Oumer and his family had plenty of supplies and the necessary paperwork to start their new lives in Burkina. Embraces were exchanged all around, along with all the appropriate farewells.

"Thank you, my friends," said Oumer. *"I will never forget what you have done for me. I hope we meet again someday and if there is anything I can ever do for either of you, don't hesitate to find me. I owe you both mine and my family's lives."*

Oumer placed his right hand over his heart as a sign of respect and devotion. *"Be safe my friends."*

Several hours later, back at the house, Dane and Tyler sank into the couches. The mission was a success. Although, there would be a thousand reports and after-action reviews to write, they needed time to relax and enjoy a well-deserved cocktail. After all, nobody at headquarters would be awake at this hour to read their report anyway.

As the two men toasted to their success, the satellite phone rang. It was an unsecure administrative phone used for calls to and from the task force command, stationed in England. Dane reached for the phone and entered the passcode to open the call. However, as he listened to the caller on the other end of the line, his face froze in pure terror, and he dropped the phone to the floor, leaving Tyler watching in confusion.

CHAPTER 2: THE DREAD

Burke, VA

There was a light tap on the door. Dane and Jenny had been sitting on the couch, waiting for the detectives to arrive. Investigators from the Bureau of Criminal Investigation had called last evening to schedule today's meeting. It was a discussion Dane and Jenny both craved and dreaded simultaneously. The state police wanted to provide an update and finally meet Dane, who had arrived home the evening prior. A second tap brought him out of his daze. Jenny sat frozen on the couch. Her gaze was focused on the far corner of the room. Her trance was unbroken. He briefly left his wife's side to answer the door.

"Mr. Cooper? I am Special Agent Roger Patterson, and this is my partner, Special Agent Patricia Stills. We would like to speak with both of you."

He ushered them inside. The agents shook hands all around, and Dane stepped slightly aside, gesturing them forward. The two agents were nearly polar opposites of one another. Roger was clearly the senior of the two and wore that experience like an embattled boxer. Heavyset and pushing sixty, he was dressed as though his days in the ring were ending. He was not necessarily sloppy, but he appeared drained from a lifetime of fighting. His one striking quality that Dane noticed immediately was the glaring determination in his eyes. *This one does not quit*, he thought. He could see an active and brilliant mind behind those eyes; eyes that did not miss any details. He saw it often with the young men and women with whom he served.

Stills, on the other hand, seemed almost too young to be a special agent. She was neatly dressed, tall, and slim when compared to her partner. Athletic build. *Looked like a marathon runner*. She exuded confidence but also the desire to succeed. Dane also saw a spark in her eyes, but they were erratic and unfocused. This one has brilliance but not patience. She is trying too hard not to miss any details. That is exactly how details are missed. *I just hope she learns from her elder*, he concluded to himself. They entered the small foyer and proceeded into the living room, where Jenny still remained frozen in place.

Special Agent Patterson nodded a greeting to Jenny as he removed his hat. The group stood awkwardly around the coffee table for a moment before Jenny invited them to sit in the two chairs opposite the couch. Dane returned to his place at his wife's side. The agents sat across from them in two overstuffed leather chairs and used the table between them for their notes.

"Can we get you anything? Coffee? Water?" Dane asked.

Both agents politely shook their heads.

Patterson began, *"I know how awful this is for both of you. Agent Stills and I wish we could give you some comforting answers."* He then directed his focus to Dane. *"I am sorry to have to meet under these circumstances, Mr. Cooper. Time is crucial here, so we want to go over everything again with both you and your wife. Any little detail, no matter how insignificant it may seem, could prove important. Ma'am, if you could, please go over the day again in as much detail as possible."*

Both agents removed notepads from their jacket pockets. Jenny began to recount the events of the day. She explained how Angela went through her normal morning routine. She was excited and bubbly, thinking about school starting soon and, of course, looking forward to her daily walk with Daisy.

"As I said before, there was nothing out of the ordinary that day. Angela came downstairs around eight o'clock for breakfast. She had been upstairs putting some clothes away and packing a bag for Goodwill ever since she woke up. She wanted to head over to the new Springfield Mall for back-to-school shopping. Well, it is not a new mall, but it has been remodeled the last couple of years, and she really liked some of the new shops. I told her that if I got her new clothes, she would have to donate some of her older items to charity. I had promised her that I would take her that afternoon. Angela then went upstairs and changed. She came back downstairs and told me she was going to take Daisy for their morning walk. She had been doing it every day this summer, unless it was pouring rain. I encouraged her to take morning walks with the dog," she said between sobs. *"I never thought, never imagined...."* Her voice trailed off as her emotions overtook her.

Patterson paused and let her regain her composure, then asked, *"What was she wearing, and approximately what time did she leave?"*

Both Agents peered at their notes as Jenny answered to make sure they had the correct details.

"She was wearing a yellow short-sleeve blouse that snapped up the front and light blue jean shorts. Her shorts had a bunch of holes in them, which I never understood. Her hair was in a ponytail, and I think her hair tie was red. She put on a blue pair of low-cut Converse shoes before she grabbed the leash. She is always wearing Converse. She has a million different colors. That was around eight thirty. And then she and Daisy were gone." Jenny started sobbing softly again and fell into Dane's arms as though a great burden had been lifted from her shoulders.

"Daisy. German Shepard, correct. Approximately five years old," Patterson read from his notes.

"Yes. Daisy is black and tan, about fifty-five pounds. Angela's best friend. Daisy had a purple collar with her name on it and tags. One silver for contact information if she were ever lost, and a second green one for her rabies vaccination. The leash was one of those rope kinds. Black and purple," she added.

"Have you noticed anything out of the ordinary in the neighborhood in the last few weeks other than the two vehicles you described to us earlier?" asked Agent Stills.

to retrace her steps. He had identical applications on his phone that were linked to her apps. Apps that were now worthless since the device never collected the information he required and now lay useless in some forensics lab.

Patterson added, *"We haven't found any unusual contacts on her phone, and it doesn't appear that she was using any chat rooms online. Does she have access to social media like Facebook, Snapchat, etc.?"*

"We didn't allow her to have any social media until she got older," said Dane, speaking for the first time. *"We thought it best she waited until she was in high school. We did the same thing with her older brother, John. She also had limited access to the internet. That laptop in her room has parental controls installed. It is for schoolwork, research, and emailing her friends, and that is all."*

Both agents continued to write in their books.

"Do you mind if we look in her room again?" Asked Stills.

"Of course not, but I have a few questions first," replied Dane. The initial shock had begun to wear off, and his mind was analyzing every angle.

"The first is cameras. Have all the traffic cameras in the local area leading in and out of the park been pulled and analyzed? There are multiple entrances to the park by vehicle. Ox Road, one-twenty-three has a main entrance by the golf center. There aren't any traffic cameras there since there is no light, but just north of it is Canterberry Road, which should have some. There is also a second

entrance that most people don't realize, which is farther south and heads east to the boat ramp. Again, no light, but someone coming from the north or south would have to pass by some cameras. Then you have the entrance to the campgrounds from Burke Lake Road. Dane Road, I think. There are no cameras either, but I am pretty sure there are cameras where Burke Lake intersects with Ox Road and Fairfax County Parkway, Dane Continued, *"Lastly, you have South Run Recreation area. That is probably the least likely option since Angela certainly didn't walk that far, and a kidnapper would have a hard time getting her to move that distance without someone noticing. I think the entrance to the boat ramps is the most likely option since it is rarely used and is the closest vehicle access point to our house."*

Stills and Patterson exchanged a glance at one another. *"We are reviewing all the camera footage we were able to obtain and looking through all those scenarios,"* answered Stills. *"Some of the footage is useless since cameras break all the time, and the Virginia Department of Transportation or VDOT only has so much manpower to fix them, but we are reviewing vehicular traffic along Ox and the Parkway around the timeframe of Angela's disappearance to try and locate a possible suspect."*

"Good, how about cell phone records?" Dane continued. *"Have you gotten records from the nearby cell towers and panels? I have data from her phone on previous walks in the park. I can give you data on which towers and panels are utilized along her route. Those may tell you who was in the area. They may have seen something.... may have done something. We should also contact the Virginia*

Department of Transportation, the garbage company, landscape firms in the area, etc. to find out if any crews were in the areas on those days."

"Mr. Cooper, we are pursuing all angles. I assure you, we have teams going over every detail. I completely understand your frustrations," Stills continued. *"We have a team of professionals that will stop at nothing. We will extract the tower information from Angela's phone concerning previous walks in the park."*

Dane visibly relaxed as Jenny gently placed a hand on his leg. It was her subtle way of calming her husband, knowing the depth of his distress and feeling of helplessness. With Dane, seemingly satisfied, the two agents climbed the lonely staircase to walk through the little girl's room once again, searching for anything they may have overlooked. Anything. The room was just as they had left it after previous visits. It was a decent size room on the second floor, with full windows on the back wall overlooking the yard and the woods of the park beyond. *Damn it*, thought Patterson. *Did this monster watch her from those woods?* The two agents began a systematic search of the room. This was, however, not a typical search conducted by the police during the execution of a warrant.

They showed care and compassion and gently searched the room for any hint of her whereabouts they may have missed. They checked all the usual places. They lifted and examined the underside of her mattress, gently rifled through the contents of her small desk, and turned out all the pockets of her tiny clothing. Cases like these leave marks on all men's souls.

They returned to the downstairs living room. Dane and Jenny had remained frozen in place, as if too scared to move for fear of missing their daughter's return. Both agents had seen this scene too many times before. They thanked them both and promised to keep them abreast of any developments. Without a word, they showed themselves to the door.

Once in the car, Patricia broke the silence. *"I didn't think of the cell tower panel records. Can we even do that?"*

"I am not sure, but we are definitely going to try. Surprised you didn't think of that, Ms. tech genius."

"I thought about it, but I am not sure it is legal or if we even have the analytical capacity to search through all that data. What does this guy do? He seemed to think like an investigator."

"No idea. The records just say he works for the military. In the D.C. area, who knows what that means?"

"You have seen way more of these cases than I have, boss. It has been four days. Is there even hope?"

"There is always hope, kid. Always. Now, we have a short drive back to the station. Start reading me the case file from the beginning."

CHAPTER 3: THE AFTERMATH

Washington D.C.
1 year later

Pupil: *Are you There?*

Keeper: *Yes.*

Pupil: *I still got one. Having issues. Need your advice.*

Keeper: *Contact me later tonight and remember what I taught you.*

Dane slowly opened his eyes, the pounding in his head fueled from the previous evening and the blaring alarm clock. The device was purposely located across the room, forcing him from his bed, lest he continue his sleep, damning the world. He willed himself to rise and silence the alarm, while slowly making his way to the tiny bathroom in his apartment.

Dane had lived in this place for nearly six months yet was still not used to the emptiness. The apartment was actually a basement space, separated from the D.C. townhouse above. Each day, he would descend the exterior basement steps and enter his own personal hell. The place consisted of a small bedroom, barely large enough to fit a mattress, and an attached bathroom that made turning around difficult. The remaining space was filled with a straight-line kitchen and bar area tracing the top edge of the meager living room, and a tiny over-

and-under laundry closet. Barely five-hundred square feet in all, but enough for Dane's simple needs.

The loss of Angela had broken an already strained marriage. At first, he and Jenny stayed strong in their hope that one day their little girl would come walking back through the front door. However, as the days turned to weeks and weeks to months, the two watched as their individual grief turned on one another.

Resentment, guilt, and shame all combined, along with the failure to control those emotions, tore the marriage apart. The separation had been amicable. Jenny and he both agreed that their relationship had become toxic. Trying to stay together for John was really only having an adverse effect on the boy, and the home they shared was scarred by too many memories.

The house was sold, and Jenny and John resettled in a small ranch home in Manassas, while Dane sought refuge in his D.C. dungeon apartment. A small mattress lay in a corner of the living room for when John came to visit. He knew it was impractical for John to visit during the week with school and sports. The commute from anywhere in northern Virginia into the nation's capital was insurmountable.

Weekends, however, were their time together. Dane would normally pick John up from school every other weekend. They would find a place to eat in the local area, waiting for the stream of traffic to die out before returning to Dane's apartment. Occoquan was their normal hangout.

Washington D.C. is considered by many a cesspool of politicians, lobbyists, and lawyers. He could not agree more. However, John had taken after his father by adopting a love of history which D.C. has in droves. Plus, the location fit his budget and was closer to work.

The pair would spend the weekend exploring not only the famous Smithsonian museums but also the less well-known spots. Bonding with John and being there for him was all that remained in Dane's life. A multitude of family, friends, and co-workers bombarded him with welfare checks.

Suicide rates among soldiers were a major issue since the start of the wars in Afghanistan and Iraq, especially among combat soldiers. He had lost many friends and colleagues, both from visible injuries sustained in battle and the hidden ones upon their return.

Dark thoughts often permeated his subconscious, especially after losing Angela. But it was that spark of hope that she would be returned to him and the knowledge that John needed him more than ever that kept the demons at bay each and every day.

Dane finished cleaning up for work as best he could. He swept the empty Jamison bottle into the trash, mentally noting the need to pick up another bottle before he returned this evening. Cup of coffee in hand, he exited his apartment. His location on Independence Ave Southeast was conveniently close to his work. It was about a three-mile walk which occasionally he enjoyed since it gave him time to think. More like time to drown himself in guilt. But on mornings like this when he wasn't exactly on time, he would take his motorcycle. It was an old Honda Nighthawk that was reliable but not much to look at. His move to D.C. necessitated less driving time to work but also prohibited any sort of large vehicle. No parking and narrow, old streets did not facilitate anything larger than a Prius. Public transportation was the only way to efficiently maneuver through the dense city. However, buses didn't go out across the Anacostia River and into the industrial district where he was headed. So, motorcycle it was.

Dane proceeded around to the rear of the townhome. The owners had allowed him a small space to store the bike underneath a tarp which he removed before starting the ancient vehicle. With a puff of black smoke, it started quickly, and he rolled it down the yard and into the street. He climbed on the bike and was soon heading east on Independence toward the river. Once across, he turned north along Anacostia Ave and entered a more industrial part of the city.

The unit where Dane worked was not located on a traditional military base. The members wore civilian clothing to avoid drawing attention at the complex. The building was typical of those in the area without any particularly redeeming qualities. It was nestled in with other warehouses and office complexes offering automotive repair, towing, aluminum siding, etc. It looked like all its neighbors, yet quietly and professionally hid the secrets of the soldiers inside and the mission against which they were tasked.

The Unit was comprised of various Soldiers, Sailors, Airmen, and Marines from throughout the Special Operations community. The operatives were the top one percent performers across the Department of Defense formation and were specially selected for the unit based on unique qualities. Invite only. Most people think Special Operations and immediately identify with Navy SEALs, Army Rangers, and Special Forces. Rough and rugged soldiers resembling famous movie characters like Rambo or Commando. That couldn't be farther from the truth. Physical prowess is a must in the community, but the general public is often ignorant of the intellectual competency required for Special Operations.

Anyone can lift weights until their muscles bulge out of their T-shirts while spraying the enemy holding a machine gun with one hand, the belt of ammo in the other. Well, that was a little far-fetched, Dane thought. The truth was Special Operations Soldiers needed to think on their feet. React to complex and ever-changing battlefield conditions. They had to make quick decisions in an environment where hesitation often led to failure or death.

The unit went a step further. They wanted Operatives who could think two or three steps ahead. They would have to be physically capable, but that wasn't enough. SEALs were tasked with parachuting into the ocean in the dead of night and swimming several miles to secure a beachhead and wipe out an enemy force. That took incredible physical conditioning and stamina. The unit, on the other hand, needed operatives to remain in the shadows and solve the hardest of problems, not always through might, but more often through cunning, stealth, and subterfuge; and normally alone in the field.

A SEAL team may conduct that direct-action raid against a terrorist camp full of twenty hostiles. Dane and his peers on the other hand would target a specific influential figure. They would terminate that individual in a clandestine manner and then remain in the country after the fact to determine the political, social, military, and economic consequences, if any. That took incredible mental conditioning and stamina. Dane knew more than one guy who had popped. The guy just couldn't take the stress, the unknown, and the complete lack of the secure embrace of teammates.

A team leader had once broken down the mission for him in simple terms concerning the F3EAD cycle which is Find, Fix, Finish, Exploit, Analyze, and Disseminate.

"Dane, we are the whole cycle. Other organizations have entire teams on the battlefield to complete this cycle. We have you. You find the target, fix their location, and eliminate them. Blend back into the environment pretending nothing happened, to exploit the aftermath, analyze any additional intelligence, and then disseminate it to those that need to know. You are a hitman for the Department of Defense. In the immortal words of Doc Holiday, 'and this time it's legal.'"

It made sense to him.

Once inside the gates, Dane steered the bike to the rear of the complex and parked among the other vehicles, out of sight from the main road. He entered through the small rear lobby. It was tastefully decorated with several comfortable chairs and a two-person receptionist counter. After running his I.D. through a vertically mounted reader, an adjacent door clicked, approving his entrance without having to verbally engage with the front office staff.

He continued down the narrow hallway beyond, toward the rear stairwell. The hallway was barren and contained several doors along the right side only. Dane knew that behind those doors were team storage lockers, gymnasiums, an Olympic-size pool, training areas, and even a soundproof rifle/pistol range. He used to enjoy countless hours behind those doors, but that passion had faded during the last year.

Ignoring the elevator, he proceeded to climb the stairs. He passed the second floor, which was full of administrative staff sections; a place he rarely visited. His destination was the third-floor operations center. He was already fifteen minutes late for his meeting with Command Sergeant Major (CSM) Reynolds.

After a light tap on the man's door, he was ushered inside.

"Close the door Dane."

He gently closed the door and took a seat across from the CSM and his massive desk.

"You wanted to see me, Sergeant Major? Sorry, I got hung up in traffic."

"Cut the shit, Dane and stop with the ridiculous formalities. We have been friends for a long time. Hell, you should be a Sergeant Major by now and looking to replace me in a year or two. You should be on the shortlist again, by the way but you are going to get passed over and if you don't get it together, possibly relieved."

He studied the man he had once called a good friend. They had grown up together in the unit, but Jeremy had been a few classes ahead of him and higher in rank. He was pushing fifty years old and was nearing retirement after nearly thirty years of service, but he looked like he could still run circles around guys twenty years his younger.

"I'm sorry, Jeremy. I am really doing my best to keep it together."

"Keep what together, Dane? I have watched you slowly destroy your life and career while drinking yourself into a stupor on a daily basis. I am sympathetic. I can't imagine what it is like to lose a child."

With that comment, Dane's posture stiffened, and his eyes keenly focused.

"Easy Coop. I am not trying to take advantage of your grief," said Jeremy as he softened his tone and gestured for calm with his hands. *"I spoke to Jenny yesterday. I know she wants to pronounce Angela deceased with a funeral to try and find some*

closure for all of you and I know it is tough with John. There I can relate. I only see my girls about twice a year after that demon mother of theirs moved them to California. Fucking courts. Nevertheless, you have him close by. He would be lost without you. You have to get your shit together, if not for yourself, but for him."

Dane could only nod. He had spoken to Jenny last night about that very issue concerning Angela. That probably explained the empty whiskey bottle on the counter. She wanted to hold out hope that somehow Angela would be found. But she also knew that the family needed closure. The police still had no leads, and even though the case was still open and Angela would not be officially pronounced deceased for another six years or so, Dane could see the dejection in their eyes every time the police provided an update. They knew the cruel statistics as well as Dane regarding the timeframe of a missing child. Jenny saw the same look in the agent's eyes. Unlike him, she was ready for family and friends to grieve for the last time at a small ceremony for Angela to celebrate her short time in this world. Dane still would not budge.

"The truth is, Dane, I am about out of rope to throw to you. I may be your boss, but you know I am also your friend. Here, take this." Jeremy handed him a notecard. The Humane Hands of D.C., Pennsylvania Avenue Christian Church, 2500 Pennsylvania Ave SE, Washington D.C. 20020

"What is this?" Dane asked.

"It is a support group run by one of the churches downtown specializing in grieving parents that have lost a child. I don't want any pushback," said Jeremy as Dane's body language began to alter again into protest mode. *"These are good people, Coop. I can't stand by and watch you throw your life away. You won't talk to your friends, and you won't open up to the psych. You won't even entertain talking to the chaplain. Maybe you can find some sort of peace among strangers and, for the record, old friend.... I am not asking."*

Dane could only stare at the paper in his hand.

"I want you to take some time off. When you get back, we are going to make some changes. Shuffle the deck a bit. I will let you know where we are going to put you." Upon the obvious dismissal, he stood and exited the office. As he moved down the hallway heading to his Troop's area, he heard a call from an intersecting hallway.

"Hey, Coop, wait up," Tyler called out as he jogged down the hall to catch up with his teammate.

He stopped and watched as Tyler approached. The two hadn't spoken in nearly six months. Once they returned from Mali last year, Dane had been off the road and manning a desk in the Troop operations center. He was still a very senior operative in the organization, and many of the junior officers and non-commissioned officers looked to him for advice and guidance. But his heart wasn't in it anymore, and he knew that he was mentally checked out of the game. Tyler, on the other hand, had been busy over the last year. He was finally promoted to Master Sergeant and had taken over the team leader position Dane had left behind. Tyler had just returned from a successful mission in Kurdistan, and Dane was eager to hear about it since he had worked on that project in previous years and knew many of the major players.

"Hey Tyler. Welcome back. How was Kurdistan?"

"It was fine, man. We can talk about it another time. I wanted to talk to you if you have a minute." Tyler gestured toward an open team room, not giving Dane a chance to protest. *"All of my guys are out west at the training site supporting selection so nobody is here."*

He remembered that the unit's biannual selection course was set to begin in a few weeks. Most of the guys were out supporting as cadre, which explained why the place was empty. Damn, he thought, my head really isn't in the game at all. I love going out there. I should have volunteered. It would have been good to hang with the guys and clear my head for a bit.

Tyler grabbed a seat at the conference table in the center of the room, leaving the chair at the head of the table open for Dane in deference to his former team sergeant status. There were three operational Troops, and each had four teams. The structure was similar to most Special Operations type units, and each team was assigned their own room. They were typical office-style spaces with cubicles and desks along the wall and a large conference table at the center where teammates could hold meetings, collaborate on projections, or, as most normally was done, sit around with a couple of beers after a training exercise or day at the range.

"I wanted to see how you were doing, man. Please don't think I am trying to get into your business, but I haven't seen you in a hot minute, and I have heard through the grapevine that you haven't been doing so well." Tyler appeared to be hesitant with that last statement.

Dane sighed. Here was one of his oldest friends in the unit trying to reach out, yet he was afraid he would bite his head off. Have I sunk that low? He thought. *"I appreciate it, Tyler. Things have been rough. You heard Jenny and I split, right? Sold the house. She and John are in Manassas. I'm in D.C."*

Tyler nodded.

"It has been really tough on John. I am trying to keep it together for him but...I am dealing with it. I just need time."

"I totally understand. I just.... listen, we have always been pretty tight. But only as much as you allow. You have always held things pretty close to the chest. Just remember that you have friends here that you can talk to. All the guys look up to you and would help out in a heartbeat. I just do not want you to think you are alone. I talked to Jenny and she mentioned the funeral. Now before you get upset, I want to tell you that I understand. Completely. I am not saying to give up hope. Simply reminding you that others are hurting as well."

Dane paused for a moment. *"I really appreciate it buddy and I know you guys are here. I am trying, but I am not ready to move on. I don't know if I will ever be ready. Some part of me certainly never will. But I have to work through this."*

"I get you, man. Just please remember I am here and others as well. Don't let old Reynolds put on the gruff act. He is more worried about you than anybody else. I am on the road a lot, buddy, but my phone is always nearby."

"Thanks, means a lot."

Tyler rose and clapped Dane on the shoulder. He made his way to the door and looked back briefly before he left, as if afraid this would be the last time he would see his friend. Dane watched him slowly close the door affording him privacy. He had once found comfort in a team room just like this one. It was alien to him now. *"Keep it together.... keep it together,"* he mumbled as he slowly laid his head on the conference table. *"Keep taking it one day at a time."*

CHAPTER 4: THE SCOUT

Washington, D.C

Dane stared at the microwave clock in the dingy kitchen while he cleaned up from dinner. He used to enjoy cooking, always trying new foods and styles. Most combat soldiers try to find some sort of calming hobby to help alleviate the stress from work. For Dane, that was cooking for his family and expanding their culinary experience using recipes from the various countries he had visited. John and Angela had endured dishes from the African continent as well as the Middle East and Southeastern Asia. Sometimes he was able to replicate the delicacies he had sampled overseas, and other times they had to make a last-minute pizza order.

This culinary expansion also included distinct cultural restaurants that populated the metro D.C. and northern Virginia area. Somali rice dishes, Iraqi kabobs, and thick ostrich steaks all graced the Cooper family's plates. Trips to the zoo would prove embarrassing for the Cooper children, as Dane would loudly proclaim which animals tasted good and which were wretched, loudly enough for other patrons to hear. Angela would roll her eyes as her father described the sweet taste of freshly boiled camel meat or the chewiness of zebra beef jerky. One of their favorite zoos had been Busch Gardens in Tampa, Florida. The amusement park boasted an endless supply of roller coasters and attractions that were woven throughout a vast African themed zoo. Dane had dined on nearly every animal in the exhibit in one form or another, but that was over. Over the day, some monster destroyed his family and stole his baby girl.

Dane could feel his blood pressure rising as sadness and guilt converted into pure rage. *"Calm down,"* he muttered to himself. *"This will not help."*

In the first few months, these emotions would weigh heavily and morph into severe depression. Booze fueled the downward spiral and normally offered him the sweet release of sleep as the alcohol content shut down his mind and body. However, in recent months, those manifestations changed. Dane would tap into his anger instead, something he normally kept in check and only reserved for the enemy when overseas on assignment. Untapped depths of anger would crash over him like waves on a stormy beach. Thoughts of revenge, of extreme violence acted upon those that took his little girl, would consume his thoughts. Knowing that he needed to keep this at bay, Dane tried to limit his consumption of alcohol. Proving impossible at best, he instead hid himself away from the world. When the angst emerged while in public, normally a local bar or pub, he would flee to the safety of his apartment where the anger would be hidden from the world. He was already in enough trouble at work as it was. Dane did not need additional complications due to an altercation in public or an encounter with law enforcement. He was hanging onto his job by a thread as it was.

He re-checked the clock as he swept the microwave dinner wrappers from the counter into the trash. His meeting tonight was at six p.m. He had no desire to attend, but Reynolds had been pretty adamant. *I wouldn't put it past him to call over there and make sure I attended,* he thought. It was five-thirty, which gave him thirty minutes to walk over to the church on Pennsylvania Avenue. Maybe the walk would help clear his head and mentally prepare for the sharing of souls that would surely happen. Dane did not understand how hearing other people's stories of pain and loss would help. His imagination alone would replay various versions of Angela's kidnapping, which would deliver him to the brink of madness. He didn't know the details of her abduction or the events that came after, but his imagination would fill in the blanks with horrors beyond anything he had ever seen. Although, he had seen horrors throughout the world, never once believing his daughter, or even his family, would ever be subject to the depravities of man he had witnessed. He was certain that similar stories from complete strangers in a church basement would not do anything to provide him solace.

The thirty-minute walk did help with tamping down the rage that would bubble up inside him. Several times a day, these feelings would tear across his soul, and he would look for solutions. During the day, Dane found solace in the gym at work. The unit had several fighting areas with kickboxing bags and mats, which he frequented several times a day. Although not the gym rat Tyler was, Dane enjoyed working at the bags with his feet and fists whenever he found breaks throughout the day. In the days since Angela, this place had become his church. Bruised knuckles and bleeding feet and shins were his penance. In the past, he rarely used to lock up the building for the evening. With so many folks working at the unit, it was inevitable that someone had to burn the midnight oil. However, these days, he found temporary peace that was unavailable in his tiny apartment. Sometimes late into the night, the satisfying crunch of bones on the bag was his form of confession. Since he was a soldier and fitness and training were key to his profession, nobody would find fault with anyone working out throughout the day and into the evening. Several of his peers held odd hours, but they still often stared at Dane, as if he were a man possessed.

The Ranger Regiment had a structure Dane had to follow when he was a younger trooper. Runs, road marches before the sun came up, and strength training in the afternoon. This routine was conducted by squads or platoons of soldiers, which meant he had no say over his daily workouts. The team or squad leader set the agenda. Now at the unit, everyone followed their own personal routine based on their needs. He was able to swim in the mornings, which was better on his knees and hips, while conducting short sparring sessions to vent his rage. Mentally he might see himself still in his twenties, but the years of deployments and combat had taken its toll physically and told him otherwise. The strength coaches and physical therapists referred to the operatives as aging athletes. Most of his peers were seasoned Special Operations warriors with similar backgrounds. Everyone had some sort of lingering injury that would rule out traditional physical exercise. Blown knees, broken backs, and strained ligaments prevented strenuous running and certain strength training. Dane was fortunate that he had traditionally enjoyed biking and swimming. The trainers had long advocated that he conduct non-impact activities lest he find himself confined to a wheelchair at an early age. After all the surgeries, that prediction was probably already a forgone conclusion.

Long walks through the city had a similar effect on that rage although not as satisfying. The walk to the church took Dane south and east of the capital across the river. Everyone always associates Pennsylvania Avenue with the White House not realizing the boulevard bisects the entire southeast portion of the capital, ending in Maryland. He headed south to that famous avenue and then proceeded east across the John Phillip Sousa Bridge. The bridge had biking and walking paths, which made it a popular venue with outdoor enthusiasts who wanted to enjoy the various parks on either side of the Anacostia River. It may have been easier to just leave from work for this meeting since the unit was also on the east side of the river. However, Dane could stare at his office clock no longer, and even though he was not really hungry, he knew that he needed to go home and eat first if he was going to be able to get through this meeting.

He arrived at a historical old church seated prominently on a corner of the avenue. Several people were mustering around outside feverishly finishing that final cigarette. Dane noted their coping mechanisms but held no judgment. Nicotine had been his answer to stress at one point in his life. He now coped with the gym or the bottle. Who was he to judge? He climbed the steps and entered the lobby of the church. Bulletin boards and wooden placards gave vital instructions and locations for a variety of meetings. Every anonymous category must have been here this evening. He located his group and followed the sign down the steps and into the basement. He entered a drab space underneath the chapel. The overhead lights provided a soft yellow glow augmented by basement windows along the left and right side of the room. Row upon row of cold, impersonal metal chairs faced a small podium. A young minister was arranging his notes and checking the microphone. The space easily accommodated sixty people, but only about half were taken.

He poured himself a cup of coffee from a side table and took a seat in the back third of the rows. As if on cue, the minister spied the newcomer and paused his preparations. As he made his way over, Dane began to feel that familiar dread that blossomed whenever he was asked about Angela.

The minister extended his hand. *"I am John Anderson, one of the junior pastors here and coordinator for this outreach program."*

He took the man's hand. *"Dane Cooper."*

"I am glad you were able to join us tonight and I hope we can assist you with your grieving. Everyone here has experienced a tragedy that is often beyond words. We come together to cope with

that grief and lean on one another with our stories to ease our burdens. Are you willing to share your story with us tonight?"

"Thank you, but I plan on listening for my first time. I am not ready to share my story publicly just yet."

"Completely understandable. We are here to assist with recovering, not force it. People often have a difficult time opening during their first session, but, once they do, healing begins at a previously unknown level. Please let me know if you change your mind or need any additional assistance. Nice to meet you, Mr. Cooper."

The young pastor then greeted several other attendees as he made his way back to the podium. He adjusted his notes, tapped the microphone once, and opened the meeting. He began talking about grieving and the effects on the soul. A few Bible passages were inserted as well, but Dane was hardly listening. He looked around the room and saw so much suffering. After the young minister's words, grievers were invited to speak. One after another, attendees took the podium to tell their stories. Heartache after heartache, he listened to the misery.

Dane heard stories about children taken by disease or others killed in car crashes. There were more stories about tragic violence in the city and children being caught in gang crossfire. Stories such as these and other violent acts seemed to increase every year and dominate the nightly news cycle. Big cities across America were plagued with this disease, and D.C. was not exempt. Gun control versus the preservation of the second amendment was viciously debated, each side not willing to give an inch of ground. Dane himself was an adamant supporter of constitutional rights. It angered him at times to hear politicians and ordinary Americans call for the banning of guns. He served to uphold the security of all the people, and that included protecting them from the government. Dane knew what happened when a government had unlimited power over their defenseless citizens. The genocide, imprisonment, suppression of even basic human rights led to immense suffering. He did, however, understand that some measure of accountability had to be in place to protect the people. Unfortunately, no matter how many laws you enacted, and regardless of enforcement, man would continue to kill his fellow man. Guns were not the problem. People were. Dane remembered reading the crime section of the local newspaper in Nairobi, Kenya. Perversely, he would laugh to himself when he read about murders with spears and bows and arrows. The world gone mad.

Dane refocused on the individual speakers. There were no stories of kidnappings until the last one. A frail, defeated-looking woman, somewhere in her mid-forties, began talking about the abduction of her son five years ago. Five years, he thought. He had barely survived one year without Angela.

The woman told a story of how her son had been on his way home from school. As a single, working mother, she had trusted that he would arrive home safely after walking a few short blocks from the school, but one afternoon, that had all changed when witnesses claimed to see her son forcibly taken less than a hundred yards from their home and thrown into the backseat of an awaiting vehicle. Descriptions of the car and the abductors had proved useless in the ensuing police investigation. An investigation that reached a dead-end when the remains of the little boy were found in a nearby park only days later. Another broken family with no closure. No justice.

The young pastor concluded the meeting, inviting everyone to stay for coffee and have private conversations with one another if desired. He stated that he would remain as late as necessary in the event anyone would like to have private counseling.

Dane headed over to grab a coffee for the walk home. He did not intend to talk with anyone yet, but the last speaker intercepted him at the table.

"*Hi, my name is Jill,*" she said to Dane while extending a frail hand.

"*Dane,*" he responded.

"*I don't mean to pry and completely understand if you don't want to talk, but...*" she paused. "*I noticed your reaction to my story. It seems like you are struggling with an issue that I can relate too.*"

"*It is difficult to talk about. I am still working through a lot of emotions. I lost my daughter in a similar way. It has been a year.*" He struggled to keep his emotions in check. "*It has been a year, and the trail is cold. She has not yet been found.*"

"I understand," she responded. *"It took me years working through those emotions over losing Charlie. I was over-wrought with guilt that I could have done something to prevent the abduction of my son. Then sorrow, then horror at how some animal could do that to a child. I landed on rage. That emotion consumed me for a long time. I am probably still not completely done with rage, but I have at least found some sort of peace and acceptance of the things I cannot change."*

"I still have all those emotions, but rage is definitely where I am currently at," said Dane.

"Are you a religious man Dane?" she asked.

"I was once. But not anymore."

"I was prior to the loss of my Charlie. Religion isn't for everyone, but it was how I was raised," she continued. *"I believed in all the good book had to offer. The New Testament, that is. God's love for his children, yada, yada, but I couldn't come to grips with the fact that if that were true, how could a benevolent God allow this to happen to children?"*

"I have many of the same thoughts," he responded. *"It's not that I don't believe in something. It is just I don't understand it all."*

"Exactly," Jill continued. *"Well, I finally did find my way back to the church, but this time, I found some comfort in the eye-for-an-eye theory."*

"God as the punisher for sins rather than the forgiver. The Old Testament God?" he asked.

"I see that you have an understanding of the books. Yes. I find comfort in believing that if man on earth does not punish these monsters, they will at least find eternal damnation in hell."

Dane pondered what Jill had just said. *I have read nearly every religion's book, lady,* he thought. *They all say essentially the same thing but only offer salvation if you worship and obey according to their specific set of rules.* He, of course, did not confront the woman out loud since she seemed sincere and was being genuinely thoughtful. However, it was hard to accept any form of religion after seeing what was done to people by those who claimed to follow whatever book they held dear. His thoughts drifted back to his Catholic high school upbringing and the lectures he received from the Jesuits about the wrath of God. They were, after all, responsible for the Spanish Inquisition. They also talked about God's love and forgiveness for his children. The Old and New Testaments seemed to be a different God completely. One was fire and brimstone, while the other advocated turning the other cheek. Dane always found these polar opposite demonstrations of God's governance of his children confusing.

"Let me ask you Dane, do you believe in the death penalty?"

"It is strange you ask. I used to want rapists, and murderers, and child molesters taken out back and hung or shot. But my attitude changed over the years when I witnessed pure evil throughout the

world. Death was too good for some of these people. Too easy. In some cases, they needed to be killed if it is too high a price in friendly bloodshed to take them alive. But, if capture is an option, I want them caged like animals spending eternity locked away. I want them isolated. I want them broken. I want them to be a shell of who they once were and when they are reduced to absolutely nothing.... then I want them to face judgement in the afterlife. Whatever that afterlife may be. I am rooting for Satan on that one."

Jill gave the faintest of smiles. *"Sounds like you might just be an Old Testament guy after all. But remember, both books apply to our Heavenly Father and our judgement at the Pearly Gates. The laws of man do not supersede the word of God. He wants the wicked punished. However, he forgives those that repent. It was nice meeting you Dane."*

"You too, Jill."

With that, Jill placed her coffee cup in the trash and found her way to the exit. Dane stood looking at the single cross mounted above the doorway. It was a simple adornment making a simple statement. Yet powerful at the same time.

"Everything ok, Mr. Cooper?"

He hadn't realized that the pastor had come up beside him. *"I just question sometimes where we as a species went wrong. What makes people do the things they do? Is this what God intended?"*

"It is often very difficult to understand God's will. His reasoning is beyond our comprehension. We just have to trust in him and have faith. "

"I am not entirely sure I can that. Some things may be God's will, but didn't he also give us free will?"

"He did indeed, but free will does have consequences if one chooses to violate the word or as some would put it the command of God."

"I guess I am just looking for a sign."

"Aren't we all?"

Scout: *I made contact.*

President: *And?*

Scout: *He is ready.*

President: *Thank you. I will notify the Recruiter.*

CHAPTER 5: THE SUICIDE

Fort Hunt Park, VA

The rain pounded the windshield as Roger Patterson slowed the vehicle's speed around the narrow off-ramp leading from the George Washington Parkway. Agent Patricia Stills beside him, sipping on some sort of coffee blend that smelled of vanilla and pumpkin. Patterson could never understand the appeal of those fancy coffee shops that charged a small fortune for a bizarre concoction of flavors and spices. He preferred the Styrofoam cup of gas station coffee that rested in his middle console but Still's was in that younger and obviously more hip generation that disdained the archaic notion of coffee-flavored coffee. The two agents could never find a compromise. Normally Patterson drove, so he purchased his drink of choice before arriving at Stills apartment and then let his younger partner choose her poison on the way to their assignment; Starbucks drive-thru as usual.

He slowed again for the turn into Fort Hunt Park. The rain and wind cut visibility next to nothing. Not to mention that strict restrictions of the department budget seemed to apply specifically to their vehicles, and that budget never accounted for annual updates to the windshield wipers. The agents both worked in the General Investigation section, and although missing children and possible abductions were their main focus at the State level, more often than not, they were called in to assist local police with various crimes including mysterious deaths. That was the call they were answering this morning. Patterson had been notified at his home early this morning that a man was found dead in the park under strange circumstances. Local police had the location secured and were awaiting city detectives and agents from the states. Another crappy Friday to end the week, lost in the name of duty. He would have envisioned cancelled plans for the weekend that this case would bleed into, but then remembered he had no plans.

The battered sedan meandered through the park, finally locating the scene in one of the many small parking lots in the southeast corner. Patterson remembered visiting the park once before, years earlier, when reports of a missing child had been called into the state police. The park boasted a huge recreation area with minimal vehicular traffic. It was basically a one-mile, one-way loop around playgrounds, trails, and picnic shelters surrounded by an untouched labyrinth of trees. The history of the site was extensive and varied. It once was part of George Washington's Mount Vernon estate, housed cannon batteries to protect the Potomac, and was even used as a military base where questionable practices were employed while interrogating German prisoners during World War II.

Currently, the site was extremely popular with cyclists who did not have to share the road with cars and joggers but only had to watch for the other maniacs on twelve speeds. A family had rented one of the shelters for a birthday party. A child from the party, no more than nine years old, had wandered off. Frantic parents and relatives had scoured the park for any sign of the child and after several hours, had called the police. Roger had arrived with several other officers as a full court press to find the missing child. This proved easier than they thought when it was discovered that the boy wanted to see the water. So, he just walked in the direction of the Potomac. He exited the park through the woods and somehow managed to cross the parkway without injury and was found by a patrolman among several fishermen. The men casting their lines figured the child had come from a nearby park along the river and since nobody was actively looking for him, they figured his parents were content to let him stay and watch them reel in catch after catch. Thankfully calls like this were more the norm, and Patterson had been relieved that the day had ended on a successful note.

The flashing of red and blue lights snapped him out of his reverie. He pulled the car off the side of the road about thirty meters short of the yellow tap, so as not to interrupt or contaminate the scene. The rain had finally started slowing as he and Pat exited the vehicle and approached the nearest officer.

"Special Agents Patterson and Stills," Roger told the officer as he showed his badge firmly attached to his belt. The officer nodded and handed him the clipboard he was charged with. Roger signed both his and Pat's name along with badge numbers. The clipboard was used to log everyone in and out of a crime scene. Roger knew the drill. It was standard to rule out any evidence found that could be contributed by investigating officers. No matter how careful the police were at any crime

scene, trace material was always transferred and had to be ruled out during the course of the investigation. The two agents continued underneath the tape and toward the plainclothes officers near the vehicle. They would be the local detectives. Patterson introduced themselves to the closest one and asked for an update.

"What have we got," he asked the detective.

"White male. Mid-forties. Apparent carbon monoxide poisoning. We opened the windows to clear the scene and get rid of the fumes but left the hose in the back-passenger side window just as we found it. There doesn't seem to be any signs of a struggle," the detective answered. *"We identified him as Arthur Camp. His current address places him in some crummy little house in Pohick, up on Route One. He doesn't seem like the outdoor enthusiast type, so we have no idea yet what brought him to the park. Not exactly a scenic day. He also has quite the rap sheet."*

"You have a printout?" Stills asked, speaking for the first time.

"Right here. He has a history of molesting kids. He did ten years on one count of child molestation down in Georgia. Once he was released, he moved up to Virginia. He has been here for about three years, and get this, he works as a school janitor in the Fairfax County school district. Apparently, even though he is a registered sex offender, they somehow overlooked this and let him inside a damn school. He bounced around between several locations, normally elementary schools, which apparently is his preference since his

conviction was for inappropriate contact with a ten-year-old. He has had a few complaints made by parents whose children claimed that he would stare at them and seemed to be taking pictures occasionally. Apparently, he creeped out some of the teachers. One even went so far as to report him to the state office. Nothing came of it. Never any proof. Schools choose to move him from time to time instead of dealing with it. Lazy bastards. Fucking sicko. Good riddance."

The detective handed Patterson a sheet of paper with the details of one former Arthur Camp. Roger read through the detailed information despite the cliff-note version just relayed to him. *"Mind if we take a look,"* he asked.

"Be my guest. He isn't going anywhere. The scene is a nightmare to process, and the medical examiner on-call is still at least thirty minutes out. He was on another call up on route one. Bad car accident."

Roger handed the sheet to Stills as they both approached the vehicle. They were provided with shoe coverings from the duty officer with the clipboard which they already donned to avoid extraneous footprints at the scene. Both Agents put on latex gloves as well. The vehicle was an older-looking, tan sedan with no discernable markings. It looked well-worn but not completely out of place in the park. People from all economic walks of life visited this area, so older used cars were just as prevalent as new Range Rovers and Mercedes Benzes. The driver's side window was lowered exactly as the detective had described. Camp was slouched over in the driver's seat, leaning partially on the center console. His face was blue, and his swollen tongue was extended as if to jump out of its owner's mouth As Stills studied Camp's lifeless form and began to take notes, Roger walked around to the vehicle's passenger side. He carefully opened the door and studied the body from the opposite side. He paid particularly close attention to the face and the one hand not tucked underneath the body. Hands were always points of contact during any sort of struggle. Camp's hand and face were free from injury. His right hand was calloused and covered with tiny scars, but that was not unusual for someone working in manual labor. Roger did not move the body to observe the left hand since this wasn't his scene, but he expected the same condition as the right

Roger moved his attention to the glove box without any fresh cuts to observe. The medical examiner would retrieve any trace material from the fingerprints back at the office lest a struggle did ensue without any physical signs. The glove box bounced open upon release and was filled with receipts, napkins, and trash. The obligatory owner's manual laid on the bottom beneath a current registration and proof of insurance card. Patterson began to slowly dictate all the material he found so Stills could create a proper written record. The findings were probably nothing, but every detail was annotated since an unanticipated break, later in the case, could be predicated on the most innocuous piece of evidence.

With the front seat complete, the two agents moved to the back. The rear passenger window appeared to have sustained damage recently and was covered with a thin plastic tarp secured with duct tape around the window edges. A black hose running from the exhaust pipe had been pushed through the small rear corner of the tarp to allow the deadly gas to enter the vehicle and kill its occupant. Stills approached Roger's side and removed a small digital camera from her purse. The crime scene photographer would take professional pictures for the case file, but both Agents liked to take personal photos of items that interested them. Stills met Patterson's eyes and knew what the older man was thinking yet withheld any sort of opinion this early in the case in front of the local detectives. The agents did not want to taint their investigation. Next was the trunk. It was devoid of any personal effects, minus the spare tire and jack. It was clean. Stills was finishing up her notes when another vehicle arrived at the scene. The government vehicle screamed Fed when compared to the state sedan Patterson and Stills arrived in. Roger could practically smell the new car aroma from here. Why are the Feds here? He wondered.

Roger began walking the ground in the immediate vicinity. He sent Stills to confirm some final details with the detective on scene and see who the newcomer was. As the team's junior member, it was her responsibility to capture all the details in a written report with input from Roger. It wasn't their case, but they would consult with the local team if requested. She also began to sketch the scene for their internal report. This type of scene would not rate a forensic sketch artist, so the investigators would rely on pictures from the scene. But Stills knew Patterson would want some sort of simple sketch to help jog the memory where pictures themselves could be deceiving. Once complete with the immediate area, Stills headed over to catch up with her partner, who seemed to be searching the tree line and adjacent recreation areas. Stills knew better than to interrupt her partner and waited patiently.

"Who is that?" Roger asked.

"FBI. Special Agent Carl Blanchard. He works out of the main office in D.C. Gave me his card. He really didn't go into detail about why he was here and I didn't ask. That is the locals' problem. We are just here to advise and assist. I assume he is doing the same."

Patterson thought about it for a moment. He took the business card from his partner, glanced at it, and placed it in his breast pocket. *"Look over here,"* Patterson said, gesturing to a row of tall bushes.

"I don't see anything boss."

"It could be something, or it could be nothing, but it looks like somebody may have recently walked through the bushes here when they were still wet. They were careful, but when a bush is wet, their limbs will fold easily, even if brushed against gently. Once they dry, they normally will return upright."

"But it could be anything.... a hiker, a deer, maybe even a dog."

"You're right." Patterson straightened and gestured to Stills for the camera. She took several shots of the area, returned the camera, and began to head for the car. *"Come on. Let's go."*

Both agents returned to the immediate crime scene area. They thanked the detective, signed out with the duty officer, and headed to their vehicle. The newcomer was examining Camp's vehicle and broke away to approach the agents before they reached their vehicle.

"I met your partner, but we haven't met," the man said as he extended his hand toward Roger. *"Special Agent Carl Blanchard, FBI."*

Roger shook the man's hand. *"Roger Patterson. What brings you here?"*

"Advise and assist. I am sure the Virginia State Police is doing the same."

"We normally consult on cases like this. The locals usually have a good handle on these types of investigations, but the state likes to provide resources whenever possible."

"It is the same with us. The FBI is not all-knowing but having a second set of eyes on the scene never hurts. We all have different perspectives that can aid any case."

"I concur completely. Just odd that you guys would be notified of a suicide." Roger responded.

"Actually, I was called since it involves crimes against children. I should have stated that upfront. My department tracks child predators, and any crime involving someone on the registry gets our attention, no matter how trivial. It looks like another one will be

crossed off our books. Speaking of which, I believe I am meeting with you both later today. The Cooper case?"

Roger nodded. *"We are updating Angela Cooper's parents at 10am. We don't have much of an update, but we like to touch base in case something new develops or they remember something. I don't believe in cold cases."*

"I like that. I don't, either. Thank you both. I look forward to talking with you more later today." Carl shook both agents' hands and turned back to the crime scene.

With one last look around, Patterson entered the driver's side and started up the vehicle. Once Stills was onboard, he backed out and then continued around the one-way loop to the northern entrance/exit. They exited the park and began to backtrack to Fairfax, where they would finalize their initial report while it was fresh in their minds. Roger was lost in thought for several minutes.

"Want to let me in on what you are thinking, boss," asked Stills. *"FBI involvement seems a little odd for a suicide."*

"It is out of the norm, but I can understand their interest. Child sex trafficking has become a huge issue as of late and they are following every possible angle. Let's focus on the case at hand."

"Ok. Want to review the draft case file I have so far?" Pat asked.

"No. Let's brainstorm and capture initial thoughts based on what we have seen. I think we can agree that this went down one of two ways, yes?"

"I think suicide is the most likely way it went down, but I guess this could be an old-fashioned murder. Pretty difficult to pull off, but not impossible."

"Correct," Patterson continued. *"So, suicide looks like the obvious answer. Since the victim is deceased, and so far, there haven't been any immediate witnesses, nobody can tell us for sure. Therefore, we still have to consider another explanation of events and rule it out if we are going to unequivocally close this a suicide. That second explanation is murder."*

"Murder seems a pretty far stretch here, but I see where you are going with this train of thought," Stills answered.

"So, tell me what you saw that could indicate that this was a murder."

"Ok, well, the first thing is the hose. We have no concrete proof that Camp put that hose in himself. I guess someone could have approached the vehicle and quietly punched the hose through that plastic. I guess it wouldn't be very loud."

"Did you notice the radio dial," asked Patterson.

"I didn't even notice. The car was turned off," admitted Stills.

"The radio was very old. Probably original with the car. That sedan was made in the eighties. Today's vehicles have no marking on the volume control. That is why you sometimes forget you were blaring music when you shut the car off, and when you go to start it the next day, you blow your eardrums."

"Hah, I may have done that once or twice."

"Those dials in his car have indicator levels. It was turned up nearly two-thirds of the way."

"So, he might not have heard someone punch through the plastic," Stills answered. *"Still, that is hardly enough to go on."*

"How did he cut the tube to the length he needed? Where are the cutters? Where is the extra line of tubing he cut off? Did he find the exact length necessary to go from the exhaust to the window at the local hardwood store?"

Stills gave her boss a puzzled look.

Patterson continued. *"Let's say he did this. He drove out to the park with the intention of killing himself. His trunk or interior of his car should have contained the materials necessary for the job. He should have acquired the tubing somewhere and something to cut it with. He would have measured the length, cut the necessary piece, and then inserted both ends. Where is the cutter and the extra piece of tubing? There was a small break in that bush line I showed you. What if someone approached on foot and under the cover of all that rain? It would certainly be hard to see someone approach, especially from the blind spot on the typical car side mirrors. They would have to take a quick measurement, cut the tube, and insert it without being heard because of the radio volume. With the monoxide coming directly into the vehicle, Camp would have passed out in a few minutes and probably died in ten minutes, start to finish."*

"He could have measured at home. Had everything all prepared and then drove out and set everything up. The police may find all of this stuff at his house."

"True. But I don't think that is guaranteed."

Stills was thoroughly confused. *"What do you mean?"*

"What was the weather like all this morning?" asked Patterson.

"It has been pouring rain non-stop since about 6 a.m. Thankfully it slowed and eventually stopped when we got there."

"Why weren't Arthur Camp's clothes or shoes wet?"

And what was the Fed's interest? Patterson thought to himself.

CHAPTER 6: THE BOTTOM

Fairfax, VA

Pupil: *Are you there?*

Keeper: *Yes*

Pupil: *I have two now. My collection is growing.*

Keeper: *Just remember that more dolls mean more people are looking.*

Pupil: *I have been careful. Nobody will find me out.*

Keeper: *Never be too sure. One mistake is all it takes.*

Dane ducked down behind a large rock outcropping just outside his driver's side door. Everything was loud. Even the smoke seemed to emit a unique sound of its own. He ejected his mag into his left hand and quickly stuffed it in the dump pouch he had on the rear of his belt. These mags were cheap, but he couldn't afford to lose them. He may have to re-load later on. With a fresh mag in, he peered over the small barrier right as one of the guys slammed into the earth next to him. The man was bleeding profusely from his left arm. "Holy shit Randall, hold still!"

As the man used his good arm to stabilize his rifle on the rocks, Dane reached over and grabbed Randall's tourniquet from his medical pouch. He quickly secured the device about two inches above the man's elbow and cranked it down until it would cinch no further. The flow of blood retreated to a trickle from the right side of Randall's left hand where his thumb and pointer finger once were.

Several chunks of dirt peppered the two men as enemy rounds struck dangerously close to their position. "Doc! Over Here!" Dane yelled above the noise.

The platoon medic had just finished attending to another casualty on the other side of the vehicle. The entire convoy had been ambushed, and they were in a fight for their life. Normally, they would have sped right out of the ambush, but the dried-up riverbed they were traversing made that nearly impossible. Boulders the size of cars slowed the movement to a crawl. And that is why they chose here to hit us, he thought. Doc saw Randall and prepared to rush to their position. He was holed up only twenty feet away, but under fire, it might as well have been a mile. Doc stepped from behind the vehicle and .....CRACK!

Dane snapped awake by the squawking of his cellphone on the nightstand. The sound clearly not belonging on the battlefield had forced him into consciousness. Still in a haze from the night before, he struggled to remember why he had set an alarm. After leaving the church last night, he had taken a circuitous route home, ensuring he could visit as many bars as possible. Ugg, the meeting with the BCI this morning, he remembered. This will not be fun. He and Jenny were to meet with the two agents from the Bureau of Criminal Investigation at the Fairfax office this morning. Apparently, the Virginia State Police Commander of the unit was also going to be there to provide an update along with some Fed. Dane was not hopeful.

He jumped in a cold shower to wash away the rest of the cobwebs from his head. He donned the cleanest pair of jeans he could find, something that could pass for a collared shirt, and headed out the door after only a single cup of coffee. His body was not quite ready for anything else. He went through his normal routine of retrieving the motorcycle from the backyard and started off toward Fairfax. Thankfully it was not raining any longer, and the roads were nearly dry. He had a beat-up old truck, but since parking in downtown D.C. was an absolute nightmare, he kept it in the unit parking lot for when he needed it. He was thankful that he didn't need to go to the unit and retrieve the truck today. He was barely going to be on time as it was.

Dane once more crossed over the Anacostia River to jump onto Interstate two, ninety-five south. He traveled along the river before it dumped out into the Potomac as he passed Joint Base Anacostia Bolling. He was headed toward National Harbor, Maryland. Before the harbor, he crossed the river again on the Woodrow Wilson Bridge into Virginia and headed west toward his destination in Fairfax. He always hated crossing that bridge since the metal grooves in the road made the bike wobble. Riding the motorcycle was a form of therapy for him. People complained about the traffic and the carelessness of motorists in the Northern Virginia, D.C. area when it came to bikes. Dane however, had no issues. He was rarely in a hurry and certainly was never one of those clowns weaving in and out of traffic like a maniac, barely missing the bumpers and fenders of all the vehicles. He preferred a nice smooth ride in the right lane and would even take side and back roads if it meant avoiding the constant stop-and-go of traffic. Jenny had never been fond of riding so normally moments spent on the bike gave him time alone to think. But Angela had always begged him to go for a ride. He would never go far and never enter the freeway, but he would take her around the neighborhood or over to the mall for ice cream. She loved the pink and black helmet he had bought for her covered in skulls. Angela would tuck it under her arm and strut like a Hell's Angel through the food court with a Superman ice cream cone.

Dane pushed down those memories and focused on finding the BCI office. It was just off the freeway and was easy to find. Traffic was light, and he had made good time, but of course, Jenny was already there and waiting on him. He saw her little red jeep in the lot as he pulled in, her sitting on a bench by the front entrance. He turned off the bike and approached the set of double doors by which she sat realizing the toll this was also taking on her. Clearly Jenny would have been more comfortable inside, but she needed him to help her with presenting a united front when getting the news from the investigators. She probably doesn't want to get the news alone.

"I see that old bike is still running," she commented.

"Hopefully, she has many more miles in her," he responded.

They stood awkwardly for a few moments, neither comfortable with the silence nor able to initiate small talk. Even though they were once husband and wife, they found themselves at a point where they had nothing left to say. He knew that the dissolving of the marriage was not solely the fault of one or the other. The pain of losing Angela had torn a hole in each of their souls, and instead of coming together in their grief, they pushed each other away. Jenny immersed herself in her work. They had met in college when she was a nursing student. Her focus as a college student was much sharper than his. She knew exactly what she wanted to be when she grew up and how she wanted to help people. Dane, on the other hand, bounced between majors, never really finding his niche. The Army had always been in the back of his mind followed by a career in law enforcement. Upon graduation, they had married and agreed upon a short enlistment in the Army, whereas, upon completion of his service, he would look into a federal law enforcement career. Of course, since nurses were needed all over the country, Jenny easily found a rewarding career from duty station to duty station as the short enlistment turned into a career for Dane.

Dane had done the exact opposite in his grief. He completely lost focus at work, as evidenced by his meeting with Reynolds the other day. He found grief in a bottle as helplessness overtook him. He had conducted his own informal investigation right after Angela's disappearance. He spoke with neighbors. He re-traced every possible route Angela could have taken. He talked to garbage collectors, park employees, maintenance workers, bus drivers, and anyone who was working within ten miles of their house that day.

Dane soon began to realize that without access to precious resources, or more accurately intelligence support, this was one mission that was bound to fail. He never gave up hope. He just gave up on himself. Jenny stayed positive but focused on John and her career, determined to move on. Dane stayed positive but focused on the past. The marriage had lingered for five more months and then collapsed. Legally speaking, they were still married. The state of Virginia required couples with children under eighteen to wait a full year before the state finalized the divorce. They both knew that they were simply running out the clock. Reconciliation was impossible.

They both turned and entered the building as if by some unspoken agreement. They had never been here before. The agents had normally scheduled a visit to their house or a public place nearby, such as a library. Dane assumed it was to put them both at ease in the comfort of their home if possible, so they would relax and hopefully remember an important piece of information not previously disclosed. The agents were aware that they no longer shared a dwelling, and the office was about as neutral ground as they would find. This conversation would be inappropriate at an Applebee's. Both he and Jenny showed identification at the front desk, and soon were escorted into the back offices. The receptionist led them through a maze of cubicle farms overwhelmed with noise from phone conversations and the clicking of keyboards. The office was alive with activity and offered a sense of urgency. The officers were clearly focused on whatever task they had at hand. Once near the far wall, they were ushered into a smaller hallway with several glass office suites that afforded more privacy than the cubicle farm. At least audible privacy. They entered the second office on the left, and the investigators in the room all rose to greet them. He and Jenny were both acquainted with Special Agents Patterson and Stills. The third man introduced himself as Captain Ivers, who was the Commander of the Fairfax office. He expressed his condolences to them both and wanted to meet them and personally ensure that he was energizing the full resources available to him by the state police to find their daughter.

"I know this has been a horrendous experience for you both," Captain Ivers offered. *"Special Agent Patterson and Stills are two of our best. They will leave no stone unturned. We take all crime seriously, but nothing more than crimes against children."* With that, he excused himself with other business leaving them in the capable hands of the Special Agents. The fourth attendee waited patiently throughout the awkward introductory process until the captain had departed.

"Mr. and Mrs. Cooper. Special Agent Carl Blanchard, FBI," stating his normal opening phrase during investigations. He offered them both his hand.

Patterson gestured to the table and gently shut the door as everyone was seated around the conference table. A large carafe of coffee with cups and a pitcher of water stood at attention at the center of the table, ignored by everyone present. Roger cleared his throat and began.

"I appreciate you both coming here today. I know it can be difficult to continually relive this event. We have been updating the case periodically as often as possible, but without any new leads, it

is difficult to offer any progress report. This by no means is an admission of defeat or a recommendation to cease looking. However, I want to be upfront and honest with you both. I don't want to offer false hope." Patterson paused to get a reaction from the Coopers, but they both remained rigid and emotionless. It was Blanchard that broke the uncomfortable silence.

"If I may, Mr. and Mrs. Cooper, I want to share my background and maybe help explain the Bureau's involvement in this case."

"It's Dane and Jenny," Dan interjected. *"No need for formalities here."*

"Certainly. Mr..... Dane, Jenny, I work for a department that tracks and monitors known and suspected child offenders. We concentrate on repeat offenders, serial molesters, for the lack of a better phrase. We track known offenders through the national database, to which they are all registered upon committing a crime. When they move, we make sure we know when and where. We monitor all reports from Federal, State, and local police when an abduction occurs. We use this database as a kind of starting point to provide authorities with potential suspects and help narrow the field. For example, one perpetrator may have a certain MO, modus operandi. That is a particular method by which he commits his crimes. The police may investigate a crime, and our database has several offenders that match that description. If possible, we can locate and quickly eliminate several suspects based on alibis and other factors and then provide investigators with a reduced list of possible perpetrators. Or these suspects may indeed be guilty and thereby prosecuted."

"So, you play defense?" asked Dane. *"You are there to respond after the fact, is what I am hearing."*

"Dane," warned Jenny.

"It is quite alright Mrs.... Jenny. I understand Dane's frustration. To answer your question, unfortunately, that is somewhat accurate. However, we do offer insight into prevention as well by keeping tabs on these convicted criminals. We do unannounced welfare checks. We occasionally will surveil some of our worst offenders to ensure they are not violating the parameters of their paroles and/or acting in a manner that would indicate a return to their previous lifestyles."

"That is the most roundabout answer I have ever heard." Dane's temper was slowly rising. *"Government-speak for what? Do you have any information about our daughter? Do you have a suspect? Suspicions maybe? Anything to add? One Goddamn lead!"*

"Mr. Cooper," Patterson interjected. *"I know this is emotional for you. Special Agent Blanchard is simply trying to demonstrate his assistance on this case and several others. The FBI has resources and analytical manpower we simply don't have at the state or local level. And they assist in every way possible."*

"I appreciate all you and Stills have done. But none of that brings my daughter back or, at the very least, brings her abductor to justice. All of this means absolutely nothing. I am hearing the same old story month after month, and now you have simply brought in a new voice actor to say the same old tired lines. It doesn't change a thing.

You have my number, gentlemen. If there is a development, give me a call. If not, I will just assume you are all doing the best you can at the state, federal, or whatever hell level you want to call it, but stop wasting my time and energy."

Dane stood from the table and exited the room, the glass door nearly shattering with the force of opening. He stormed through the maze toward the front of the building and the exit. Jenny rose as well, apologized for her ex-husband's behavior, and quickly followed him to the front door.

"Well, that went well," offered Blanchard.

"I don't know how often you deal personally with the families of the victims, Carl," answered Patterson, *"but until you can fully understand their grief, place yourself in their shoes. You need to work on your bedside manner. He didn't want false promises or smoke and mirrors. He wanted theories. He wanted a detailed plan of action for what comes next. He wanted answers. And since we don't have any, I really can't blame him for the outburst. I would have reacted the same way."*

"Well, I wish I had some sort of clairvoyance. I wish I knew where these monsters lived and when they would strike, but I don't," Carl answered. *"Going on the offense, as he inferred, is next to impossible. You agents know as well as I do, that in nearly all the cases we do solve, the perpetrator is usually considered a normal guy. Neighbors will be shocked and surprised at his actions, claiming they never suspected someone like that could do such a horrible*

thing. How could he have children trapped in his house? He was such an upstanding citizen. Blah, blah, blah."

"So why are you really here, Carl?" Stills asked. *"I mean, what is your interest in some dead pedophile in the park and now a year-old abduction case?"*

"Like I said before, we at the FBI track and monitor as many cases as possible. We look for patterns. Try to be predictive. We all want the same thing. So please do not read anymore into this. The FBI is not trying some subterfuge or playing according to some secret agenda playbook. We are looking at every angle. And that's it." Ending the conversation, Special Agent Blanchard stood, collected his things, and walked out of the room.

"Am I missing something, boss?"

"I think we both are Pat. There is always more to it when the FBI starts poking around."

"You think the dead pedo is more important than he is letting on?"

"I am not sure yet. But I do know that we need to dig a little more into Mr. Arthur Camp. Maybe he is more than just some local pervert. We need to see his arrest report from Georgia."

Jenny caught up to Dane as he was donning his helmet and preparing to start the bike. He felt better after leaving the building but was far from suppressing the rage inside of him.

"What the hell was that in there, Dane?"

"That was a song and dance. They have nothing, Jenny. Nothing!!! And them some flashy ass fed shows up with fanciful anecdotes about all the federal government is doing to protect the world from these monsters. They aren't doing shit!" He could feel the rage building and did not want to take it out on Jenny. She deserved better.

"They are trying. They don't have a magic crystal ball that tells them when all the bad people are going to do bad things. They also have these things called laws, and unfortunately, even these monsters have those little things like rights. I am pretty sure you have lectured me about that in the past."

Dane visualized where this conversation was going. It was certain to end in an even bigger fight. This was something he had to avoid. *"I am leaving Jenny. If you want to sit through those pointless discussions, I am in no position to stop you. But every time we talk about this... every time, another little piece of me dies. I want answers but will not subject myself to that torture when they have nothing. They have done nothing, and they will continue to do nothing!"* Dane donned his helmet, clearly ending the conversation as he kicked the starter. The engine roared to life, and he sped out of the parking lot, hoping the ride home would quell the rage inside.

Spotter: ***He is home.***

Recruiter: *Let me know if he goes for one of his long walks.*

Spotter: *I will. He does nearly every day.*

Recruiter: *Thank you.*

CHAPTER 7: THE PITCH

Washington D.C

The ride did little to temper the rage. He considered heading over to the office and maybe working on the bags a little, but Dane realized that now was not the time to be around people. He needed more time to cool off. Heading home was the better option. He was sure the place was a mess and should probably take the time to clean up. John wasn't coming over until tomorrow since he had a function tonight, so the afternoon and evening were free.

Dane entered his dungeon apartment and put away his motorcycle gear. He tried straightening up for the next hour, but his heart wasn't in it. The bathroom and kitchen were as clean as they were going to get. As he was picking up clutter in the small living room, he noticed some of the photo albums on the bottom shelf of his book cabinet were in disarray. In the world of digital images and computer displayed photo-albums, there was still something comforting about collecting images from the past in a tangible form. He was not a complete dinosaur. Digital cameras were the norm now, but he still liked to print out shots from memorable occasions to place among the real pages of a book that he could touch and see as he held cherished memories from the past. Without thinking, he retrieved one randomly and sat back on the sofa. Florida.

The album re-told the story of that adventure when he and Jenny decided that the best way for the family to bond would be a cramped trip to Florida with everyone tucked away in a small RV for seven days. Although the lack of personal space and privacy had touched off nerves throughout the trip, he wouldn't have traded it for the world. It had started with renting a small RV, which in itself had been a royal pain. The paperwork was endless, and Dane had spent nearly three hours at the rental agency before returning home. The family was already anxiously awaiting his return, bags in hand. The next hour was spent trying to put the proverbial twenty pounds of crap in a ten-pound sack. Every crevice was stuffed with clothes, food, toys, and electronics and when they finally hit the road for their first leg of the trip, the heavens opened up without sparing a single drop. While the kids bickered and Jenny questioned every turn he took, Dane squinted against the constantly fogging window for a glimpse of the road. The spigot in the heavens seldomly closed for the duration of the trip.

They had reserved a spot on the beach down in the Florida Keys, but warmth and sunshine escaped them. Nearly the entire trip was spent inside the tiny vehicle reading books or playing board games that nobody was very interested in. However, although the days were brutal, the storms cleared nearly every evening for some reason. So, a vacation of swimming in the waves and basking in the Florida sun was replaced with cool evenings around the campfire. A burnt hotdog in a bun. A warm marshmallow on a stick and quite possibly the most incredibly vivid skies coupled with family conversation, stories, and jokes.

Bonding occurred, not how they thought it would, but it did nonetheless. They talked about that vacation for years. He knew that it could never be repeated.

Sitting alone in the apartment dredging up old memories was not having a beneficial effect. Dane decided that maybe a walk through the heart of the city would help. It had been a very emotional day. He quickly replaced the album on the shelf and grabbed his wallet and keys. As he emerged from the basement, he could already feel the sun washing away the grime of the darkness that had been enveloping him all day.

This time Dane reached the street and headed west which was the direction of the capitol. He had toured the monuments and memorials a million times. He could provide professional tours through nearly every Smithsonian Museum. Yet he never tired from those walks through history. He and Jenny often joked that he should teach once he retired from the military. Wear a tweed jacket with patched elbows and learn to smoke a pipe. He could use his experience in the military, along with his unique way of relaying historical facts, to entertain an entirely new generation of learners. He would, of course need to soften up a little around the edges. Jenny always joked that his delivery would need a little work.

Talking to college students was not like talking to fellow grunts. This generation was quite a bit more sensitive. Hell, the other faculty in this dream world would probably also take offense to Dane's sense of humor and straightforward speech. Non-military people would never understand the banter in the

Army. Crude banter found in all the Services. But that dream had faded, as did any energy he once had for another career.

His route took him south along Lincoln Park and then straight on to the backside of the capitol. It was a beautiful structure. Too bad it was filled with heathens and crooks. It seemed to always be under repair as if no amount of improvements could contain the greed found within. Filled with beautiful statues and other priceless art, Dane always felt it was the most expensively decorated prison on the planet. But it was beautiful inside. Since it was next to impossible to visit, and never on the spur of the moment, he circumvented the estate grounds to the north and continued on to the National Mall. This was perhaps the busiest section of the city. Life was everywhere, which helped him clear his head. People jogged through the dense crowds and rode bikes or those goofy Segway things. It was the ones that played sports however, that always entertained him the most. Twenty and thirty-year-olds dusting off their hands and pants after a vicious base run in kickball. Kickball... hilarious.

It was among all this activity that Dane first noticed a man who seemed to be paying him too much attention. He knew that this was a crowded area and that he was walking a normal route used by many other people. But years of training and employment of tradecraft did not just dissipate with his current state of apathy and sorrow. Some habits die hard. Dane thought he better keep an eye on this guy. It was probably nothing. He had been out of the game for so long that nobody would have any interest in him.

He continued through the mall but adjusted his course. It was not a textbook surveillance detection route but it would do in a pinch and on the fly. He stopped for about thirty minutes in the Museum of Natural History. It was one of his favorites. And although he wasn't particularly interested in museums today, it would give him a chance to see if the man followed or was truly of no interest. It also was telling on whether or not the man followed due to the detectors at all entrances. Dane was not carrying a weapon for that very reason. *"Let's see if this guy is armed,"* he thought to himself.

Dane wandered the halls and exited in the same manner he entered. The man had not followed. Nor had he left the area. He saw him out of the corner of his eye at the food kiosk across the street. It was still not that usual. The man looked like any other well-dressed businessman in the city enjoying a break from the confines of a windowless office or the glare of computer monitors and artificial lighting. He was average in every sense of the word, and he had not entered the museum, which in hindsight, really told him nothing. Well, that was stupid and totally non-productive. *You are getting rusty old man,* he thought to himself. So, he continued on. Time to ramp it up a little bit. Dane continued leisurely along the street, still heading west, and entered the next museum. He climbed the grand front steps of the American history museum. This time he spent only fifteen minutes on the first floor and then exited the north side of the museum onto Constitution Avenue. No businessman. Not that he expected him to be sitting with an ice cream cone on the back steps. Dane sat momentarily and pulled out his cell phone to kill the time. If the man had followed him from the front, maybe he would appear. But after five minutes it was obvious that the man wouldn't make an appearance. None of this made any sense. He was positive the guy was following him. Call it intuition, whatever. *Or is my paranoia catching up with me? What the hell was going on?*

Dane backtracked east and then headed back to the mall. Sure enough, when he reached the southeast corner of the building, the man was now idling near some street vendors. The city was overpopulated with these merchants selling everything from Make America Great Again shirts, Let's Go Brandon sweatshirts, and every other variety of apparel with FBI or CIA emblazed across the surface. The man was definitely waiting on Dane to emerge, not even thinking that there may be another exit. The man was either an armed professional looking to do him harm or a complete amateur. He sized the man up again and made his decision. This is not a professional. *Yet this is not random,* he thought. *Better let him pick me back up, and I can lead him to a place of my choosing.* And that is just what he did.

Dane made sure to be visible when he walked by the man and crossed the street north of the Washington Monument. He maintained a brisk pace past the World War II memorial which was one of his favorite stops. After World War II, most pedestrians worked their way down to the Lincoln Memorial along the southern edge of the Reflecting pool. That was the normal route. It was also a route that passed one of the few public restrooms in the area. Washington, D.C. seemed to follow the lead from New York City and insisted its tourists and guests refrain from going to the bathroom for the duration of their visit. But he was headed toward the Constitution Gardens to the north. The park was small and rarely had a lot of foot traffic, with tourists preferring the monuments during their brief visit instead of the small pond and park. The businessman was not far behind. Definitely following him. Dane slowed his pace as he entered the park, taking in the environment before selecting a location along the north side of the pond with a secluded seating area. *Perfect,* Dane thought. He headed to the nearest bench and proceeded to pull out his cell phone as he sat while turning on the video function to capture any audible conversation. As the man neared his position, Dane focused on him and patted the seat beside him.

"Why don't you have a seat and tell me what you want." If the man was surprised, he didn't show it. As he sat, Dane was able to study him a little closer. Still average; average build, average height, nothing memorable. But that was sometimes the point. The man broke the silence quickly when he extended his hand. They were soft. Banker hands.

"Mr. Cooper, my name is Andrew."

Dane shook the man's hand, *"And what is it I can do for you, Andrew?"*

"I want to tell you a story. I will try and keep it short since I know your time is precious. Nearly ten years ago, my life was changed forever. I had a loving wife, a beautiful daughter, and a booming business. I had just gone out on my own, starting a headhunter firm to recruit talent for several of the big companies and lobbyists in this town. I was a junior partner in a large firm and climbing the corporate ladder seemed impossible. I had a book of clients who were more than willing to take a chance on me. A known recruiter who was willing to give them a financial break for taking a chance. I was riding high. It felt like that line from Shakespeare. The world being my oyster or something. And then it happened. I was just leaving my downtown office and heading to the metro to catch my train home. I received a phone call similar to the one I am certain you received. My daughter was gone."

Andrew paused. Dane was not sure if he was trying to fight back emotion or pausing to let the story sink in. Or both.

Andrew continued, *"The days and weeks that followed were torture. Then the weeks became months, and months turned into years. My wife left me after three years and my business was ruined, and my liver seemed to be the only organ I could rely on. My heart was broken. I tried therapy. I tried support groups like the one you were at last night."*

Dane was not surprised by that last line. Once Andrew had begun his story, he figured that maybe there was a connection between the two. But what did he want?

"Then I found the club. Well, they actually found me. They helped me sort through my emotions. Helped me deal with the guilt, the shame, and everything in between. I found a group with shared experiences where not only could I help myself, but I could help others in return."

"Let me stop you right there, Andrew. Are you telling me you have been following me for the last two hours to join some sort of exclusive support group? Support club? Sorry to waste your time, but I am not the support group kinda guy which I realized the other evening."

"Mr. Cooper."

"Just Dane."

"Dane, it is not that type of club."

"Then what kind of club is it? What do you guys do?"

Andrews had been facing forward as he told him the story about his daughter, almost as if reliving the memory without direct human contact was easier. For the first time he turned and faced Dane directly. *"We hunt monsters Dane."*

He stared at Andrew as the men sat in a moment of silence. Had he just heard what he thought he did? There is a group that hunts child abductors and molesters?

How is that even possible? He had so many questions. *"So, tell me, Andrew, how exactly does your club hunt these child predators, and what do you want with me?"*

"I am not at liberty to get into all the details, but I can tell you that we have members with all different skills. Myself, as a business recruiter? My job should be fairly obvious . And it was an easy fit. As for what job the President has in mind for you, that is up to him. We have soldiers, police, lawyers, a little bit of all walks of life working together as a well-oiled machine."

"The President? That is what you call the boss? I like the well-oiled machine part. That is a pretty good pitch. *Or is this some sort of trap or sting. Are you with the feds Andrew? I had a weird visit with one of them this morning so please excuse my apprehension."*

"Your apprehension is normal Mr..... uh Dane. I am not with any law enforcement service. I am who I say I am, and that is all. I am also not privy to discuss the finer details, but the rest of your questions will be answered if you are willing to meet the President."

He mulled over everything he had just heard. Andrew reached into his suit pocket. Dane tensed slightly, wondering if he had mis-read the entire encounter and now would be facing a barrel or a badge. He was prepared to handle either, but Andrew simply removed a business card from his breast pocket.

"My information is on the front. Email, cell, etc. On the back is the meeting location."

Dane accepted the card and flipped it over to the back side to see the Bellevue Forest neighborhood address in Arlington. Pretty upscale area. Probably out of a cop's price range.

"The information on the back is for Sunday afternoon at 2pm. If you decide to pass on the invitation, my information is on the front so you can reach out to me in the future when you change your mind."

"Don't you mean if I change my mind?"

"I have lived through this agony for nearly a decade. I have seen it destroy even the strongest of individuals. I have also met several men like you and men like you will always seek action and justice. Sometimes it just takes a little longer. I hope it doesn't take long this time. For your sake."

Andrew slowly rose. He offered Dane the briefest of nods and walked back the way both men had travelled as Dane continued to stare at the card in his hand.

Somehow the day had faded, and the first signs of the evening were approaching. He didn't know how long he had been sitting on that bench. Club. Retribution. Revenge. All these thoughts tumbled through his mind as he tried to make sense of today. It was surreal, from the Special Agents in Fairfax to the mystery man in the fancy suit. The police were helpless. They practically admitted it. *But the club? Was that the solution? Obviously, it was illegal as hell. But did that matter anymore?* Dane thought about that. He was certainly no stranger to violence. No stranger to death. But that had been war. Senior military leaders had given him targets. *Then again, who were they to play judge, jury, and executioner? What moral authority did they claim that this club couldn't?* The bottom line was that he was sent to punish bad people in the Army. It seemed like the club was doing the same thing. And why shouldn't they?

I have done all I could, but I failed my marriage to Jenny, he thought.

I am doing all I can but failing to connect with John.

I need to do all I can for Angela. And for me.

Recruiter: *I talked with him.*

President: *What was his response?*

Recruiter: *He will be there Sunday.*

President: *Thank you.*

CHAPTER 8: THE BOY

Manassas, VA

Pupil: *Who killed him?*

Keeper: *Police are claiming it was suicide.*

Pupil: *Do you think that is true?*

Keeper: *I am not sure.*

"Dila dhamaantood! Weerar! Wayoo Allaah!"

"What are they saying Ali? What instructions are they giving them over those fucking speakers?"

"I don't think you want to know Mr. Dane."

"Just tell me already! Are they giving them instructions? Like a battle plan? Telling them where to hit us next?"

"They are saying to kill you all. Attack. For Allah. No plan. Just attack. And then once you are dead, drag your lifeless bodies behind the trucks."

"That is just great! Tyler! Tyler! Cover the south side! If those skinnies get over the compound's south wall, we will be over-run! Get second platoon's remaining squads over there by the tower for

cover, and make sure they are covering the west gate with at least a fire team. The idiots don't seem to realize there is another entrance yet. Ali, where the hell are the Isaaq? Get on the phone with Awad! Tell him we need re-enforcements now! The commandos can hold them here and at the main gates, but not forever! I need his forces to attack from the rear! They probably don't know we have more guys up the road. I don't want any of those shits escaping."

"Tyler? Can you see Ahmed?"

"He is by the tower yelling at the PKM teams! Trying to get them to get the other gun back up!"

"Tell him to leave them be! They can fix it. I need those DShKs from the technicals in the fight, right now!"

"Ahmed, move that fucking truck! Move it to the front gate! Fire the DShK at that house corner! Now! I don't care what you think! Now get the second one over by the west gate to reinforce the fire team. If they bust down that gate fire on them with everything you have!"

"Dane, they are moving! They need more ammo! One of us is going to need to get down there and unlock the shed!"

"Stay where you are Tyler! I'll get it!"

"Ali! Stay here. Keep your head down! Listen for Tyler if he needs help with commands and translations!"

"Dane! Ali! DOWN! RPG! RPG! RPG!"

The truck turned over on the first try. It was even older than the motorcycle but still clung to life. Dane was grateful. He really didn't want to purchase a new vehicle. The old truck had been faithful all these years. It was a clear morning, so he decided to walk over to the unit compound instead of biking. He would be picking up John this morning, and he couldn't exactly have him hanging off the back of the Honda holding his duffel bag. Also, storms were looming and predicted to terrorize the area from late morning straight through the evening. The truck didn't always run smoothly, but it didn't leak. A ride on the motorcycle would be miserable. He also wanted to clear his head from that dream, and the walk over to the unit would help. Damn. Somaliland. That had been a shitshow. They had been lucky they made it off that roof in one piece.

The ride to Manassas was uneventful. The route was familiar now since he drove it at least twice a month. Dane reflected on his encounter from yesterday. The offer had been on his mind every moment since. He made his decision to meet with this president person and at least hear him out. More than anything, he speculated on what they would ask him to do. He immediately figured out some sort of shooter or finishing option due to his background. But maybe not. Maybe they needed him to perform some administrative function or some sort of logistics task. Maybe ask him to move weapons or vehicles around for other people. Would he be satisfied with those types of roles? Andrew seemed comfortable in his role and helped the group as best as he could. That fit with Andrew's life, but Dane wasn't Andrew. That would not be good enough for him.

He arrived at Jenny's house to find John hanging out on the front porch with his bag. He kept a few items at Dane's, but a majority of the time; he lugged his bag between the two parent's homes. He always felt guilty watching John traverse two worlds but kept reminding himself that two happy homes were better than one toxic one in the long run. He would have to work on his so-called happy home. Maybe someday, get a bigger place so John could actually have a room to store his belongings.

"Hey Dad," John called out as he walked over and jumped into the truck. *"Mom feels like crap, or she would have said hi."*

"Absolutely no worries." Dane put the truck in gear. *"Hungry? Where do you want to eat?"*

"Let's head over to Occoquan before it starts to pour. Sit along the river."

Dane steered that way, and they were off. The short car ride was filled with their normal father-son banter that occurred every two weeks. It was usually more one-sided since he didn't have a lot of news to share. He rarely talked about his work among his family members. He never had. He would talk with them about the unique places he visited, the cultures, the customs, and everything, but never the job. For one, it was always classified at the uppermost level. Secondly, leaving work at work helped Dane separate the two parts of his life. He did not want the man he was at work coming home to his family. He much preferred to listen as John talked about school, sports, sometimes girls, and always about driving. John tapped the dashboard of the truck.

"Still going to give this to me at sixteen?" John was currently enrolled in driver's ed at school and would have his permit soon.

"That's the plan," Dane responded. *"You need to get that permit so we can start driving."*

"I have driver's ed next semester and then I can apply for the permit. You going to show me some of those cool moves you learned in all those driving courses you talked about? Skidding around corners. Knocking people off the road. I want to learn how to do a one-eighty!"

"Easy. Let's get the basics down first. Then the cool moves."

They lunched at one of their favorite places in the little river town. Madigan's boosted a large outdoor deck and on the weekends was normally crowded with boaters, tourists, and a heavy dose of local day drinkers. Bands played on the deck and inside as well. However, the weather began to turn as soon as they arrived, and the activity level dropped rapidly as people scurried for shelter. He and John still enjoyed lunch, watching the rain dance upon the water. The outdoor dining area was covered, and the little moisture that found its way inside only provided relief from the hot weather. This was the first time

Dane felt any peace in weeks, and the first time he didn't feel anxious.

After lunch, during the ride back to D.C., Dane let John know that he had to drop him off around noon on Sunday since he had a meeting. A work thing.

"Dad, that is totally fine. I am exhausted from last night. Let's just chill out. Stay up late and sleep in late. You remember Kevin from school?"

Dane nodded.

"For his birthday we went to this cool place out in Winchester. It was night paintball and it was so cool."

He enjoyed listening to John's recap of the night's adventure. The dimly lit playing field, shacks scattered about for cover and eerie music playing from speakers mounted throughout the woods. The kids were all issued some type of black mechanics overalls so as to blend in with the night and keep their street clothes clean.

"And the paintball guns. They had these little visible red lasers on them for aiming. They were pretty accurate. I shot Scott Preston right in the butt! It was hilarious. He said it hurt to sit down later when we had pizza in this gazebo thing when it was all over. Everyone was laughing like crazy."

Dane laughed to himself, *"Sound's like fun."*

"Think we could go sometime?"

"Hell yeah," Dane responded, *"I can shoot you right in the butt."*

They both laughed.

"So, what do you feel like doing tonight?" Dane asked his son.

"I was hoping we could hang out, watch some action movies and pig out on pizza. I have run around enough. I am whooped. Oh, and the rocket launch is tonight. Jackson Lentz's company Jupiter's Moon is taking a bunch of civilians up for a ride. Also, there is a movie I want to watch. Have you ever seen Man on Fire? Mom won't let me watch it, but I checked, and it is on regular TV so it shouldn't be all R rated and stuff."

"Sounds like a plan, son."

Later that evening, Dane watched as the boy's attention was glued to the TV. John had talked non-stop on the car ride home about the launch. *"That will be me someday, dad. I was thinking about the Air Force and possibly a career later with NASA. I know they just started that whole Space Force thing, but it doesn't seem like they are really going to do anything with space. I mean, go up there. It sounds like they are just going to concentrate on the satellites and stuff while the Air Force trains pilots. Mom doesn't want me talking to a recruiter until I am at least seventeen. What do you think Dad? I know you're going to say,"* mimicking Dane's voice *"it's not the Army."*

"Was that supposed to be me? Horrible impression."

"But dad, the Army doesn't seem to be going up in space anytime soon."

Dane groaned. Well at least he wasn't thinking about joining Space Force, he thought to himself. However, Air Force was not much better.... Ugg. *"Funny guy, huh, but in all seriousness, there is nothing you can't do John, if you put your mind to it. And your mom is right. Look at all your options before you choose. Just enjoy being a kid for now."*

"And now we want to check in with our man on the ground, Andrew Newton, as we near launch time. Andrew is covering the fifth historic launch for Mr. Jackson Lentz's Jupiter's Moon company. Over to you Andrew."

"Thanks Eric and Joyce. I am here in Pecos City Texas and you can feel the excitement in the air. The final countdown for launch will begin shortly. A historic crowd is in attendance and the clapping and cheering are deafening as I am sure you can hear in the background. The crews have been loaded and the remaining safety checks are being finalized. This is the fifth launch by Mr. Lentz's Jupiter's Moon Corporation, and everyone is excited as seven more people join the ranks of astronaut. The launch will take them out of the earth's atmosphere where they will spend twenty minutes in space before their return. During that time, they will experience zero gravity and witness the earth like few others have.

Preparations have been made for a gentle landing and recovery, about ten miles off the western Florida coast. The U.S. Navy and Coast Guard are both standing by to assist Mr. Lentz's crews if necessary. I will continue to provide updates as we near launch time which should be in about another ten minutes. Back to you guys in the studio."

"Thanks Andrew. We will cut back to you as soon as the final countdown commences. Exciting times Eric. Exciting times."

"In other news, we have been following the tragic disappearance of little Dana Chase from Reston. Her school held a vigil this Friday to remember and pray for their fellow student who has now been missing for nearly two months. The Reston police remain vigilant with the assistance from the State and Federal authorities. You can see her picture here on our screen. The authorities continue to scour the area for any signs of this poor little girl. If you have any information please call the hotline number on the screen."

"Just tragic Eric. It breaks my heart."

"It is terrible Joyce. I cannot even imagine what that poor family has been through."

Dane's gaze was fixated on the television until they went to a commercial. It slowly traversed the room until finally resting on the boy's enquiring stare. *"You okay, Dad?"*

"*I am*," he replied snapping out of his trance. "*I know we don't talk about it much. How are you holding up?*"

"*It gets better every day but, I really do miss her. I see things like this on the news and just can't understand how something like this can keep happening over and over again. Why don't the police stop these guys?*"

"*Unfortunately, as you get older you are going to see the ugly side of humanity son. There are a lot of really good people out there, but there are also some really bad ones. The police can only do so much. There are a lot of Americans out there and not enough cops.*"

"*I get it dad. Just frustrating and sorry about the movie earlier. I didn't even think before I suggested we watch it. I forgot it was about a kidnapping.*"

"*John. It is a really good movie. Angela is always on my mind but all we can do is hope and pray she is returned to us safely one day. I... We can't spend every waking moment in sorrow. We will always remember her but we need to live our lives. Did you like the movie?*"

"*I thought it was awesome. I mean, her being kidnapped and he thought she was dead and then he tracks down all those guys. He killed every single one of those guys. He did it in some wicked ways too. That one guy with the bomb in his a.... butt. Creasy went medieval on them, but he never seemed to lose his cool. It was a pretty good story. I have heard stories about a lot of kidnappings in Mexico, but that was crazy.*"

"Do you think he would have done all that if he thought she was alive? Would he have tried to negotiate, maybe, instead of killing them?"

"I don't think that would have worked dad. Those guys were pretty bad. They didn't seem like they were going to just give up. Plus, they really didn't seem to know if she was dead or alive. They didn't seem to care. They probably wouldn't have acted any differently."

"So, you think he was justified in what he did to all those guys? Killing them?"

"Absolutely Dad. Look at what they did. The police were even in on it. Creasy had to get justice for Pita. Nobody else was going to."

"Ok, enough of this serious talk. Let's get back to that launch."

"Eric and Joyce. The countdown has begun. 10, 9, 8, 7......"

Feeling refreshed, Dane got out of bed the next morning and made his way into the kitchen. John was sprawled across the couch, foregoing the small bed in the corner he had prepared. He could hardly believe that it was nearly ten o'clock. He felt great. No hangover, no lingering dreams. Nothing. First time in a long time. John began to stir as he prepared breakfast for the two of them. Sometimes they would venture out to one of the local greasy diners, but more often than not, Dane liked to cook a big breakfast. He had lost the cooking bug he used to contain, but spending days with John would renew his spirit temporarily. He didn't spend nearly enough time with the boy. Not entirely his fault since John was growing into a young adult and was doing so much. Between school, sports, and a part-time job, he wondered how he found time for all of it. But then he remembered being that age once. The energy was limitless. Hah, he could use some of that nowadays.

They climbed into the truck for the trek back to Manassas. John was still half-asleep, probably due to the enormous breakfast. But that was fine. Dane was already thinking ahead to his meeting later today. The mysterious president and his secret club. At times he thought the whole thing sounded ridiculous. A bunch of dads' running around playing judge, jury and executioner. Hah. Over the hill heroes. They would be lucky to avoid a heart attack. But then again... why not?

Jenny was waiting for them when Dane pulled up the drive. Both of them jumped out of the truck, and he threw John his duffel from the rear bed. After a quick hug and thank you, John bounded up into the house hugging his mother on the way in the door. *"I see your other relic is also still running,"* she said as she indicated toward the truck.

"This old truck hasn't let me down yet."

"Sorry I didn't come out the other day. I felt like crap. Double shift at the hospital and I was completely drained. It was all I could do to keep my eyes open on the way home. One glass of wine and I was out for the night."

"No worries. I get it."

"I talked to Tyler the other day. Just so you know. I am not snooping... just worried. He said you guys had a pretty good talk the other day and I am sorry about the whole funeral thing Dane. It is just...I think we all need some sort of closure."

"I get it. I really do. Tyler mentioned it as well. I just feel like having a funeral is letting go. And I am not ready to let go."

"I understand that. I really do. I will not push anything right now. You let me know when you are ready. However, at some point, we need to start the healing. I think that starts with acceptance. The funeral is that acceptance. I am still holding out hope Dane. Please, don't think I am giving up. I will always dream of her walking back through that door. But we need to heal. We need to help John heal. I pray the police or whoever finds her. However, for right now, it is out of our hands."

That is not entirely true," Dane thought.

CHAPTER 9: A NEW CASE

Arlington, VA

"Preliminary reports are coming in from Camp's house, Roger. It is looking like a real shit-show over there."

"What did they find so far?" Roger asked from across the desk. The two agents shared a space in the PIT that was claimed by two large desks pushed together so they could collaborate face-to-face on cases. The entire section of Violent Crimes was referred to as the PIT, short for Pit of Misery, and although the pair focused primarily on crimes against children, they discussed all violent crimes with other sections. They never knew when one case could be tied to another. There were about forty agents that shared the space on a regular basis. It was an open floor design horribly mutated by generous amounts of cubicle dividers. They did serve their purpose of blocking some of the noise that inevitably carried across a room shared by so many people. Roger's seniority provided him with ample space and a prime location in the back corner of the room. Space Patricia was grateful for since her rank did not bring such privileges. Besides the two desks, they had managed to scrounge up several dry-erase boards, and the cubicle walls provided plenty of surface for pushpin décor in the form of bulletins, photos, case sketches, etc. Each portion of the wall represented a current open case. There were five.

Patricia had the phone to her ear as she took notes with her free hand and read them back occasionally to the caller to confirm accuracy, and more importantly keep her partner abreast of the situation. The lead detective on site at Camp's residence was an old friend. Even though he would write an official report later, he provided a once-over-the-world in case the initial evidence pointed toward another active or time-sensitive case.

Patricia spoke and scribbled at the same time. "*What did you say he was doing in the park? Masturbating? You mean when the medical examiner moved him you could see his hands? To pictures on his phone? That's disgusting. We saw the phone on the floorboard but we didn't move or disturb it. Clothes? What kind of clothes?*"

"*Ask about gender,*" Roger said quietly, now beginning to write his own short-hand notes.

"*Male and female, huh,*" Stills continued. "*What else Don? Oh, that would make sense. He had access to the locker rooms and keys to all sorts of shit.*"

She covered the mouthpiece briefly and said to Roger, "*They found lots of undergarments in a box in his basement. Small closet that seemed to be his private place to uh... enjoy his trophies. Elementary age kids' clothes. Boys and girls. They think he was stealing them from lockers while the kids were in gym.*" She removed her hand and continued the conversation. "*And printed out photos on the walls? Are guys over at the school he worked at?*"

"Suicide note, cutters, piping," Roger whispered.

"What about indicators for suicide? Oh... Ok... No, it's fine. Thanks for the update," Patricia said as she hung up the phone. *"He had to run. We will get a full copy of the report. This guy was much worse than we thought."*

Roger groaned. *"Let's hear it."*

"First thing was all the clothes and pictures. The pictures were clearly taken through holes in the wall. You could see the edges in the pictures, so he obviously had no formal training or high-end lenses. Almost all the photos were found on his cell phone. Guy's not too good with a camera. He would then email certain ones to himself, and he could print them out at home. They are cataloging the photos now since they are not sure why he printed those particular shots."

"Potential victims I would assume."

"Agree with you there," she responded. *"Don is heading over to the school now to meet with the team there. Also, get this... Arthur Camp isn't the only janitor that didn't show up at work today. Another Janitor, a,"* she glanced at her notes. *"David Bell. Working there for about three weeks and then nothing. Gone. No notice. Staff said he was quiet and kept to himself. He never caused any trouble or issues. But it was strange as how he, and I am quoting here, 'he wasn't the janitor type' end quote. That came from the assistant principal to the first officer on scene at the school. Claimed Bell did his job, kept to himself, and never caused any sort of trouble but he*

just stood out as a fish out of water. They are going to conduct a more thorough interview later today with supervisors who had direct or indirect daily contact with Bell."

"Do they have any sort of preliminary theories? Is this guy part of this whole thing?" Roger asked.

"They are not sure about this Bell guy. May be nothing. I think Bell is just one of those coincidences. Probably nothing more than a drifter, working when he has to, and moving on when he can, but crime scene guys are finding a lot of DNA samples in Camp's house. They will eventually need to rule Bell out if some sort of history comes back on him that warrants digging. If he is in any of the databases and they get a hit, he will definitely move up the list for questioning. Right now, they are concentrating first on processing both scenes. The house and the school."

Both agents paused for a second in thought as if a necessary moment of silence was warranted based on those gruesome details. It was Roger who broke the silence. *"So, do they think he moved past peeping and may have started bringing kids home?"*

Patricia nodded. *"It is a distinct possibility but too early to tell."*

"How about a suicide note?"

"They have not found a note so far, but they did find tubing that matched the stuff at the scene and some cutters thrown on a shelf in the garage. It looks like he got everything ready at the house and then drove out to the park. And get this, he had been suspended last week from the school and was supposed to turn in his badge this

week. Apparently, a fresh batch of complaints found a principal finally willing to stand up for the kids. Principal contacted the local PD and was supposed to have a follow-up with them a few days ago. The PD wanted to talk to Camp, but like I said, he never showed up, and never surrendered his badge. He disappeared and now this. So far, a canvassing of the neighborhood hasn't turned up a thing. Suicide is looking really strong right now."

"Let's see where the evidence goes, Pat. I do agree with the theory. Suicide is the strongest one so far. However, they need to go down every rabbit hole. What do they need from us?"

"Let's head over to the school. Don liked the tubing angle we brought up at the park. Even though it didn't add up to an obvious involvement of somebody else, he liked our perspective. And if this Bell guy is anything but a coincidence, we may see something that ties him in."

Both agents began to pack up their things to head over to the school when this time, it was Roger's phone that rang. *"Special Agent Patterson, BCI."* He listened for a moment as Patricia slowly sat down recognizing her partner's body language, indicating that this was an important call.

"Ok, listen, can I call you back in five minutes? I would like to call from a private conference room. Lots of noise here and I want my partner to be on the call. Ok, great," Roger hung up as he finished scribbling down the number.

In answer to Patricia's look, he continued, "*That was the Pennsylvania State Police. They had a girl taken recently. They heard about the Dana Chase case. From an initial glance, they think theirs is very similar to ours. Grab the file and meet me in the Grady conference room. I am just going to let the Captain know. Oh, and grab Cooper's jacket also.*"

"*So, what we have is the disappearance of Holly Jones,*" the Pennsylvania State Trooper's voice relayed over the conference line. "*Thirteen years old. Last seen in Marsh Creek State Park just outside of Glenmore. You guys are probably not familiar with Glenmore. It is west of Philly off Interstate seventy-six. The Pennsylvania Turnpike. Similar to the Chase case you have down there. Out walking her dog in the morning. Very normal routine. Parents thought nothing of it. She does it all the time. The park has a lot of walking trails, all accessible from the surrounding neighborhoods. Middle-class subdivision. Low crime rate. Holly's routine was to walk along the trails and stop at the dog park. It wasn't crowded that morning, but at least one witness confirmed she stopped by the park. Gave us a basic direction she walked when she left. Then nothing. Girl and dog were just gone.*"

"*I agree that they are similar. Dana was twelve.*" Patricia flipped through the case file while Roger read through the basic details from his notes. "*She was walking her dog in Baron Cameron Park here in Reston. It's about twenty miles west of D.C. Same thing. Hiking trails. Small dog park. She was seen in the park by a few people but after that, both she and the dog vanished. She has been missing for nearly two months. We turned that park upside down. Pulled any camera footage we could find, talked to anybody that may have been in the area. Still came up with nothing."*

"What about the Cooper case? That is about a year old, right? Any similarities beyond what we saw on the news?"

This time it was Patricia that answered. *"The two cases are very similar, and we have compared them both extensively. Angela Cooper leaves her home in the morning to walk her dog in the park. Very routine. Heads into the hiking trails and is never seen again. She went missing from Burke Lake Park. Probably about twenty to thirty minutes from where Chase was abducted. The major difference is no dog park there and nobody came forward claiming to have seen her in the park. Once she left her street toward the trails through the woods, she simply disappeared."*

"A lot of similarities but nothing concrete to tie them together. We are not exactly close neighbors, but close enough. There may be something. We have absolutely no leads. I can send you a copy of what we have and if you can do the same with the Cooper and Chase case files, maybe something will jump out at one of us. We know this is a stretch, but something feels off. Like we are chasing the same ghost."

With the call disconnected, the conference room was silent. Both agents, deep in thought, stared at their notes. They eventually rose and headed back to their space, grabbing a lousy cup of lukewarm coffee on the way. *"What are you thinking Roger?"*

"I am having a hard time putting the pieces together. All these cases seem similar but then again, we really have nothing to go on. We have almost zero evidence."

"True."

"But maybe that is what does tie them together."

"What do you mean?" she asked.

"The scenes are too clean. We have worked way too many of these cases. And me a few more than you due to my age. I have never seen so little evidence. This abduction was textbook. It was methodical. Planned to a tee. So, what is that really telling us?"

"So, you think it is the same person? "

"Person, or persons."

"Persons, Roger? I have never heard of such a thing. But not out of the realm of possibility."

Roger continued his train of thought. *"I am brainstorming here Pat but look at the facts so far. Normally these assholes fall into one of three categories. Well, loose categories. Right? It is someone in the family, an acquaintance, or a complete stranger."*

Pat was looking through her notes. *"Neither Chase or the Coopers really even had any family to investigate. And the little family they did have, lived far away with airtight alibis."*

"True and remember, molesters who are family almost never kidnap. Right? They are compulsive about the abuse but rarely take it a step further and actually abduct the child. Where would they go? No need. They have continued access without anyone knowing and want to keep it that way. Threaten the children into not talking, etc. The next is an acquaintance."

"Ok, but we ruled out anybody close to the families."

"Yes and no," he responded. *"We ruled out those that we know about, or at least the list of names the families provided in the interviews. I would say it is safe to pause on that angle, but we still can't rule it out."*

"So, we are talking about a complete stranger, and we are probably dealing with a highly intelligent person. They committed the abduction with virtually no evidence. This was not spur of the moment."

"And remember Pat, he or she... let's just say he for ease here since this is typically a male crime.... he has also successfully concealed one or more additional crimes. If the children are deceased, the bodies have yet to be found. Unfortunately, they may never be found. Or this psychopath still has one or more of these children and has been able to escape detection. Extremely rare but it has happened."

Back in the PIT, Patricia began to furiously scribble on the reversible dry erase board they had along one wall of their cramped space. The whiteboards were a recent addition, something the department could apparently afford. They must have been cheaper than windshield wipers. Previously, she had to endure the countless reams of butcher block Roger had preferred. A reminisce of his early Army days, the paper stands were an antiquated system of flipping huge sheets of paper on a free-standing easel before the day when anybody cared about the decimation of the Rain Forest. Today's technology provided smartboards that even interface with computers in order to capture digital notes. Roger knew the new systems were more efficient, cost-effective, and all that crap. But he secretly still kept all his old easel notes safely stored and preserved in his home basement.

"Ok, Roger, let's map this theory of yours. Multiple perps working together."

"Easy Pat. I was just talking through scenarios. Looking at it from all angles. I never said I had a theory about multiple kidnappers working together. Just threw it out that the cases were similar and if it wasn't the same guy, then it could be different guys with the same MO."

"Exactly, but you may have something here worth exploring further." The excitement in her voice grew. Pat was writing on the board. When she stepped back, there were three names written across the top. Charles Clancy, Jimmy Gatter, and Sam Mitchell. Underneath, she had written city and state and a single number on the third and final line. *"In the academy, I wrote my thesis about serial killers and linkage. You know, how they may have influenced each other. Copycats, and stuff like that. These are three*

different killers across several decades. There are more but these are the first three off the top of my head. Clancy in Chicago killed fourteen. Gatter in Fort Lauderdale killed four. And Mitchell killed six in Cleveland. Do you know what they all had in common?" Roger shrugged realizing that he had always studied the here and now and didn't really look to the past for answers in the present, unless it affected a case directly. He recognized the names but he was never a student of serial killers. He was curious about where this was going.

"All three were either mentors or mentees of other serial killers. Technology was different at all these junctures but the bottom line is that they communicated with others in a variety of ways. Charles Clancy studied the police reports from H.H. Holmes in Chicago. Holmes was one of the first recorded serial killers in America. He had at least fifty murders. Many actually believe it may be double that number. He would skin his victims and then sell the skeletons to medical colleges. Sick. Had something like three wives. Built that murder hotel. This was going on around the time of the world fair in Chicago at the turn of the century."

She continued, *"Erik Larsen wrote a historical fiction book about him,* ***The Devil in the White City****. Good book, by the way. There is plenty of evidence that he shared his techniques with Charles. In person. The next guy. Gatter. He was in prison with Ted Bundy. Somehow, they found a way to have contact in maximum lockup. He had asked Bundy how to select victims and Bundy has passed him a newspaper article with the personal ads circled. That was how Bundy found some of his victims. He theorized that since they were* *single it was much more likely they lived alone. Gatter was doing time for manslaughter but was eventually released. He was obsessed with the Bundy killings and would go on to kill four women before he was caught. He was using the same technique. They found articles and news clipping all over his apartment. And the last one? He followed two different sickos in Ohio in the early 2000s. Madison and Swell. Remember those two? Sam Mitchell followed their lead and killed six women himself. Rumors were that he was in contact with both Madison and Swell during his killing spree which coincided with their murder timeframes. There are others duos over the last several decades that had the same urges. The same sense of purpose. Deranged, but purpose nonetheless."*

"And you think this somehow applies to the kidnappers and molesters we may be dealing with now?" Roger stared at the board as Patricia scribbled facts about each killer.

"I am obviously no psychologist, but these murderers were abducting woman for the most part. Abductors. They did it for sexual gratification. Sadism. Because they hated their mothers or fathers. Whatever. They were psychos. So are our possible suspect or suspects. They have the same impulses, which are clearly not acceptable to society, hell, even worse since it involves kids. Even some criminals have standards. So, they must keep these impulses hidden or at least close hold. But they want to share with like-minded individuals. With the internet these days and the so-called dark web. Shit. Communication would probably be easier than in the past between serial killers. The only difference between our possible guys? Sexual attraction." She pointed to the board. *"These*

animals like woman and some men. They communicated on police tactics. Hunting grounds. Disposal methods. Places to avoid. All of that. Our possible suspects? Same thing. Same mentality. Same desires. Same impulses. Just different sexual preference."

Fixer: *It is done.*
President: *No trace?*
Fixer: *Clean. Nobody will suspect anything.*
President: *Excellent.*

CHAPTER 10: THE OFFER

Arlington, VA

Dane stepped from the backseat of the aging Prius. The afternoon was surprisingly cool due to the recent storms, which had finally tapered off. His appointment was in about twenty minutes. Plenty of time to cover the remaining distance on foot and possibly spot anything out of the ordinary. Of course, everything in this neighborhood was far from ordinary. The Bellevue Forest neighborhood screamed of money with its flowing lawns and manicured landscaping. These were the homes of the rich, and those with power. Not necessarily physical power or a position such as a Senator, Judge, or CEO, but the people behind the scenes pulling the strings. The consultants, the advisors, the aide-de-camps. It was hard to imagine that some sort of society of assassins, or whatever they were, called this neighborhood home. Dane knew of the area from previous passes through but could not fathom the scope of these dwellings. Crazy.

The address was clearly marked on the gatehouse at the end of the drive. The post long abandoned in exchange for current technology, the guard was now an electronic squawk box that interrogated visitors. After a quick exchange, the pedestrian gate at the side of the stone booth clicked open. After passing through, the robot master slowly shut the gate behind him. Dane continued up the long drive toward what could only be referred to as an estate. Well, he thought to himself. It does kinda look like Wayne Manor from all those Batman movies. This could be the real deal. The driveway was at least fifty meters long, with the main dwelling set back far from the prying eyes of anyone. A scattering of other structures was partially visible through the thick tree line. *Sheds? Small cottages?* He really couldn't tell. There was at least one barn.

Once on the porch, the front door was opened before he even had a chance to rap the ornate knocker centered on the wooden door. *"Good afternoon, Mr. Cooper. My name is Jack. Please follow me. Mr. Thornton is waiting for you in his study."* Dane followed the man into the house.

Jack did not seem at all interested in chit-chat, so he kept to himself as he studied his surroundings. He had been in many wealthy estates over his career, and he normally found one of two designs. The first was what he called modern crap. Those were the homes with all the fancy art-deco stuff. Everything was ornate. Golden statures. Expressionist art on the walls that looked like they were painted by a three-year-old rather than some thirty-year-old starving artist who painted in the nude with only his left foot. Those types of art somehow fell into the six figures price range. Nearly all these owners also had some sort of miniature designer dog in the house that was either biting at your ankles or secured in someone's purse. Everything was painted gold. The second type of design was the wannabe hunter's home. Everything was deep shades of brown. Wood covered nearly all the walls, and any available open space showcased grand oil paintings depicting some dude on a horse in the woods with his hunting dog scrambling around the hooves of his steed. Each room had some strange animal fur rug like a polar bear or zebra. There would be a huge dog living here. Some sort of exotic European breed designed to hunt polar bear and elephants or some crap. People with money did strange things.

However, Mr. Thornton's home was that rare third category that Dane thoroughly enjoyed. The entire space felt like one big smoking lounge nestled in a massive library. Not cigarettes. He could envision men lighting up pipes with sweet tobacco or giant cigars, reclining in one of the overstuffed chairs, cracking a book about the Battle of the Bulge with a roaring fire, the only sound emanating throughout the home. It was a house of study and reflection. It was comforting. Once through the front great home, they passed a large stone kitchen. It was larger than his entire apartment. Probably about three times larger. You could feed a small army in here. A large oak table was the centerpiece, capable of seating at least sixteen people. Probably more. He was aware that his mouth was agape. Thankfully, Jack had not once turned until he reached the study door and opened it for him. As Dane passed through, he heard, *"Please bring up some coffee, Jack,"* as the door was gently shut behind him.

Dane paused as he took in the room. The study had shelves from floor to ceiling encircling both main walls, with an alcove at the far end constructed of nothing but wrought iron and glass. Several more, large leather couches and chairs, like those in the front room, were scattered about the vast space creating various seating areas to facilitate simultaneous small group meetings. The room's only occupant rose and moved to meet him halfway across the enormous space.

"Charles Thornton. Thank you for agreeing to meet with me, Mr. Cooper," he said as he extended his hand. Dane accepted the greeting and studied the man for a moment. Charles Thornton was a fit man, probably somewhere in his mid to late sixties. He couldn't have stood over five foot six, but somehow had a commanding presence. His dialect betrayed a slight Southern drawl, and his composure screamed Southern aristocrat. It was his eyes that were the most striking. They were a bright blue and Dane felt them searching his very soul.

"Are you from Georgia, sir?" he asked.

"Good catch. Savannah but that was a long time ago. I am not surprised that you recognized the slight drawl despite my best attempts to suppress it over the years. You did of course spend nearly six years in Savannah yourself."

He was slightly taken aback. *"Relax Mr. Cooper. Please come sit. We have much to talk about."*

After they were both settled, Charles began. *"I spoke with Andrew. My recruiter. He told me you had an encouraging conversation. I know he gave you very generic information and I am sure you would like to know more."*

Dane simply nodded. He had mentally prepped for this meeting and decided that he was going to play his cards close and do more listening than talking. He thought, *I don't need to tell these guys everything.*

Charles retrieved a large folder from the table at his side. He slipped a pair of reading glasses from his breast pocket as he opened the loose pages. He began to read in a dead even tone as though he were a parent attempting to soothe a child before bed with a story.

"Mr. Dane Cooper. Born and raised in the Boston metro area. Graduated from the University of Boston and married Ms. Jennifer Harken. She was a nursing major and you seemed to bounce around finally settling on history. Shortly thereafter, you enlisted in the Army and were whisked away to basic training at the ever-popular Fort Benning School for Boys. Your drill sergeants saw something in you. They offered you a chance to try out for the Rangers instead of heading off to some infantry unit. You accepted and headed to Airborne School and then Ranger indoctrination upon graduation."

Dane was a little unsettled, but his basic bio was certainly available to anyone with fifteen minutes and a Wi-Fi connection.

"Indoctrination. Funny that they used to call it that. Sounds like a cult. Well, it says here you did all the Ranger things, moved up the chain of command, took more and more responsibility, etc. Squad Leader, Platoon Sergeant. You conducted two deployments after our nation was attacked, conducting operations in Afghanistan and

Iraq. Two Bronze stars for meritorious actions. One for each theater. Your men loved you. Not to mention your superiors. All your evaluation reports here are top-notch. Also, two children along the way, Johnathan and Angela. Very impressive." Charles paused there.

"Is that what you are interested in? My Ranger career? That was a long time ago. I was much younger than," Dane sarcastically asked.

"Not exactly. Your earlier career is a solid base. A launching point for the second half of your military service to this nation. You checked all the right boxes. Passed all the tests if you would. It was when you decided to attend selection and after successfully completing that hellacious course, to begin your illustrious career as an operative for the unit that captured my attention. Conducting those terminations, for lack of a better term"

This time, Dane's jaw did hit the floor. Apart from many thoughts and questions that wandered his mind, some were screaming for answers. *How the hell does he know all that? What else does he know?*

"Shall I continue?" Charles began to read again. "It appears you made a few more trips into Iraq. Well, Kurdistan to be more exact. Rubbing elbows with Kurdish, it seems. During the first stint, you were hunting a particular Al Qaeda bomb maker. Removed him from the chessboard, I see. Second time around, it was an ISIS leader that needed attending to. It seems you and the Peshmerga, along with some other American associates, were quite successful during

that operation as well. What is really interesting to me and us, is your work in Africa. Same enemy as you saw in Iraq and Afghanistan, but it was a different environment. You were a gentleman soldier. Working with statesmen and military leaders alike. I was especially impressed with Somalia. Nobody ever really knew that you and Mr. Johnson were working with the Isaaq clan leader, Awad Mohamad Abduwali. I always found the family lineage fascinating. Their name, their father's first name, followed by their grandfather's first name. I personally never did like it when people named their kids after themselves. Seems pretentious."

Looking back at the file he continued, *"And then we have Mali. What a disaster. Very unfortunate that the military decided to remove the legitimate government. Right before elections. AQIM certainly stirred up a hornet's nest, getting the Tuaregs' blood boiling. As you probably know, the country is still a mess. The French are trying to intervene, which is probably just making it worse. Hopefully, your friend, Mr. Oumer, will be able to come home and fix it one day."*

"You are reading and alluding to quite a bit of classified information, Mr. Thornton. Where are you getting all this from?"

"I am well aware of the fact, Mr. Cooper. My associate the Colonel, was kind enough to provide the details. We wanted to ensure we were approaching the right kind of person for this club."

"I still do not know what the hell this club really is, and I really don't appreciate all the cloak and dagger. Can you please just get to the point?"

There was a slight knock on the door, and Jack entered with a tray. He placed the carafe and two cups between the men. When he offered cream and sugar to be left behind, Charles thanked him, *"It is fine Jack. Mr. Cooper takes his coffee black, but every so often he enjoys just a hint of agave, which, unfortunately, we do not have on hand at the moment."*

"I guess I really shouldn't be surprised by anything at this point," Dane remarked as Jack exited the study.

"We are thorough in our research." Charles placed the closed folder back to its original location and turned his attention to the refreshments. He poured each man a healthy cup. He retrieved his, settling back into his chair, indicating that he would continue the bedtime story. *"What would you say if I told you that our current criminal justice system in this country is antiquated, corrupt, and incapable of responding to the current human threats that our forefathers could not have ever conceived of when they wrote our constitution?"*

"I would agree with you. I have traveled all over the world on paid vacations, courtesy of Uncle Sam. I have seen inhumane abuse. I have seen criminals beheaded. Subjected to a loss of limb without even a shred of evidence, they had committed a crime. Then I have seen the exact opposite. A complete breakdown of any semblance of a system. Some real Mad Max type of stuff. No laws and absolutely no enforcement. The powerful continue to seize whatever they want, while the poor eke out a miserable existence. Our system is far from perfect, but it is far better than anything else out there. Our Constitution has stood the test of time. So, I would argue it is our

laws and the way we enforce, or rather not enforce, that is the real problem."

"Exactly. Far from perfect, our system does at least yearn for equality and justice. It just falls short sometimes and quite frankly it fails when it comes to protecting our most important citizens. Children. One could argue that we actually suffer from too many laws trying to preserve this right or that right. It seems criminals have more protection under the law than the law-abiding society they hid among and that is where we come in."

"How exactly do you accomplish what the cops, the feds, hell, even investigative journalists, are unable to do? With all their combined resources, they still can't stop these animals. It seems to get worse every passing minute."

"I will answer your second question first. We actually are very well resourced. I would argue better when it comes to a specific task. Our benefactor is quite generous. The police receive an annual budget, correct? Well, that entire budget gets spread over a million different categories. First, you have all the other crimes they must address. Then you have the overhead. Cars, offices, radios, and equipment that exhaust quite a large chunk of the money. Lastly, you have human capital. Salaries, health care, dental, retirement, I could go on and on, but those are the largest costs. Therefore, all that money is spent and not for fighting child predators but for all criminals. They must police the prostitute on the corner as well as the drug king importing fentanyl into our neighborhoods. We have the luxury of a single focus. And we have free labor. Motivated individuals. I am by no means accusing the police of not being vested

in their work. Far from it. But our people have a stronger motivation to succeed."

Dane found himself nodding in silent agreement with Charles.

"And to your first question. We can do this where others cannot, for the simple fact that those three examples you provided don't work well together, and they must focus on other tasks. There is also blatant distrust among those groups. The local police fear the federal officers will try to take control of an investigation. The federal officers feel intellectually superior at times to the locals and fear that they will make mistakes. Journalists attack them both for the slightest misstep. And nobody trusts the media. Our members have a single focus. One. Plus, we come from all different walks of life. Businessmen like Arthur. Ex-soldiers like Jack. We have judges, police, military, accountants, and even a florist. We bring talent together and focus on one single problem. Different perspectives from different walks of life. All of our members have lost a child, which provides that single focus. They all play a role. And there is no small role."

"I am assuming this is the part of the interview where I get to ask you questions."

Charles provided the simplest of nods.

"My first is how do you stay off the radar? You can't exactly go around killing people and rescuing children without someone noticing. If you have this many people working on cases, how do you

keep a certain degree of separation. For instance, what if someone gets arrested? How do you know it won't link back to you? To me?"

"First, we do not just go around killing people. At times we do remove chess pieces from the board. When we do that, it is with methodical planning to obscure the actual cause of death. If death is even necessary, sometimes it is not. I believe you have expressed a desire to see some of these men rot for the rest of their lives in a cage."

Who are these people? How are they getting all this information? They have people everywhere, thought Dane.

"We also have a very compartmented system in place. We communicate as little as possible. Decentralized control. Something I believe you are familiar with in Special Operations. We also don't know each other."

"Don't know each other. I know you are Charles. I know he is Jack," Dane said as he indicated toward the other side of the door. Hell, I even met Andrew."

"And those are the last people you are likely to meet unless absolutely necessary. At least officially and by name. We all work together, but all communication goes through me and Jack. We are the only two with the full knowledge of members. Everyone else goes by their codename. You never met the Scout, but that person reported to me about you. You never met our Spotter. Surveillance expert. How do you think Andrew was able to find you in the city? And you will never meet the Colonel," he added, touching the

folder on the table as a reminder to Dane of the depth of the organization and its access to sensitive information. *"But you will work together, and you probably won't even know it. You need a piece of equipment? It will be provided for you at a secure location. Information. Your assistance will be a digital ghost. It goes both ways."*

"So, nobody will know about me? Just you and Jack. Oh, and Andrew. So, what happens when Andrew gets pinched and is going to talk?"

"Jack will take care of it."

"If you talk?"

"Jack, once again."

"And since he seems a man of few words, am I to assume Jack won't ever talk?"

This time Charles simply nodded. He studied Dane as if trying to read his mind. *"What I am offering you are resources beyond your comprehension. Resources even the state and federal police do not possess. By combining our efforts, we are able to solve many of these problems."*

"So where do we go from here? What do you need me to do?"

"You will track these monsters down. You will assist others to come in to eliminate them but, you will have to be prepared to strike

as well. Your role will be as a Shadow. A sort of Deimos if you would."

"The Greek God of fear and terror? It has a nice ring to it. Let me ask you. Have you rescued any children?"

"Yes."

"How many."

"Fifteen thus far."

"Did you have the sickos arrested?"

"We ensured the authorities were notified most of the time."

"What about the other times?"

"We punished."

CHAPTER 11: THREE WEEKS LATER

Washington, D.C.

Pupil: *Are you there?*

Keeper: *Yes.*

Pupil: *I have to get rid of one.*

Keeper: *The more you have, the more responsibility.*

Pupil: *I am trying. This is hard.*

Keeper: *Practice makes perfect. You can always try again, be careful.*

The light recoil pushed back predictably against his shoulder as he settled the optic back on the target after his first shot. The rifle was sleek and practically weightless in his hands. It had been his faithful companion on many missions. Once the carbine's magazine went dry, he dumped the weapon to his left side, letting the sling take over as he drew his sidearm from the holster on his right hip. Two shots rang out before he even extended his arms to a full bracing position. Thirteen more shots rang out. It was at this point a decision had to be made. Which weapon do you reload first? Opinions vary, but the general consensus is to reload the pistol if the target is still a threat. Reload the rifle when you have a pause. Either way, the paper silhouette out at twenty meters was not shooting back today. He quickly reloaded the pistol from the ammo pouch on his left hip, reacquired the target, and then cleared and holstered the Glock. That was enough for today.

Dane depressed the retrieve button on the range control panel to bring the target to his station. His noise-cancelling muffs reduced sound to a minimum but couldn't completely drown out all the shots of his teammates, duplicating his efforts. All ten shooting lanes were in use this morning. God, it felt good to be back on the range. I haven't shot in forever.

The unit's range was unlike any shooting establishment in the civilian world. Not due to its state of the art equipment or ungodly distances to shoot. It was only fifty meters in length that you could find at nearly any range, and it tended to get smoky with too much use due to a filtration part on backorder. Its uniqueness was due to the professionals utilizing the space and the complete lack of interference from staff or other shooters. That is not to say civilian ranges were unprofessional. They simply had a different purpose. They had standards and processes for safety designed to encompass first-time gun owners as well as lifelong enthusiasts. The patrons ranged from competitive shooters to casual gun owners to students in gun safety classes desiring to learn. They acted professionally but were there for one single purpose. Sport shooting.

That type of shooting required quite of bit of safety oversight. Dane's peers were with him on the range for work. They practiced drills, checked and re-checked sight zeros, and adjusted gun belts and kit to ensure maximum effectiveness on the battlefield. They used concealed holsters and a variety of pistols. And rifles. This was more than sport shooting which several of the guys did in their spare time. No. Time here was work. As George Patton had once supposedly said, the object of war was not to die for your country but to make the other bastard die for his. Dane had been to civilian ranges where he was outshot when it came to precision. That was fine with him. His purpose was to shoot with efficiency. Get as many rounds on target as quickly and accurately as possible. The enemy could be the best pistol shot in the world. Shoot the wings off, butterflies, but that would do him no good if he was struck three times in the torso by Dane before he lined up his first shot. Hard to mimic that kinda of training on a range where you normally didn't receive incoming fire unless the backstop was shot out and the rounds ricocheted back. Hah, I remember that time Clint and I were in here shooting in the old days with the crappy traps. Those rounds seemed to come back at us just as fast as we fired.

Dane remembered one of his early instructors on the range. *"I don't care if your first round is not a kill shot as long as you hit your target and hit him first. That is step one. You have reduced his ability to shoot back. It is round two, three, and four that need to be precise and lethal and never stop until he hits the ground. Humans are amazingly hard to kill."*

He left the range after ensuring both weapons were clear. A room off the side of the range provided an area for the shooters to clean and service their weapons. Solution tanks and high-top work benches were scattered along the walls, with plenty of Q-tips and rod patches for everyone. The space could easily accommodate twenty people or more and normally did in the late morning like today. The guys liked to work out in the gym to around eighty-thirty or so and then drive a few rounds down range before cleaning up and heading to the team rooms. Nothing started before ten anyways. This was also a great opportunity for shit-talking after targets were compared.

"Man, Jones, did you forget your glasses this morning? Or are you too hungover to shoot straight?"

"Fuck you. Gunny put a new sight on my ten-inch barrel. I was dialing it in."

"Is that what you call that?"

"Screw you Hawkins. Let's talk pistols. Need me to show you how one works?"

Dane smiled, listening to the banter. He remembered the days working out with the team, dreading having to head into the office for some boring meeting. Or worse yet, some bullshit semi-annual online training that was designed for a six-year-old. They had the most ridiculous animated classes about security and not conducting classified work on cell phones or plugging stuff into computers. Well, no shit, he thought. But that was his life now. The staff part, anyway. He finished his maintenance, checked his weapons into the armory, and headed to the first meeting of the day after a quick shower.

It had been several weeks since the meeting with the President. Dane knew that he needed to be ready when the call came, hence the change up to his morning routine. Hell, his whole routine, for that matter. He ate better. He slept better. He just felt better. It was as if a purpose was all he needed. He was not naïve enough to believe he would be prowling the mean city streets every evening, gunning down local pedophiles in dark alleys. But to him, shooting had always been one of the strongest building blocks for every other task. Well, along with land navigation. Shooting taught discipline, concentration, and, most importantly, situational awareness. Whether alone or as part of a team, you had to be alert while controlling your weapon with discerning shots. Flyers, as they were called when you missed the target, were completely unacceptable. That was an unaccounted-for deadly projectile that could kill a teammate or an innocent bystander. The whole concept of tactical firearms training was situational awareness but really much more. It was tactical decision-making. Operatives often had to make decisions in the blink of an eye that could mean life or death.

Once he had returned to the unit after his mandatory time off as per the CSM's instructions, he was moved from the troop into the Operations shop. Staff. The S3 shop, as it was called, was the brains of the organization and controlled everything from missions to training, intelligence analysis, and even logistic coordination. Dane was not the senior NCO in the shop. That was the Sergeant Major. He provided oversight of each staff section along with his Lieutenant Colonel as a counterpart. Dane was the NOCIC, NCO in-charge for future operations or simply FUOPs. He worked on all the plans for future missions down the road. He attended briefings, wrote proposals, and staffed concept slides for the big bosses to either accept or decline. If it was accepted, Dane's staff would continue to build the project until about three months from the anticipated execution. Then it would pass to the Operative conducting the mission and be coordinated by the current operations folks. The Operative would own it from that point forward. Even though it was not the most glamorous position it did keep him employed and his mind occupied. It also was not the busiest section which meant that Dane found the time to brush up on other skills that had laid dormant over the last year.

The first floor of the building contained a training area, the size of which most people could not fathom. Besides the state-of-the-art gym, indoor range, locker rooms, and individual storage cages, there existed the Maze. The area was accessed by several different points and was laid out like a labyrinth fulfilling almost every training need. Two large roll-up doors on the south end provided vehicle access. Cars, trucks, and/or vans were met inside by re-enforced four-ton lifts for performing modifications on the undercarriage when necessary. Cameras, audio devices, and Tagging Tracking and Logging (TTL) installs could be rehearsed ad nauseum until the act of sliding under a parked car and finding the optimal install points in the dark were second nature. Additionally, racks of car doors and vehicle ignition switches were scattered about, with rolling chairs available to sit at ease and master the door locks and ignition keys of the make and model vehicle of choice. Three by five cards were taped to each door with instructions for common defeat techniques. It was, of-course, unfeasible to have every car represented in the room. The bookshelves lining several walls above workbenches contained volumes of every known car manufacturer. Key blanks filled plastic bins alongside grinding and cutting machines for both vehicle and residential key duplication. It was a car thief's paradise and really any other type of thief as well. Though not as helpful for most operations, areas were dedicated to motorcycles, heavy machinery and even boats. All sorts of transportation were found on the battlefield.

The shop continued with arrays of even more workstations to rehearse delicate soldering of electronic installs. There was a section dedicated to the molding and modeling of concealment devices for collection equipment. These collection devices could be used in plain site or hidden in almost any environment. Everything from common everyday rocks to electronic devices and even food containers that could hold a camera or audio device. Two rear doors on the opposite far wall provided entrance into the main portion of the Maze itself. It equated to a trip to Disney's Epcot center in that it was globally represented.

Behind each cascading door were individually tailored rooms with locks from around the world, grouped by region or sometimes country specific if necessary. For instance, one room contained common locks and safes from Europe while the next was centered around northeast Africa. However, the sheer magnitude of an enemy such as Russia and China warranted their own separate spaces. Nearly all the rooms were arranged identically. A twelve-foot-long table with stools commanded the center of each room. Safes were arrayed beneath, mounted on blocks with wheels for ease of access. But it was the walls that captured the attention of any visitors from outside the unit. Floor to ceiling shelves dominated all available wall space and were adorned with small wooden blocks mounted with every lock imaginable.

Labels identified each type of lock with stickers on the bottom, like the auto-shop recommending particular defeat techniques. They were easily accessible for retrieval to the center worktable by sliding ladders found in some medieval monastery libraries. Common everyday locks that could not be mounted such as padlocks, bike locks, etc. could be found in each table drawer along with extra equipment for their defeat. This maze wound the entirety of the building, making occasional space for utility rooms necessary to keep the building afloat with power and water.

The final room connected to the Northside of the building with two doors similar to its southern twin. It was here that the Operatives had their individuals metal cages to maintain their equipment. The space was convenient for dragging new kit or old into the maze for testing. Each had a wide door for access to bulky items. Shelves adorned both sides and reached nearly ten feet into the air. Gear always seemed to be overflowing behind each gate. Operatives in the unit had a lifetime of collected gear in addition to the copious amounts the unit provided. Dane remembered his first day at the Unit. His equipment was delivered literally by forklift. Each new Operative was issued a pallet of military gear and then given additional funds for civilian clothing or equipment they would need. They often needed to refrain from personifying a military presence depending on where their target was located. Many of these individuals lived out in the open away from the battlefields, believing they were immune from the reach of the United States.

Dane spent his free time in the maze practicing three fundamental skills. Vehicle entry, lock picking, and TTL. In his mind, those were three of the main tasks he reasoned would serve him best in his new role in the club. Find someone. Exploit their vehicle. Tag their vehicle. Find their bed down location. Exploit that location and develop a pattern of life to determine the ideal moment to strike. Simple. Plus, all the tools he needed were right there. The accountability of equipment was dismal. Most of the tools were off the books, purchased in unique ways to make the owner virtually untraceable. Big ticket, and expensive items were stored behind locked cages and inventoried monthly, but tools, lock pick sets, small cameras, etc., were readily available for all to use. Operatives were even encouraged to build their own kits for training missions and deployments. The custodians simply wanted to know what you took so they could order more inventory. Dane already had a sizeable collection both in his cage and at home. But it never hurts to keep your eyes open for new toys. He didn't ignore his other tasks knowing full well that things like photography, long-range surveillance, and camera installs might become necessary as well, but those were specific tasks that he could refresh quickly before any mission.

Dane slugged it out for a couple of hours in office meetings watching the digital minutes tick away. He was meeting Tyler later for lunch and was looking forward to catching up. He also had an appointment with the President this evening with a hint that his first assignment would be forthcoming. The hours in the day couldn't tick by fast enough.

He found Tyler easily in the greasy diner a few hours later. To ensure that the lunchtime crowd would be nearly exhausted, they chose one o'clock. Food would come out fast, servers would be too tired from the rush earlier for continuous check-ins, and the place would be deserted, offering some measure of privacy, Perfect.

"What's up, Coop? I keep missing you at the range," Tyler said as Dane slid into the booth opposite his old teammate. *"Word on the street is you've been hitting the range pretty hard lately. Drilling some nice sets is what I hear."*

"Just getting in a little practice. You never know when you may need it. The office can be a rough place."

"You finally got caught up in staff man. Tough break, but they ain't going to let you go now."

"We'll see. What about you? What do you have coming up Tye?"

They paused momentarily while the tired-looking waitress took their order. The appreciation showed on her face as they ordered simple items quickly and without any fuss. She left the table and Tyler continued telling Dame about his upcoming trip. He had not been around the office since he had to get some specialty training that wasn't even available in the maze. He had been up in Maine for a couple of weeks working with a company that develops unique solutions for particular operations. Dane was familiar with the mission since his new job owned the portfolio. He knew the product Tyler had been testing and would probably get to use it in the near future. He was jealous, and it must have shown.

"So, what about you, Coop? How long are they going to keep you in purgatory?'

"Reynolds told me a year and then possibly a year up at Brigade. He thinks I have a good shot at nine if I do the right staff time."

"Sergeant Major? You?" Tyler said with a smile. *"I can't believe they even let you be a Master Sergeant. Take the nine man. Do a few more years and retire. You have more than earned it. Maybe open a bakery....no, no, no.... a flower shop,"* Tyler laughed out loud as Dane just smiled.

"Jackass."

The food arrived. They keep the conversation light, and Dane tried to steer away from his staff work and what he was up to in his free time, as much as possible. He always enjoyed the younger man's company, friendship, and loyalty. He had to keep his membership in the club secret for the time being. However, Dane certainly reflected on the fact that someday he might need a trusted friend. Tyler would never let him down. One phone call in the middle of the night, and he would show up with a shovel and a six-pack of beer. Tyler was correct. He should punch a few more tickets and then get out. However, what he could not tell Tyler is that the move to staff was actually proving valuable. He had found the young soldiers in the intelligence section more than eager to give him a crash course in data analytics. He had always focused on operations, and he could do that part of the staff job in his sleep. Although, he was good at putting together an intelligence picture on missions, he never truly understood the number of databases and information that was available to the analysts. He had been provided with reports from them to build upon when planning a mission. Now, he was learning how to use those systems for his own purpose. Now he just needed to learn how to cover his tracks.

Later that evening, he once again climbed the long driveway up to the president's front door. Like clockwork, Jack opened the door before he could even knock.

"He is in the study. I believe you know the way."

CHAPTER 12: THE VICTIM

Jones Point Park, VA

The jungle was thick with dampness. It was everywhere with no relief. It was almost always the same whether day, night, rainy, or clear and that dampness drained a man. Physically. Emotionally. Spiritually. Days became weeks, and weeks became months. Every village they passed through looked the same. The Thatched huts of each community surrounding a central cooking area consisting of a meager pile of rocks spewing wisps of smoke. Clay pots and pans were scattered about while every insect known to man buzzed about. Animals roamed throughout the village, looking for any sign of nourishment for their hollowed frames. These were the scavengers. The dogs, goats, etc., any spare piece of food providing sustenance for their only source of survival. The meal is often the slimmest of rotten leftovers. Electricity and refrigeration were unknown concepts here. There was normally a cow for milk and eventual meat and/or an Ox to plow the rice fields. The rice fields were the worst to cross.

When soldiers reminisce, many of the details vary. Vietnam's northern and southern portions were vastly different, and the countryside was nothing like the urban centers. But what was always the same was the suffering. The dampness bred insects of every variety that never ceased their incessant buzzing. Much like the suffering of tinnitus, he would never stop hearing that sound. It would stay with him forever, along with the children. Barely skeletons with loose folds of flesh, they wandered, they cried, they simply gave up hope and sat among the dirt and mud. The fighting affected them the most. The brutality of war was never easy for any human, but the world required it of man. Politicians would swear to bring about peaceful change. Leaders would rise up and call for the cessation of arms in the name of peace. However, man, never listened. Bound to repeat these horrors once the previous mistakes were forgotten. Although they speak of suffering sacrifice. It was the children that truly witnessed the cruelty of man in all its forms. He had certainly seen it that day for himself. The jungle was thick with dampness. It was everywhere with no relief. And that dampness drained a man. Physically. Emotionally. Spiritually. Days became weeks, and weeks became months. Every village they passed through looked the same. Until it didn't. Was it friendly? Was it hiding foe? Did it really matter? They were dead. All of them. Their tiny little bodies at impossible angles among the rocks. The dampness. It engulfed all.

Her tiny body was entangled at impossible angles among the rocks. Her limbs broken and bruised. The water rose and fell every few seconds, gently rolling the little girl. Her hair was fanned out in the water and moving with the gentle current. Silence permeated the scene as investigators internalized the horror. That silence only broken by the gentle lapping of the water against the shore and the passing traffic above the bridge. The sirens of the first responders had been silenced once it was apparent that urgency was no longer required. She had already passed. Patterson and Stills stood stoically aside as the crime scene technicians took photos and made sketches, awaiting their turn to examine the scene. Dawn was fast approaching, yet the fading of the darkness and shadows did little to ease the grisliness of the site.

Both detectives had been called in early. The report of a child washed up at Jones Point, delivered by an early morning fisherman. They had arrived at blue and red flashing lights pulsating erratically against the steel and concrete pillars of the Woodrow Wilson Bridge. The bridge connected the two-states of Virginia and Maryland, arching over the Potomac River, a drawbridge at its peak to allow the free passage of vessels into the District of Columbia. Beneath this behemoth structure along the Virginia shoreline was nestled, Jones Point Park. It was a unique mixture of early Virginian history and modern pastimes.

The entrance was a concrete jungle filled with basketball courts and parking lots. Trails interspersed the area providing routes for cyclists that spanned from Virginia to Maine. This was where the officers parked their vehicles before proceeding on foot to the scene to preserve the second portion of the park. Jones Point was the site of one of Potomac's first lighthouses. Built in eighteen, fifty-six, it was placed in service to aid in navigation for the traders traveling to and from Alexandria. The city once was one of the busiest seaports in the Chesapeake region. The lighthouse itself was the latest in design that year. It was called a unified plan which combined the beacon with the keeper's home. The round top rose from the middle of the two-story dwelling providing aid to seafarers in darkness and fog.

No longer in use, the lighthouse provided no aid to the investigators during their initial hours on site. Portable lights were initially brought in but now removed as the two state special agents were ushered up to the victim by the medical examiner. Roger had already spoken with nearly a dozen agents, investigators, and detectives from multiple agencies. Maryland and federal responders as well due to the unique boundaries regarding the Potomac and jurisdiction thereof. Federal involvement was to be expected. U.S. Fish and Wildlife services managed the resources in the area and patrolled these waters with great abandon. Maryland was involved since the little girl was within their state boundaries. In a unique turn of circumstances dating back hundreds of years, the Potomac River was not divided down the middle between the two states. Instead, Maryland owned a majority of the waterway, including a portion along much of the Virginia coast. Captain Ivers had arrived on the scene before the detectives and worked with all interested parties about jurisdiction. Maryland state police had conceded to Virginia with regard to the current victim since it was Patterson and Stills' case, but they requested to be involved with the investigation since it appeared the child washed up from the river and was not dumped at the Point via land.

"Roger. Patricia." The medical examiner nodded to them as they approached. *"So, initially, I am ruling out drowning. I will*

confirm later during the autopsy, but none of the usual signs are present. I doubt there is even water in her lungs."

"So, all the bruising and broken bones are not from slamming into the rocks?" Patricia asked as she scribbled notes and sketches in the book she always carried.

Roger remained silent, staring at the tiny corpse.

"No," he answered. *"Whoever did this may have thought we would assume that is how she received all these injuries. But if you look closely at her limbs you can tell that this was done with a blunt object. A hammer or piece of metal."* He pointed to the abnormal angle of the joints and the multiple bruises around them. *"The joints were broken and then the lower portion of each limb was bent back on itself."*

"So, what is your initial estimate to the cause of death?" Roger asked, speaking for the first time.

"Blunt force head trauma. The back of the skull has been shattered. Same sort of blunt object that was used on the limbs. It looks like one powerful strike was all it took." The man rose from his squatting position and gave the state agents the scene.

"We have all we need right now. Let me and my guys know when you are done, and we will collect her. I will be up at the van," he said while departing the area. His vehicle was alongside the lighthouse, and the only one allowed down to the water's edge.

"This is definitely Dana Chase." Roger felt the wind knocked out of him for the second time today. First, when he received the call that a victim had been found matching her description. The second, this very moment confirming that dread. He had failed again. The two agents soundlessly examined the body and the immediate area for the next several minutes. Both taking notes and processing not only the scene but also their internal emotions, looking for any indication of how this became little Dana's final resting place. Stills finally broke the silence.

"What are you thinking, Roger? The area is not disturbed, and this would be a pretty difficult place to dump a body without anyone noticing. There are joggers and bikers all over the paths up there. Plus, the guy would have to park and then drag her body all the way down here. Not very practical if you want to remain unseen."

"I agree. She was definitely dumped downriver and floated up here."

"Down river?"

"I checked the tide charts on the NOAA site while we were waiting. Flood current up until about an hour ago, and then it went slack." When Patricia gave him one of those looks telling him that he needed to speak English, he explained further.

"Sorry, flood current is when the tide is coming in. Ebb is when it goes out. Slack is the pause in the middle between the two. Since it was flood current, that means she floated in from the south."

Roger pointed down the coastline away from the city of Alexandria.

"What I don't understand is why her limbs are like that. I can see the psycho torturing the poor thing, but breaking all her limbs? And it seems the water really twisted them around in an unnatural way after. Broken limbs would not settle at those angles. Why do any of this if you were going to just kill her anyway? I don't understand the torture."

"The water didn't do this, Pat. He did and I bet the autopsy will show it was postmortem."

"So, what? He has a violent temper and kept beating on her even after she was dead?"

"I would guess the exact opposite. Look at this head wound. One powerful shot. Just one strong enough to kill her without needless suffering. That shows control. He was not interested in torture. This kill was out of necessity not cruelty. Quick and powerful so she didn't have to suffer."

"But the limbs?"

"That was also done out of necessity. He broke and folded her limbs. Rigor mortis is why they are still at odd angles. He had to make her as small as possible for transport and disposal."

"Holy shit. That is disgusting. So, we need to be checking piers, docks, anything like that where he could have dumped her from?"

"And boat launches. She is small enough to fit in a bag or even a cooler. The only people that don't draw attention around here in the early hours are fishermen and joggers. I doubt he was jogging. There was a murder case like this up in Seattle in the nineties. Adult woman, very petite. I forgot the killer's name. Doesn't matter. They eventually caught him. He killed and butchered this woman. Then he placed her in a cooler with large holes in all the sides. Once weighted down with rocks, he tossed it overboard in the Puget Sound. His thought was that once it sank to the bottom, crabs and other sea-life would drag the bones out of the holes and scatter them once the flesh was removed. He did this thinking the body would never be found."

"That is probably the sickest thing I have heard so far. Times like this I really hate my job."

Roger moved closer to the shoreline, away from the body. The Ferris wheel at National Harbor stood silent as a guardian along the eastern shore. Commercial airlines continued their approach north along the river in two-minute intervals, their destination Ronald Reagan Airport. The bridge was even starting to come alive as commuters began the daily grind of traffic. All went on with their lives, clueless to the horror that lay beneath them. It was then that he heard the familiar slapping of rotary blades against the damp air. A helicopter was preparing to touch down in the open field behind the lighthouse with FBI blazoned across its side and belly. Had to be Blanchard, he thought. He called up to the medical examiner. *"You need to wait on the Feds before you move her."*

He received a thumbs up from the man and then turned to his partner not wanting to engage with the fed just yet.

"Hey Pat. You get seasick?"

Twenty minutes later, they were trawling down the coastline in a small Fish and Wildlife Boston Whaler. The agent was more than willing to help his passengers widen their search. Fairfax County had offered their assistance as well. Their large rigid inflatable boat could easily scour the entire area quickly. And that is exactly what Roger asked them to do with the Maryland police on the eastern shore. He preferred the federal whaler. The first reason being the smaller boat was less noticeable or rather less intimidating to the early-morning anglers he wanted to question. The country still showed quite a bit of animosity toward law enforcement. But even though they were in the law enforcement community, Fish and Wildlife were deemed protectors out on most waterways rather than enforcers. The second reason was that people always assumed the local police had better connections to the community than the feds. They were wrong in this instance.

Although normally true regarding feds and locals, Fish and Wildlife had a unique role in these waters. As Bob put it, the only name the officer gave them when they climbed aboard, the county and state action on the water were strictly enforcement. Speeding in no-wake zones. Outdated registration. Drunk Driving. They were good at it. He on, the other hand, did very little actual enforcement. These hard-core fishermen always had their licenses up to date and stayed within their catch limit, most simply releasing the fish anyway. He never had to check registration because their decals were always up to date. Instead, Bob worked with them. They would let him know if something wasn't right on the water. If they found garbage drifts, saw people stealing crap pots, spotted dangerous boaters, or really saw anybody doing harm to the waterway. They then informed Bob. And Bob talked to them nearly every day and Roger was hoping these relationships would pay off today.

They trawled down the western shoreline. Bob pointed out small tributaries and coves. Canoes, paddleboats, and bass boats spread across the area as the anglers cast their lines, searching for their morning catch and Bob introduced Roger and Pat to nearly every single one of them. As agreed upon departure, Bob would open the dialogue with the often-reserved fisherman, breaking the ice for the two state agents. They worked the waterways for nearly two hours until their first break.

"Morning, Steve. How are they biting?"

"Not bad, Bob. Snagged a few so far, up north a little way. Working back down south to where I launched."

"You must not have any early jobs," Bob commented.

"It's good to be the boss. So, are you going to tell me what is going on up at the point and why you are not riding solo as usual, Bob?"

"Sir, my name is special agent Patterson. This is special agent Stills. We are from the Virginia State Police Office. I can't get into details, but I am sure you will hear later today on the news that we found a young girl this morning washed up on the shore."

"Shit. That's just awful. Damn. How early?"

"She was found around five this morning."

"Makes sense you are down here. It was approaching high tide, so the current was flowing in. If she was dumped in the water, she would drift that way. Damn!"

"Steve, did you see anything odd or out of place?" Bob chimed in.

"I actually did now that you mention this, um, this thing. Didn't really think much of it until you asked. New boat out this morning. Well, a new weekday boat. Maybe the guy is normally a weekend boater and finally got a day off. I don't know. Never seen him."

"Is that normal to know every boat out here?" Patricia asked.

"Well, of course not every boat. You kinda get to know the regulars. Therefore, a new boater stands out. Especially since there isn't a whole hell of a lot of us crazies out here before sun-up."

Patricia was scribbling away in her book. *"Did you get a good look at him? At the boat?"*

"Sorry, it was dark. I couldn't even see the driver to say if it was a him or her. Too dark, but what I can say is that it was a standard

bass boat. Sixteen-footer or so but dark. Maybe Brown or black. But no design on the hull. They normally have some racing stripes or glitter on the side of the boat with logos but not this one. And the engine looked smaller than normal. You see a lot of two-fifties nowadays. This one looked to be a one-twenty-five or less. A lot smaller."

"Anything else unusual about this boat?" Roger asked.

The man named Steve peered out at the bay behind the whaler. *"Come to think of it, yeah."* He held his hands above his brow to ward off the rising run as he squinted his eyes. *"It looked like he was dropping crab pots over the side. That was around three in the morning."* He looked at his watch. *"You can't leave them more than about six hours, eight at the most. Bait will be gone. Any crabs in the pot may then start attacking one another."*

"How is that odd?" Patricia asked.

"Because" as he pointed out to the near-center of the river just outside the main channel, *"the buoys are still there."*

Reporter: *They found a little girl at Jones Point Park this morning.*

President: *Have they released the identity?*

Reporter: *No, but my sources say it is Dana Chase.*

President: *Ok. Please gather as much information as you can. Thank you.*

CHAPTER 13: THE FEDS

Washington, D.C.

He both loved and despised public transportation. On the one hand, driving in Washington D.C. was a nightmare. Every state claimed the title of the worst driver, and although each may have a legitimate claim to the throne, D.C. was a conglomerate of shitty drivers from around the country, where all state contenders vied for a shot at the belt. His seniority earned him a place in the parking garage as well as a government sedan for business use. But why fight all those drivers at the two worst times of the day? You had the early morning commute when the dread of going to work was overwhelming or the sweet release of the workday when the accelerator could not be depressed fast enough to arrive home. Nope, he preferred the bus.

However, he had become increasingly frustrated with some of his fellow passengers of late. Human courtesy seemed to have vanished. People believed that every commuter desired to hear their mindless phone conversations or listen to the latest release of some crappy song from the newest crooner. Political stances were not only strung across shirts and messenger bags, but would-be-lawyers argued everything from race to war in Ukraine and cancellation of student debt. *Pay off your own debt, you little shit, he thought. I did it in the Marines and I did not get some worthless 16th century French art history degree.* Humanity was doomed to fall like the Roman Empire due to the simple fact of entitlement and selfishness.

Carl tried to relax and enjoy the last fifteen minutes of his morning ride to work. He transferred from the Omnibus, which whisked him from beyond the beltway, to a local intercity bus that would take him to headquarters on Pennsylvania Avenue. The commuter bus was filled with D.C. professionals, quietly minding their own business and heading into the hornet's nest of the capital. Those rides were normally peaceful. The city bus, however, was a stark contrast. All walks of life found their way here. Some are on their way to work, while others are on their way home from a night of festivities. Kids were going to school. Workers were coming off a graveyard shift. Sometimes it was amusing. Sometimes it was depressing. Today, however, it was aggravating. A woman brandishing a shirt that suggested defunding the police with quite a few vulgarities thrown in had boarded near his final destination. If she could have held her tongue for five minutes his day may have begun on a brighter note, but as fate would have it, Carl was denied the reprieve. The woman selected a seat in the row opposite his. When she caught a glimpse of his shield on his belt, the berating began.

"Hey there, Mr. Policeman. Kill any innocent babies today?"

Carl glanced briefly at the woman and then returned his attention to his phone.

"I see. Is that how it is going to be? You think you too good to talk to me? Well, tough shit, asshole! It's a free country and I can say whatever I want." The woman's voice became increasingly louder.

"Ma'am. Please lower your voice. This is not an appropriate place for your protests. There are children on board that don't need to be exposed to this type of language." He immediately regretted responding to the woman. She was clearly intoxicated. He could smell it across the aisle. She was only going to become more determined now to get a response out of him. Just four more minutes.

"You can't tell me what to do. I will say whatever the fuck I want, you pig. I pay your salary. You work for me. I pay taxes that go toward your salary!"

"I doubt that." He heard a few nearby passengers chuckle. He returned to his phone, desperately trying to refrain from being dragged into a mindless discussion, but the woman became even more enraged if that was even possible.

"What did you say to me asshole! I will have your job. I will get you fired in a second. What is your badge number?"

Carl didn't take the bait. It would only get worse. People had started to retrieve their phones to record the scene hoping for an escalation.

"Oh, I see. Big man. Above us common folk. Just texting on your phone when a citizen you work for is talking to you. I am talking to you!" She virtually screamed the last part, spitting on his shoes as if to make the final point. But divine fate finally intervened, and the bus pulled to the curb. Carl pressed send on his phone, pocketed the device, and rose to the aisle. Emboldened the woman stood as well and followed him to the exit. Yelling obscenities, she must have felt like a conquering hero chasing the villain from the lands. But as Carl stepped off, two agents stepped on. The woman was seized and pulled off the bus.

"You are under arrest for public drunkenness, disturbing the peace, and assaulting a federal officer."

Carl smiled to himself as he entered the doors of the building. "*Bitch,*" he muttered.

His status in the grand hierarchy of the FBI was tenuous and often misunderstood. Carl Blanchard had been a special agent for over twenty years, yet he did not sit among the executive officers on the senior staff. Administrative functions were completely undesirable. Instead, Carl found himself in the unique position of creating his own investigations and task forces. His seniority and record of success allowed him this latitude along with a spacious corner office on the fifth floor. He, of course, had masters to answer to as well as reporting requirements up through his branch chief to the director of the Criminal Investigation Division. But, as long as he pursued goals that coincided with the agency's mission statement, he was free to pursue his chosen path. That current path was beginning to unravel, but he still did not fully see the bigger picture. It was there. It just remained in the shadows. His assistant entered after giving his boss several minutes to get settled in.

"Here you go boss. I heard about the little incident on the bus and figured this may help," he said as he handed Carl a mug of coffee.

"Thank Ken."

Ken was a junior agent that served as his assistant, but more importantly, his sounding board. The young agent was intelligent and extremely dedicated to the task at hand. The mentor/mentee relationship benefitted them both. Carl's experience and Ken's naïve perspective actually melded well. Carl realized that he had become jaded over the years, resulting in a narrower perspective on certain cases. On the other hand, Ken questioned everything and often provided just the right challenge to a set of circumstances that allowed Carl to see the bigger picture. Ken walked over and turned on the television. He sat behind his massive oak desk as his computer whirled to life.

Behind him was a set of built-in bookshelves that collected his achievements over the years. Awards and gifts from his time spent in the Marine Corp adorned each shelf along with department commendations and medals. He didn't keep any personal photos or memorabilia, that was reserved for him and him only at his home office. In contrast, none of his military memories decorated his home. He kept the two lives separate, which he credited to the retention of his sanity over the years and the reduction of stress. He was as passionate about the job as anyone, but you had to shut it off at the end of the day, or it would consume you. He had seen too many fellow agents and Marines succumb to the job, nothing outside of this life to center themselves. To his right was a massive expanse of windows, another perk of his seniority. Life continued outside of those windows and helped balance him as he worked to protect that life and bring the monsters who walked among us to justice. That view reminded him why he witnessed the horrors that he did.

"You are going to want to see this boss."

Carl was absentmindedly scrolling through his endless supply of emails when the local news captured his attention.

"We bring you live to Jones Point Park in Alexandria Virginia where a horrible tragedy is unfolding. Early this morning a young child was found along the shore of the park. A fisherman alerted the authorities upon this terrible discovery. Details are still unfolding as law enforcement is conducting their investigation. Any updates Arthur?"

"This is anything but a good morning, guys. There are limited details as the police continue to canvass the area hopeful for any witnesses. As you can see behind me law enforcement from both Virginia and Maryland are here together as well as representatives from state and federal agencies. What we do know it that around four this morning one of the local fishermen spotted something along the shoreline in front of the historic lighthouse. John Glenmore was fishing these waters from his kayak as he has done

nearly every morning for the last ten years. He knew these waters well and recognized that something was not as it should be. Upon closer inspection, he realized that it was the body of a young girl. He immediately notified the Alexandria police department who as you can tell, responded with all available resources. Additional details are forthcoming but at this point we have very limited information. The Captain of the Virginia State Police has called for a press briefing later this morning. Once we get further details, I will make......"

Carl snapped off the television. *"Ken, can you order up a ..."*

"Already on it boss. I put in a standby order when I saw you badged into the front building entrance. They will notify us when the helicopter is ready. Flight plan is already logged. Thirty minutes max."

Damn, Carl thought. This kid surprises me more and more every day. *"Great. Thanks. Way to plan ahead."* Carl closed his laptop and approached the wall opposite the bank of windows behind his desk. It was his working wall. When he took over the office, he requested the entire wall painted with magnetic whiteboard paint. It was way more expensive than the standard low-grade paint utilized in most government facilities. He fought tooth and nail with the bureaucrats and bean-counters until he finally called in a few favors to approve the requisition. The wall was one giant dry-erase board with the added bonus of magnetism to allow neodymium magnets to hold pictures, files, and virtually any piece of paper. After all these years, nearly every office or team collaboration space now utilized this paint for its versatility. Ken followed him to the board, checking his watch as he did so. Hah, Carl thought. He doesn't want me getting lost in thought here.

The Thought Wall, as some of the others in the office took to calling it, was filled with Carl's latest investigation. Whenever he approached an investigation, he fell back on techniques that he used as a young Marine officer. Modified techniques. Military mission planning was similar across all the branches. It was always thorough and designed to plan for every contingency, but he found it lacked efficiency. There were too many steps that were often unnecessary. He had devised his own, which had served him well. Now, like then, he had divided his wall into two sections. The first was theories and assumptions. Sometimes, just gut feelings. When agents referred to the Art and Science of problem solving, this was his Art. This is what may have happened or what may currently be in existence. The second section was his Science. These were facts. Data moved from Art to Science only when the fact was proven. The Art section contained nearly four times as the Science one for this investigation.

His theory was a simple one. It was the first line of writing on his Artboard. Someone was killing and/or capturing pedophiles and molesters. Ironically that statement was also written on his Science board. Over the past five years of his investigation, he had gathered enough evidence to prove this fact. Recovered children were the first source of validation. Arriving at local churches or shelters in the dead of night, telling stories about a sort of hero saving them from the bad man.

One little boy even insisted that Batman had saved him from the Joker. Carl didn't doubt his honesty in the least as told through the eyes of a nine-year-old boy. All the children had been reported missing from the Northern Virginia area and as far north as New York and south to North Carolina. And the net was growing larger. The children could never fully provide details about their saviors. Except for Batman, of course. But the other descriptions were never quite the same. Although he had found that children often do not make the best witnesses, the odds of something similar in their description were just too great and led him to the conclusion that it was not only one man. The Art told him it was multiple men. And these men were methodical. The crime scenes were immaculate. There was almost never any trace evidence.

The recovered children were also normally able to give accurate locations of where they were held captive. That would be nearly impossible. Someone made sure they could remember a location they probably never knew in the first place. Art becoming Science. Upon arrival, the scenes finally provided some sort of similarity, and that was the aftermath. The victim, ironically the accused, was found either incapacitated or deceased. Every time. No possibility of evading authorities for prosecution or the undertakers for burial. Death, however, was their normal sentence. They were only left alive if it was clear they had more victims yet to be found. Unmarked graves that were not located on site or easy to find. The superheroes left them alive. Alive to succumb to police interrogation to recover other victims and provide closure for families allowed to finally lay their children to rest. But they never talked about their attackers as if they feared for their very lives. These incidents were not circumstantial and almost every death was inconclusive. An official ruling was always made, and it was normally some sort of suicide or accident. But as a seasoned investigator, Carl knew that the rulings were never clear-cut. Doubts remained not only in his mind, but in fellow investigators as well.

Keeping these anomalies out of the news cycle had been imperative over the years. More than once, Carl had used the federal powers of the FBI to suppress case details being released to the press. Ongoing investigation was the explanation. The details had to be close hold if they were ever going to catch Batman and his friends. These were not the only scenarios Carl and his team investigated. The Camp case was a perfect example. That one was weird. Convicted molester and known pedophile. He was found dead in a park, apparently by his own hands, suicide. Literally, found with his manhood in his hand while looking at photos he had taken of elementary school children in the locker room. The scene looked like suicide. Screamed of suicide. However, smelled like something else to Carl. Why go all the way to a park? Why not just do it in your garage? He knew that criminals were never completely logical, and Camp was a definitely a criminal. But why the park?

As he stared at the Science side of his wall, he stopped on the name Dana Chase. Innocent young girl. Her life taken, probably, and her family's lives destroyed by some monster. Was her abductor next to make it on his board? Current board member was Johnathan Hunt from Baltimore. Victim of a hit and run in his own neighborhood. He was leaving a local convenience store with some cigarettes and beer. Run over as he crossed the street, apparently against the light. A young boy was found nearby at a Baptist Church. The boy was able to identify a picture of Hunt and even recite his address. But his description of his savior was jumbled and vague. The only information he provided was that he was locked away in a bedroom with nothing but a mattress and a bucket. He had no idea how long he had been there, only that the bad man would visit twice a day. However, he knew the address.

Charlie Diego. Dead on Staten Island. Apparently hung himself in his garage. He had apparently climbed up on the chair, slid the noose over his own neck, and then used his teeth to tighten a zip tie around his wrists. Lest he change his mind. The rope had enough slack to support this theory. The ceiling was the vaulted kind with an open loft above for storage. The distance and the math worked for suicide. He left a note about two kids hidden in the wall of his basement. He was overcome with guilt. He never would have made the board except for his confession of the two violent crimes in the basement, but is that what really happened? Carl was not convinced.

Carl often thought about the people who were not on his board. These cases were examined due to the recovery of children or admittance of bodies buried by the subdued suspect. What about other criminals that were killed but their death did not come up on their radar? There were hundreds of deaths through accidents, violent crimes, and even health problems every day. Was this group responsible for any of these victims as well? If they had no prior history as a child predator, then there would be no reason to believe they fell prey to whatever sort of group this was exacting justice for children. He looked again at Dana Chase's name. There is going to be another name. I am certain sooner or later someone is going to come after whoever did this. If we don't figure this out first, there will be another accident. Do I really care?

"Sir, the helicopter is ready."

"Thanks Ken. I need you to sit this one out. The scene won't give us anything that the Staties and locals won't provide. I just like to get a feel for scenes. While I am gone, I need you to pull some files. Let's start with Virginia and go back fifteen years for now. Pull all the reports on missing children. Not known runaways, but honest to God abducted children. I want information on their parents. Specifically, what they do for a living."

"I can do that boss, but that is bound to be hundreds of cases."

"Let's start with kidnappings for now. That should shorten the list. We will look at other violent crimes against children on the next go-around."

Tech: *I have the equipment you asked for.*

President: *Were you able to get the specific items requested.*

Tech: *The Panasonic is an older version, but I was able to upgrade the software.*

President: *Excellent. Thank you.*

CHAPTER 14: THE FIRST JOB

Washington D.C.

Pupil: *I got another toy for my collection.*

Keeper: *I saw the news. Are you sure you are safe?*

Pupil: *Yes. Can't lead back to me.*

Keeper: *Ok. Don't get sloppy. All it takes is one mistake.*

Dane walked around underneath the Ford Taurus currently residing in the bay one lift in the Unit's maze workshop. The lift gave him the opportunity to study the undercarriage and find the ideal location to place the tracker. The device itself had a magnetic surface on the bottom, but it was so hard to find actual metal on cars nowadays. He would use zip ties as well for secure fastening, but he needed at least a partial metal surface for the magnet in a location that wouldn't be seen by the owner or easily shaken loose while driving. The potholes of northern Virginia could swallow a car whole.

It had been difficult to find the Taurus. Ford had stopped making the car years ago, and most had aged out of rental fleets. Rental cars themselves do not normally last as long as vehicles owned by private citizens. Everyone who rents a car seems to drive them like they stole it. But he had been able to find it at one of those Mom-and-Pop rental places south along Richmond

Highway. It had been a pain, but he needed this exact model. This was the car he needed to tag.

His first mission was to develop a pattern of life for a suspected trafficker of child pornography. He needed to know where he went and who he met with. Charles had explained that the distribution of child pornography remained on the dark web, but it was getting more and more difficult to avoid exposure due to increased security on the internet. Agencies at the state and federal levels have made huge strides over the years detecting and exposing these crimes. So, many of these pedophiles had gone back to safer methods.

There was a correlation with drug dealers in some of the major cities in the early 2000s. Law enforcement was so skilled at tracking and eavesdropping on cell phones that dealers began to use public pay phones to coordinate deals. It finally led to the removal of those phones in major American cities to fight the distribution of drugs. The pedophiles downgraded to personal exchanges as their new method to avoid detection. Small data drives and even CDs were still available to most consumers. They would simply burn their obscene content onto one of these external storage devices and then physically pass it to the end-users. It was safer than trying to set up fake accounts, obscure MAC or machine addresses, and/or utilize virtual private networks. All these things relied on a technology company that may or may not acquiesce to a warrant from the authorities. Nope, hand-carrying was the safest.

Since Dane was a one-man show on this operation, he had to be practical about the amount of time he could watch his target. John Grange was some mid-level executive at a large accounting firm. Single, mid-forties. Lived alone. He had a normal nine to five job, five days a week. Unless he was getting the porn from a co-worker, Dane was fairly certain that he did not have to keep eyes on him during normal business hours, which was good since he needed to maintain his own work presence. The tracker would help him find John after he left work. His office was one of those large buildings over by the Springfield Mall. That would be a little challenging to get there when Grange left for the day, since he would have to leave D.C. right during rush hour and travel with everyone else heading south.

Last week he and Charles had discussed the operation and the equipment that he needed. Charles informed him that his supplier could normally meet any request in five to ten days unless it was exclusively from the military and/or the intelligence community. Those items would take upwards of a month. Dane had requested two simple, commercial, off the shelf trackers. The kind anybody could purchase. He also needed a rugged laptop made by Panasonic, often referred to as Toughbooks. Virtually all computer companies made some sort of rugged computer in today's current marketplace due to the demand during the wars over the last two decades, but Dane preferred the Panasonic brand. He was loyal to a product that worked well for him in the deserts of Iraq, mountains of Afghanistan, and the jungles of Africa. That kind of product should hold up to the mean streets of northern Virginia. Hopefully.

He had used a hotspot puck that provided internet service over the cell phone tower network, retrieved from his storage unit, to download the required program onto the Toughbook. The program was designed to work with the two trackers to integrate their location with mapping software to provide location data in real time. Real-time meant anywhere from a ten second to one-minute lag due to connectivity. The signal had to travel through the cell phone network and then down to the computer into the program. Depending on the time of day and cell phone use by the public at large the network could be busy, resulting in a delay. Dane had always lived by the military adage that, two is one, and one is none. Always build in redundancy when possible. Plan for Murphy's luck striking at least one of the trackers in this scenario. He always placed two trackers whenever possible.

Dane was not entirely clear how this child pornography distribution ring was discovered, only that another club member had done most of the legwork but was called away on other business and could not finish. Grange was identified as the leader of a cell of some sort. The other club member had determined that Grange was distributing to six other men. He witnessed several possible hand-offs. However, a search of Grange's home showed no signs of production capability or electronic distribution. The member had theorized that, like a terrorist cell, Grange oversaw a small group of members and was the only go-between with the main distributor. This protected members both up and down the network. If there was a compromise in any part of the chain, only a cell at most would be lost, but the remaining collective would be secure. Exactly how terrorists throughout the world conducted business with the intent to remain hidden until showtime.

Dane had read the target package the other man had created and his findings. He agreed with this theory. A thorough search of Grange's cell phone records revealed hundreds of contacts but no direct link to known or convicted child predators. Any one of these contacts could be the head honcho. Charles wanted to find that man before the entire cell was exposed. He didn't want this ghost to go dark. He had considered leaving a vehicle down at the Franconia Springfield Metro but dismissed the notion. Any vehicle would draw unnecessary attention if left for long periods of time in a parking lot. *I don't even think you can park overnight at the metro station garage.* He decided to follow Grange as best as he could as a one-man team. The Taurus was rented for two weeks and would be better than his own personal vehicle for surveillance. Charles had provided him with a real Virginia Driver's license but a different name under the picture along with a debit card in that name. He didn't even bother to ask. The documents might not stand up to heavy scrutiny, but they were enough for the little run-down car rental agency and an aging Ford Taurus. He would review the stops Grange made on the computer program each evening ,showing where the trackers traveled. If there were reoccurring or suspicious stops, then he could duck out of work and setup a stakeout. It was the best plan with his limited resources. If he had a full surveillance team and the freedom to dedicate daily twenty-four coverage, they could finish quickly. As it was, he figured it would probably take two weeks. This was, of course, predicated on the assumption that the child porn addict receiving custom productions would update his supply often.

Dane had installed cameras in the side view mirrors; each mirror with two cameras could capture forward and to the side. A quad-cam viewing tablet was nestled in the arm rest. The Taurus was some variation of grey that was anything but memorable. Perfect for conducting surveillance. It would not stand out. He smiled to himself as he remembered a surveillance detection school he had attended years earlier. He was required to plan driving and walking routes throughout the day and attempt to identify any surveillants that may or may not be following. These runs could last up to six hours and involve multiple modes of transportation. Public buses, trains, and even bicycles were not off limits. Upon completion of a run, Dane would meet with one of the instructors at a local coffee shop. He would provide a detailed description of any vehicle or people following him. Make, model, color, and license plate. Height, weight, hair color, etc. Any detail he could remember. He had to include a reason why he chose that person or vehicle. The standard was double spotting the surveillant over time and space. The double spotting couldn't be a logical route for another person to take. If he saw a car alongside or behind him on the freeway and then twenty minutes later at a rest area, that was a logical movement for that vehicle. That car didn't do anything abnormal to indicate it was following him. Now, if he saw a vehicle heading the opposite direction from him and then twenty minutes later it was parked outside a store he shopped at... that warranted scrutiny.

His instructor, Donald, was a retired CIA station chief with a penchant for vodka, with whom Dane enjoyed working. It wasn't a pass or fail type of course but rather one that was designed to teach new techniques so students could hone their craft. Donald encouraged Dane to use unorthodox techniques, think outside the box, and push the boundaries. It was because of their close working relationship that, after one particularly brutal run, Dane had only one surveillant, but he wrestled with even that decision. It was ridiculous and made no sense.

"How did it go?" Donald asked.

"I only got one," Dane responded.

"Doesn't matter. Only need one to determine your status."

"Yeah, but this one is embarrassing."

"Hah, Ok, shoot."

"Cherry Red Mustang. Convertible. Nineteen sixties model. Arizona plate, MY6T3LV. Which I assume means my 63 love, so probably the 1963 model." Dane paused, looking for Donald's reaction. When he received none, he continued. "Driver was a thirty to thirty-five-year-old Caucasian female. Long blond hair, five-

foot-six to five-foot-eight. Slim build, wearing a light white sweater, blue jeans, and sunglasses."

Donald smiled at him. *"You are correct."* Seeing Dane's surprised look, he continued. *"Barbara got ready to leave for the morning's run to surveil you. Her car wouldn't start. Her husband had already left for work, and she didn't have time to get a rental. So, she took her husband's restored cherry red Mustang, which he keeps in the garage under some sort of micro-fiber cover to prevent dust damage or some nonsense."* Donald finished with a small chuckle. *"Not your normal surveillant."*

Both men had a good laugh.

Northern Virginia

Later that evening, Dane returned home after completing phase one. His counterpart, who performed the early surveillance of Grange, had provided his home address. Dane scouted it on several occasions. Grange lived in a small townhouse community in Springfield. Nothing special, but he was pleased by the poor street lighting throughout. It was an older community population, with very few children. Typical D.C. commuters slave away nine to five, taking advantage of more affordable housing away from the expensive Arlington or Alexandria areas. These people had to get up early. They were asleep by ten. Children were sleeping, and the dogs already concluded their final walk. Dane chose eleven-thirty to ensure solitude. He approached on foot after parking the Taurus a mile away. He was in and out of the parking lot in under two minutes. Both trackers were already prepped for installation, and he found the vehicle easily. He slid underneath, slap, zip, zip... slap, zip, zip and then he snipped all loose ends. As he slid back out, he confirmed four zip-tie ends in his hands along with the cutters. Back at the car, he checked that the trackers were broadcasting and readable on his Toughbook before heading home. Neat and clean.

The next day, after checking the computer for the trackers, he went about his normal routine at the office. He had estimated a battery life of eight days before he would have to return and swap out trackers. Their ping rate was set to slow during the day and after ten p.m.to conserve power. From 5 p.m. to 10 p.m., it pinged at a rate of once every five minutes or could be increased in frequency by a stroke of the keyboard. However, to change the ping rate, Dane had to have the laptop near the trackers to send that signal. It would be simple on a day he was doing a physical follow. He had finalized his plan for data collection for three days before any actual follows. There was no sense wasting time on the street and possible exposure of the vehicle to the target if he didn't need to. One week wasn't enough to develop a true pattern of life, but it would be a good start. Saturday and Sunday would be his physical follow days to see what Grange did with his time off. Monday would be the eight-day battery life mark. He would swap trackers the Sunday night prior. Just to be safe.

The first five days proved very mundane. Dane sat at his bar table in his apartment, reviewing the tracker program. He was not anticipating any investigation into his activities, so it was not worth the trip to a local library or coffee shop for free Wi-Fi. He used a virtual private network to conceal his online identity. It wouldn't stop the sternest of investigators, but it was fine for this assignment. Besides, following people in public was not illegal. Well, with the help of the trackers, it was, but they couldn't be traced back to him anyway. Grange would leave for work at eight-thirty sharp every morning. Very punctual. He would avoid the I-95 freeway, instead preferring backroads and parkways to avoid the traffic. His car remained in his office parking lot all day. He punched out of work at five after completing his eight hours of work with a thirty-minute lunch break. His stops were normal. Stopped at a gas station once. Stopped for groceries. The guy didn't even go to the liquor store. The car stopped movement normally around six-thirty at night. It stayed that way until the next morning. Even on Friday night, it looked like John Grange had decided to stay home. No sign of a social life. Boring.

Dane decided to do a physical follow Saturday morning, hoping for some sort of excitement. The computer in his car was powered up and ready to go. He was not sure if Grange would wake earlier than during the week, so he was in position at seven in the morning. He had positioned himself in a parking lot across from Grange's subdivision entrance. The lot was packed with cars, so the Taurus blended right in. The shopping mall here had some sort of breakfast place that drew early crowds.

Sipping his coffee, Dane settled in for the wait. Yet, not even fifteen minutes later, the computer vibrated, signaling movement. Dane adjusted himself in the seat, checked his surroundings, and prepared to back out of his parking spot, ready to follow. He watched Grange emerge from the mouth of the neighborhood directly across the street from him. This spot was perfect for surveillance. Right up until Grange pulled straight across the street into the parking lot and parked in the spot two rows over from Dane. He was going inside the trendy breakfast place. Crap. Dane patiently waited. *What are we doing here, John?* As if to answer his question, another vehicle pulled into the lot. Grange had remained in his car for an unusual amount of time, but when the other vehicle's occupant headed into the restaurant, Grange followed.

Dane had always been trained to trust his instincts and his instincts were telling him that he needed to get his eyes on the person Grange was meeting. It could be nothing but a colleague or an old friend. However, after five days of no real contact with anyone outside of work, this was breaking a pattern.

Even though the restaurant was crowded, the two men were shown quickly to a table. They must have called ahead. Dane had no such luxury. He gave the hostess a bogus name and was told it would be thirty to forty minutes for a table. But as luck would have it, there was an available space at the bar area, and he was welcome to eat there. The Gods were with him when he found a seat, providing him with a view of the men. He wasn't particularly hungry, but the first rule of surveillance, eat when you have the opportunity and never pass up a bathroom break. He ordered while simultaneously requesting the check. He had cash along with a tip ready to go, so he could leave at a moment's notice.

They are awkward around one another. They are not close friends. It is obvious. Dane had spent a career reading human behavior and he was witnessing two men uncomfortable with their encounter. Neither of them wanted to be there. It was for appearances. It was to associate in public, but not draw attention to themselves like a secret meeting in a dimly lit alley. And then he saw it. It was not very clever, but the unknown man passed Grange a book, after they had paid their tab. That may have been the passing of the pornographic material. *This could be the main distributor to various cells. Or on the other hand, it could be one weird guy giving another weird guy an even weirder book.* Dane couldn't know for sure, but he was definitely going to capture this guy's information. He had already used the bathroom while the men were eating, so he left his stool and headed to the car. As he passed the unknown man's car, he captured several photos, including the license plate, with a small, concealable camera. He fired up the Taurus and circled the lot, waiting for the men to exit. The cameras in the vehicle were already up and running. As the pair exited the restaurant, he casually drove toward them, capturing their profiles. He continued to circle the opposite side, and the side mirror caught images of the men head-on. He had what he needed and pulled away from the area to await Grange's next destination.

Grange returned home and didn't leave again until Monday morning for work. Dane didn't see any signs of life that Sunday night when he swapped the trackers. He was not looking forward to another boring week.

CHAPTER 15: THE GIRL

Fairfax, VA

"The lab guys have nothing so far on those buoys. They are really old. Their best guess is that our guy grabbed them from someone else's traps or found them washed up on the shore. All different kinds, so no way to trace any sort of purchase."

Roger listened as his partner entered their cubicle area. He was lost in thought, staring at the dry-erase boards but still heard every word Patricia said. The boards were filled with notes and pictures from several seemingly related abductions. "Dana Chase, Holly Jones, Angela Cooper. Very similar cases. Are they connected? If so, how?" Roger thought

"Did the divers find anything of value?"

"Nothing. Concrete blocks on the ends of the buoy ropes. Generic. Non-traceable. He was definitely doing it for show so he could dump the body if this was indeed him. They are doing a grid search of the bottom, hoping to find whatever container she was in but with the crazy currents around here, whatever it was could be in the Chesapeake Bay by now."

Another dead end he thought, still staring at the board. I failed another child. He sighed as he opened the Dana Chase jacket in front of him. He accepted a few pieces of paper from his partner detailing their findings. Rising, he headed to the board with Dana's name to annotate this latest bit of information or rather, lack thereof.

"The medical examiner is still finalizing his report," she continued. *"You were right. The limbs were broken post-mortem, and the lungs were free of water. Well, some water naturally from the river, but not from drowning."*

"Preliminaries on the blunt force trauma to the head?"

"Yes, actually." Patricia opened her notebook as she took her place behind her desk. *"Bear with me. Medical speak. And don't ask me to spell any of this. It should be spelled correctly in the final report if that matters since nobody can understand Doc without a dictionary handy."*

Roger waited at the board, prepared to write. *"It's fine for now. I'll do my best to transcribe."*

"One single blow to the pterion. It is the spot where several regions of the skull join." She squinted at her notes. *"The front, parietal, temporal, and sphenoid bones. Above the ear and slightly forward."* Patricia pointed to the region absentmindedly as she continued. *"Blunt object. Some sort of hammer. He thinks it was a ball-peen. Small round head on the hammer that could easily crush through bone."*

Roger wrote this information in the space under Dana's name. They were adding information but nothing substantive enough to narrow down suspects.

"Initial toxicology shows trace amounts of fentanyl in her blood. Do you think he used that to keep her complacent? Doc said it wasn't enough to kill her but enough to induce drowsiness or sleep. However, without more tests, he can't tell whether this was a single dose or indicative of use over time. Even so, it will be difficult to determine if she was drugged over time."

Roger continued to stare at the board. The marker in his hand hung loosely at his side. *"What am I missing? There must be something to point to this guy."* After a few brief moments, he returned the marker to the tray and sat back behind his desk. His eyes never left the board. After nearly five minutes of contemplation, he broke the silence. *"Ok, let's work out how this may have gone down. Put a scenario on the table. We can work off that theory and see where it goes from there."*

Patricia had her notebook out, ready to scratch notes.

"He may or may not have used fentanyl to keep her compliant. Over time, that would be difficult with dosages unless he has some sort of access to drugs. That could imply some sort of hospital employee or pharmacist. However, protocols are pretty tight nowadays when it comes to drug access. Most hospitals have those medical dispensers. Not sure what they are called, but I have seen them used. You have to enter a security code, so if you remove medicine, your name is tagged. Pretty sure our guy is smarter than that."

"The drug is effective at controlling pain more than anything. It also slows respiration which can induce sleep eventually, a coma, and often death."

"Exactly, but you would have to be careful. Especially if we assume he got the drug from the streets. No telling how potent it is. I think this was a one-time deal. Easier ways to keep her complacent without a potentially lethal overdose."

"Why could he care if he was eventually going to kill her anyway? Using it for submission would only shorten the time he had with her. I am not sure he cared."

"Maybe. Maybe not. Hear me out." Roger pointed to the book in Pat's hand. *"Let me guess. No evidence of sexual assault or molestation."*

Pat didn't even look at her notes, easily recalling that from memory. *"Not at this time. His preliminary exam of her pelvis showed no damage."*

"So why do you think he snatches children?"

"I don't know Roger. This one has me confused."

"I know, but I think her death can shine some light on his motive for abducting them in the first place. He didn't want to kill her. He had to for some reason, so he did it as humanely as possible. Like having to put down a pet in his eyes."

"Humanely? Drugs. A hammer. Broken limbs. I am still not understanding your thoughts on this." Pat showed a little more emotion than usual in her voice.

"Yes," Roger fired back. *"Look at it logically. The skull is extremely strong and has a durable set of bones. She was twelve. Her skull was fully formed and probably stronger than yours or mine. He selected the weakest point with the most probability of delivering a fatal blow. The fentanyl was to sedate her. Make her fall asleep. Once she was asleep, he placed her on the ground and took the opportunity to line up the perfect killing blow with one single strike. Nearly impossible to hit that spot if she was alert or moving around under her own will. He wanted it quick and painless. The limbs were broken post-mortem. He probably didn't want to do it, but he had to for transport. The most humane way would have been to give her a lethal overdose. However, he was also practical. He was hoping her death and injuries would be attributed to the water. You said earlier she was even found in her original clothes. He must have saved everything. He may be smart, but this was a dumb mistake. He wants us to believe that she fell into the river and died. Not very likely. And if that was the case, where has she been all this time?"*

"I think we need a little more information from Doc to flesh this out."

"Ok. Let's put a pin in this one for now. Any updates on the Camp case?"

Before she could answer Captain Ivers poked his head around the corner. *"I heard they are done processing the Chase scene. The Chief will be conducting a press briefing later this afternoon. Any updates I should provide?"*

"Sorry, Captain. Everything is still very preliminary. The medical examiner report isn't even complete. I will keep you in the loop. When we know, you will know."

"Thanks, guys. I know this is a tough one. Let me know if there is anything you need."

As the Captain departed, Patricia pulled out another file from her drawer. This case had not made it to the dry-erase board due to limited space. The case wasn't technically theirs, but they followed it closely and consulted. Camp was dead. He couldn't hurt any more children. The case now was ensuring no one else was involved. *"They have identified several of the children in the photos and have been reaching out to the parents. It is a mess."*

"I bet. Horrible news to get. Shrinks traveling with the Detectives?"

"Some. They don't have enough. Some other departments are kicking in, and our state guys have been assisting as much as possible. Over thirty children so far. Man was a monster."

"What about the other janitor? What was his name?"

"David Bell," she answered. *"Still nothing on this guy. A real ghost. They have found nothing on him. It is as if he never really existed. They have his social security, which was required for him to*

get paid. Nevertheless, there is almost no history on this guy. Home address was bogus. Guy who lived there was quite surprised when some plain clothes paid him a visit asking about Bell. Social security number was valid and simply points to him being born in Ohio."

"Ohio?" Roger asked.

"Yes. His first three numbers were two, eight, and nine. That code is in the group for Ohio. Did you not know that your first three numbers are your area numbers? Each state has a range of three-digit numbers for social security cards. You are given an area code based on your address when you apply for the number. An applicant from Ohio is given a code between two, six, eight, and three, zero, two."

"Huh," Roger shrugged. *"I never knew that."*

"For example, I was born in New York. It wasn't popular to get social security numbers back then at birth. My parents got me one later when we moved to Atlanta. I think I was around four or five. So, my number is Georgia, not New York. So really, Bell could have been from someplace else entirely. The first three numbers don't help that much. But it did give the detectives a place to start looking. However, like I said... nothing. Bell isn't on any records from the area he supposedly was living when an application for a social security number was submitted."

"Do they think he was involved?"

"They really don't know what to think. The guy did nothing wrong that they can tell. So far, the only prints at Camp's house are

his own and several children who have all been identified. It looks like Camp didn't get any visitors."

"Gee, I wonder why."

"They also don't have any of Bell's prints that they can accurately identify. He has no criminal record, no military record, and they certainly don't take your prints when you go work at a school."

"This just gets stranger and stranger."

The phone rang at Patricia's desk. *"Special agent Stills. Yes. Thanks, Doc. We will be right over."* She hung up the phone and turned to Roger. *"We are about to prove or disprove your theory. Doc asked us to come over to the morgue. Autopsy is done."*

Thirty minutes later, the pair pulled into the morgue parking lot. It was a short ranch style building that appeared anything but remarkable. The agents entered through the front glass doors and showed their badges to the front desk attendant. They were ushered into the back and shown the way to the elevator. The top floor was for administrative functions. The real work was done in the basement.

They found the medical examiner in the main surgical suite. The basement was a labyrinth of rooms for storage of not just equipment and supplies but also the recently departed. Doc was sitting at a simple metal desk reviewing files when the agents entered the suite. His recent case lay elevated on a table beyond the desk, respectfully covered in a dark sheet. I hate it here, Roger thought.

"Good morning, guys. Thanks for coming over. Sorry for the rush, but I just finished, and I know this case is a top priority." Doc rose from his desk and approached the table upon which laid Dana Chase. The two special agents silently followed.

Doc pulled back the sheet to reveal only Dana's head. The examiner had obviously opened and dissected the cranium but had put everything back together as carefully as possible, leaving only the left side of the brain exposed, as well as a portion on the top.

"All my preliminary findings proved correct. No drowning. Blunt force trauma to the head, etc. All in the report. The Physical Evidence Recovery Kit medical exam was performed by our sexual assault nurse examiner. No evidence of any type of sexual assault. But what I wanted to show you was this." He pointed to the open cavity at the top of the little girl's skull, simultaneously presenting a shallow metal dish with a lump of grey flesh.

"I removed this from the left hemisphere of her cerebrum. Tumor. Very large one. If not treated, this would have been fatal. I would be surprised if she wasn't showing some signs of its effect."

"What kind of signs?" Patricia asked.

"Memory loss. Confusion. Possibly the loss of balance. And the seizures should have been cause for alarm.'

Roger finally snapped out of his trance. *"Did you say seizures?"*

"Yes. There are a few indicators along with this tumor that infer she was having seizures. How many and how often is nearly impossible to tell. However, her Creatine Kinase levels are very high. They begin to rise an hour or two after an episode and can peak anywhere from twenty-four to seventy-two hours after. Based on her numbers, I would say she was killed between two to three days after having a seizure based on her levels."

"What else can cause these levels to rise?" Roger continued.

"Heart attack. Infections. Skeletal or muscular injury. Other disorders. Sometimes high-performance athletes can have elevated levels. But due to her age and the absence of any other disorders and infections, I am fairly certain it was seizures. And along with this." He gently tilted Dana's head to the side and used a metal tongue depressor to reveal her tongue. *"All those bite marks on her tongue are signs of a seizure. She has scarring as well."*

Just then, Roger's cellphone chirped. He backed away from the table to take the call. *Reception was terrible in the basement. I may have to go outside,* he thought, but just as he stepped near one of the tiny basement windows, the voice of the Desk Sergeant came through clear. *"Sir, we have another kidnapping, and you and Special Agent Stills are being requested at the scene. Cloverdale Park in Dale City. Units are at the scene."*

They arrived twenty minutes later at the small park. It was divided into a sporting area with several ballfields to the west and a playground with trails in the woods on the east side. The small parking lot in the center was filled with various police units. The quiet neighborhood was a scene of pure chaos. Roger and Pat approached a group of Detectives huddled around a Dale City cruiser. They were giving instructions to several uniformed officers, several with canines. Search areas were being assigned. Other officers were attempting to calm several citizens who were frantically screaming for answers. It appeared to be the family of the victim. Roger and Pat waited patiently; taking in the whole scene until one of the detectives finally broke from the huddle and approached.

"I am Detective Larsen. Are you the Special Agents from the State office?"

"We are. I'm Patterson, and this is my partner Stills. Want to give us a quick rundown? Do you have time? It seems pretty chaotic at the moment. We were told to rush over but didn't know this was an active scene."

"It is and it isn't. We had an abduction. Best guess is about two hours ago. I'll give you the basics and then I need to start working the witnesses?"

"Witnesses?" Patricia asked. *"Somebody saw whoever did this?"* Roger could hear the excitement in her voice.

"Not exactly. But someone may have unknowingly. Jon Parker age eleven, African American kid, was playing in the east side of the park with his dog. Pitbull. A few people saw him playing, and then the dog rushed into the woods. They heard some commotion but were too far away to really tell what was going on. That was around three o'clock when he got home from school. That is his normal routine, to come down to the park and play with the dog. Around four, someone spotted the dog on the side of the road on the north side of the park crawling in the street. It was a neighbor who knew the family and the dog. She called the grandmother and animal rescue. Dog was in bad shape. Multiple wounds all over its side and belly. It was sent to an emergency vet, but I doubt the thing will survive. It seemed to be crawling after the boy."

"Was anyone else home or just the grandmother?" Roger asked.

"Grandma watches him after school until his mom gets home from work. She normally arrives around six. But the grandmother obviously freaked out, called the police and called her daughter. Local units got here pretty quickly and started immediately searching the woods. Amber alert went out as soon as the grandmother gave us a current picture and a description of the clothes he was wearing. People in the park pointed out where they thought the boy entered the woods. We have the canines in there now trying to pick up a scent. Working theory is that somehow this guy lured the dog into the woods, and the boy followed. He disabled the dog and grabbed the kid. That is really all I have at the moment. You are both welcome to stay. I have plenty of hands searching the

woods, but I certainly wouldn't turn down help interviewing residents."

"Absolutely," Roger answered. *"Let me and my partner talk a couple of angles first."*

"Got it. Just let me know when you are ready."

The pair moved away from the patrol car. *"What do you think, Roger? Kinda fits our guys' MO but a boy. And a black boy at that. Serial killers and abductors normally stick with one gender and their own race. This would be highly unusual."*

"I agree completely Pat. We can't even prove yet that Chase, Jones, hell, even Cooper were taken by the same guy. But my gut is telling me to keep digging. Stalking a victim based on their pattern of behavior is nothing new. But utilizing the same approach, the distraction of a child interacting with their pet. That seems pretty specific. I feel like this is his method, and he isn't going to deviate. That is how we catch him."

"Well let's go catch him. Maybe somebody saw something. Detective Larsen. We are ready."

Tech: *I have the drive.*
President: *We have the target.*
Tech: *I will bring it by tonight.*
President: *Excellent.*

CHAPTER 16: THE NEXT JOB

Manassas, VA

Dane's route to the target was anything but conventional. Located in Northern Manassas, it was residential in nature but allowed for the unique route he was taking due to surrounding recreational, industrial, and entertainment venues. He would utilize all three to ensure he covered his tracks, leaving no trace of this nighttime home invasion. Thankfully, the President had imposed no timeline for this mission. It allowed for proper analysis and planning. The initial choice would have been a daytime entry while the occupant was at work. However, with further analysis of the neighborhood that option appeared daunting. The proliferation of teleworking, the average age of the neighbors clearly over retirement age, and the busy surrounding area almost guaranteed exposure. Someone would spot him as out of place. It would have to be at night. The target would be home. Difficult, but not impossible. All he had to do was get in, attach the electronic device he had been given to the computer tower in the den, and then leave after it had broken all encryption on the computer and cloned the internal hard drive. Easy.

He had spent the last five days preparing for tonight. His meeting with the President had provided him with the information he needed for his next job with the club. Myron

Wells of Manassas. IT specialist by day, purveyor of child sex videos by night. The capture of his license plate and picture had been enough for Charles's researchers to create a packet on him. Digging into his life had exposed his fetish for underage porn and the likelihood of distribution throughout the county. They were about ninety percent sure this was their guy. It appears that old Myron had taken a trip years ago to Thailand. There he had indulged in his wildest fantasies denied him thus far in life. The two-week holiday in Bangkok had shaped him into the man he was today. Shaped may not be the right phrase, Dane had reflected earlier in the week.

These proclivities were always there. Maybe dormant, maybe not, but either way, the trip removed any previous restraints Myron may have imposed on himself. Now removed, how would his desires manifest? He was clearly engaged digitally. They had some evidence that he was even contracting for videos to be produced overseas and sharing them with a U.S. audience. When would he take it to the next level and finally victimize someone in person? It was only a matter of time. *And what had he said to that fed weeks ago about offense and defense? Well, tonight he would play offense.* Myron, however, would have the best security possible on his computer. Apparently, he was highly regarded in the IT community. His coding was considered the best, and many large corporations and banks solicited his services. Dane had asked the President how he could be sure that this electronic device would crack Myron's computer security protocols if he was that good at his trade.

"Don't worry. Our guy is better. And Mr. Cooper, even though this assignment is for collection purposes, we do have enough on him if anything were to happen. By that, I mean if you are put into a situation that requires the elimination of Mr. Wells, please use your discretion. We need to get the full client list either from Mr. Wells or his computer."

The hardest part had been coming up with a plan to stash the motorcycle. For any clandestine activity that was a key task. A ticket, an encounter with law enforcement, or even a nosy bystander could compromise the operation. Dane did not have the option for something like a military freefall parachute insertion. No plane and certainly no assistance. Not even someone to drop him off in a car. He had to do this alone. He had taken the motorcycle for three different reasons. The first was trace evidence.

Trace evidence from himself, his environment, and even his home could never be truly eliminated. However, it could be mitigated. His truck was certainly full of dirt and dust and hair from his home and office. Unavoidable and traceable back to him. The motorcycle was different since it had no interior to collect such items. Sure, it may have some mud or dirt that could adhere to his clothes. He would just have to hope that if it did, it would either be prevented by the additional precautions he was going to take or at the very least, be common enough not to lead back to him.

The second reason was reliability. Both vehicles were aging, and there was no greater threat than getting stuck on the objective, in military terms known as the "X." The motorcycle was recently serviced and running well at the moment. The truck had been acting up lately. He silently cursed himself for not inquiring about an untraceable vehicle when the President had asked him what he needed. He certainly didn't want to come back now and ask for more resources. He would have to make do with what he had. He had considered a rental vehicle, but that came with other headaches. The last reason thought for the motorcycle was maneuverability. Dane had to plan for contingencies, including escape and evasion from law enforcement. He was under no illusion that he could simply outrun the police and their helicopters and roadblocks. Not to mention their overwhelming manpower should they wish to pursue him. The bike simply gave him more options for taking unconventional routes denied to squad cars which could provide that slim chance of escape. All it took was one small advantage to favor his odds. Slim, but he would take it. Slim advantages tended to add up over time. That much he had learned during all his years of operations.

He had ridden the motorcycle to a local bar in the Reston area. One known for being packed and staying open late. His bike could even remain there overnight if need be, the excuse of overindulgence in alcohol requiring an alternate means of travelling home if anyone asked the next day. That was very common these days. The bar was already hopping with the tail end of the happy hour crowd joined by the evening drinkers. He had scouted it beforehand and knew it would be busy. Instead of enjoying the revelries, he headed straight to the men's room. It was a single occupant bathroom, so he patiently waited his turn. When the "single-shooter" was free, he entered and locked the door. He quickly hopped onto the toilet and moved the ceiling panel he accessed the previous evening. He ensured his volume and notifications were off. No sounds or buzzing. Dane slid his cellphone into the ceiling, replacing the disturbed tile. This portion of his travel to target was complete. He had been seen at this bar, and cell phone records would place him here for as long as he needed. Contingencies. Necessary ones in case he had to use his discretion with Myron. On to phase two.

As he exited the bar, Dane pulled a small cell phone from the outside pocket of his backpack. It was a pre-paid phone purchased weeks ago in cash. When he accepted the offer from the club, he started preparing small things for operational purposes. One was communications. Dane knew that he needed to acquire alternate phones not directly tied to him in any way. He, of course desired to have no electronic signature associated with the actions he was going to undertake, but he knew that it was nearly impossible, especially without a support network assisting him. They were easy enough to purchase anonymously with cash and loaded with the appropriate programs. This particular phone had an Uber App pre-installed, and the account loaded with sufficient funds. Since the day of purchase, it had resided in a Faraday bag lined with flexible metallic fabric to block any signals to and from the device. The phone had only ever touched the network in a location far from his home and the office to initiate the device and load applications. He had also set up an anonymous storage unit that provided twenty-four-hour access. He had chosen an off-brand place in a questionable neighborhood, hoping that it provided the discretion he needed. The front desk clerk could not have cared less what name Dane provided. The pre-paid credit card was approved, and since the account was paid a year in full, the transaction did not warrant further scrutiny. Over the last three weeks, the storage unit became stocked with operational items he may or may not need. Again, he was considering possible contingencies. If he was ever suspected of a crime, or ever worse served a warrant, his home was clean and the storage unit off the books. This would be his base of operations for the time being.

The Uber arrived within the next ten minutes, and the second leg of the journey began. Dane's plan was to get dropped off at another popular nightspot with plenty of patrons in which to hide. After the vehicle left, he turned and headed in the direction of the park. Leg number three. This leg took him on a normal pedestrian path toward the Manassas Battlefield Park. He ensured his ball cap was pulled down across his brow. John and Jenny lived nearby, and someone spotting him would certainly bring up questions he wasn't willing to answer. He knew the park quite well since he and John had spent several afternoons there, hiking the historic landscape. John adopted his father's love of history and any chance they got, they swarmed over this and other battlefields with all their dwellings, monuments, and abandoned artillery pieces. Dane knew that it would be the perfect place to prepare for and begin the fourth and final leg of his journey.

The packet on Myron contained several details that provided insight into the planning for this evening. He was a methodically early riser. Lights-out in his house was never past eight-thirty. Early to bed and early to rise. Dane had selected a window for the entry between ten thirty and midnight. That gave him the time needed to work the lock on the backdoor, conduct his work on the computer, and then reverse his route home before the bars started closing at two in the morning. Normally he would plan at least an hour picking the lock on the back door. That was standard for an unknown lock when planning on entry operation. Plus, the club required what is called reliable and repeatable entry. They wanted back in the house whenever it was convenient. Dane would not have to create a key on-site, but he did need to create a copy method at the very least to replicate the key elsewhere.

Taking apart and decoding the lock or using a blank key to impression on site would be impractical, especially in the dark with limited light. Impressioning was the insertion of the key blank firmly into the lock and jiggling it up and down to make marks on the blank. With a file, those marks are then smoothed until gone. The process is repeated over and over again. Once there is no longer a mark on the blank, that pin depth is complete. Since most home locks are five pin locks that would take him all evening. Five tiny little scratches to file down. Myron would be up and making Dane a cup of coffee by the time he was finished. He hoped he could find Myron's keys so it wouldn't come to this. The actual entry should be standard since the packet also included detailed information about the lock. Someone had taken a close picture of it. Dane had no idea how they were able to get that close, imagining someone posing at a technician of some sort checking gas or water meters. Either way, the picture of the standard Schlage lock gave him plenty of opportunity to practice. He didn't even have to use the storage unit. The Maze had plenty of household Schlage locks for him to practice on. He simply pulled the two most common from the shelf in the Continental United States rooms and whiled away until he was satisfied.

He could defeat the lock in his sleep at this point. The movies overexaggerated the simplicity of picking a lock utilizing any of the standard methods. The truth was that it could sometimes be as easy. Thomas Magnum used a pick gun on hotel doors during his Honolulu investigations with lightning speed and was never at the door for more than a few seconds. But that ease and speed came with practice. Practice on a known lock. Rarely could someone just walk up to a lock and defeat it in seconds. Maybe some of the best locksmiths in the world could, but that was not him. Always plan for an hour. That was the rule. He ensured that he could utilize a standard pick gun as well as the more traditional method of picks and tension tools. The gun was modified for noise cancelation. It could be quite noisy pulling the trigger in the silence of the night. Dane had used heat shrink tubing to soften the metal-on-metal clicks. The gun was used with a tension tool. The theory was that slight tension was placed on the locking mechanism while the gun was triggered. The flat blade of the gun was supposed to strike the bottom of all the pins. The pins would rise and then become stuck in their proper slot as the lock turned. The motion would replicate the insertion of a properly cut key. The lock would then spin open.

The more traditional pick set used the same theory. Slight tension was applied, and a pike was used to push each pin up into place. It was more time consuming and required a delicate touch. Dane knew of some folks that were adept at a modified technique called raking. Same theory as the pick gun, tension was applied while a file was raked from back to front, attempting to pop each pin into place in the cylinder simultaneously. The other excruciating part of the whole adventure was when he departed. If you truly wanted to conceal the commission of the act, the door would have to be re-locked. It would have to be picked in the opposite direction. So, there was not one lock to pick tonight, but two. He carried the tools for all the techniques with him that evening. The possession of these tools by an unaccredited professional locksmith in of itself would be a misdemeanor at best. Best not to be caught with them.

During a lull in traffic, Dane left the sidewalk and began his trek into the woods. He had selected the perfect place to change. There he removed the contents from his backpack and hung the items on a nearby tree. He completely stripped out of his clothing, placing those items in the bag. He donned his new outfit that had been purchased at various locations in the last three weeks. The items have never entered his home or vehicle. Each purchase was immediately sealed in a plastic bag and placed in bins stacked at the rear of the storage unit. It was his final attempt to remove the possibility of any trace evidence that may discern his identity. His dress was appropriate for his mission this evening but also very benign if he was spotted. He was not dressed in all black like some ninja in the movies. A black sweatshirt and grey running shoes accompanied dark blue jeans. A dark ball cap sat atop his head, and thin mechanic gloves were in his pocket for donning once he was at the backdoor of the residence. A neck gator hung loosely, not uncommon for people to have. Upon completion, he would destroy the items, never to be used again. The industrial area nearby had a trash compactor which would be the final resting place. It wasn't perfect, but it was the best he could do to mitigate the risk. The only possible trace would be from the park to the target. Unavoidable but acceptable. His identity would not be tied to either location.

He moved swiftly through the woods, the slimmest of moonlight illuminating his path. The waning of the moon phase was a coincidence that favored him this evening. It was difficult to plan every aspect of an operation. Although he was not given a timeline for this evening, he knew that he could not stall and wait on the perfect set of circumstances. The moon phase just happened to be in his favor. He remembered the phrase often heard by the instructors at the schoolhouse when he was in attendance referencing the perfect plan for an operation. "*The enemy of good is perfect.*" He always tried to live by that mantra. The street he was looking for backed up to the woods of the park and the backyard of the house ran perpendicular to that wood line. He pulled the rear gate open slowly. Myron supposedly didn't have any animals, but a quick pause was just good practice. Dane did not want to sprint into awaiting jaws. The path was clear, and he had a straight shot to the patio, free from any obstacles. He would be exposed moving to the backdoor for mere seconds. He tensed and then exploded across the yard, finding the safety of the shadows near the house in under four seconds. The only lights in the yard were on each front corner fence post. The lights were guarding the two side gates to the yard. Not the back gate or the back door.

Dane hoped all Myron's security was this lax. Once inside that zone near the backdoor, he was virtually invisible. Even though the back lantern above the door was extinguished, habit caused him to slowly rotate the bulb in case the switch was activated from the inside. A quick glance through the kitchen windows told him the coast was clear. He knelt to the side of the door with his bag at his feet, the tools easily accessible. As he was preparing to remove the pick gun, muscle memory from all his years of training kicked in. No matter the operation, the technique is the same. Whether it is preparing to use a shotgun slug to blast a lock mechanism or enter quickly with a pick set, always check first to see if the door is even locked. He gently turned the doorknob.

"Well, shit," he thought to himself slowly rising to his feet and pushing the door inward. All that practice for nothing. This idiot didn't even lock his door.

Analyst: *One of the names you gave me popped up in New York.*

President: Who?

Analyst: *Henry Galfini. The Bronx. In the Fordham neighborhood in West Bronx.*

President: *Thank you. We will get someone right on it.*

CHAPTER 17: THE REVIEW

Arlington, VA

Pupil: *Hopefully this one isn't broken.*

Keeper: *That was unfortunate, but they break sometimes.*

Pupil: *I got a different color this time.*

Keeper: *Variety makes collecting interesting.*

Damn, these chairs are comfortable. Wish I had these in my apartment. Dane thanked Jack for the cup of coffee he was offered and settled deeper into the leather chair. The room was becoming all too familiar as he spent more and more time here. Charles lit a cigar as he accepted his own cup. This settling in routine had become common practice between the two of them before discussing targets and operations. Dane was under no illusion that these meetings were exclusively his. As he became more adept at intelligence analysis at work, he applied those techniques to readily available public information courtesy of the Internet. He was not the only working dog in the club. It was not obvious, but clues could be found along with mysterious deaths indicating that there was a decent size cadre of men like him.

Various stories on mysterious deaths were one thing, but sometimes what was left out of a story was more telling. The cause of death is unknown at this time. Appears accidental. The involvement of federal law enforcement was also interesting when the death did not occur on federal property. There was some story about a suicide in a parking lot. The guy supposedly ran a hose from his tailgate into his back window to off himself. Why would the FBI be interested in that? No, it certainly isn't just me. *I bet this place is a revolving door for people like me, Charles, isn't it?* He thought.

It was normally Charles who broke the ice during these little chats. He didn't disappoint today. *"That was excellent work concerning Mr. Wells the other night. The amount of data will take our people weeks to cull. However, we were able to get a lead on his contact overseas with whom he was commissioning videos. The Prime minister gave the green light, so the Royal Thai Police have already begun dismantling that operation all too... shall we say eagerly."*

"Glad to hear. It was fairly routine."

"Routine hardly seems appropriate for what you accomplished Mr. Cooper."

"It was not as hard as you would think. Myron may be some sort of data security specialist, but he lacks any prudence with physical security. Outside lights had burned out. Window shades were wide open. Hell, the back door wasn't even locked, which surprised me."

"Some people can be very careless about their personal security. Was the computer easy to access?"

"He has his home office on the first floor. He sleeps on the third. I could have turned on all the lights and watched a ballgame and he wouldn't have had a clue. The computer was right there at his desk. I plugged in the little magic box you gave me, and after five or so minutes, it turned green indicating completion. I simply removed it. The device worked quickly. I spent very little time in the office. And, since I didn't have to defeat the backdoor lock going in and out, my time on target was reduced to twenty minutes."

"May I assume then that the additional time you had to spend at Mr. Wells residence was because of the second task? A key."

"That was a little more challenging. While the little machine was doing its work, I searched all over for his keys. I checked by the doors, on the kitchen counter, everywhere. I eventually had to go upstairs. I found them on his dresser. He seemed to be a solid sleeper and didn't hear me grab them. I took them downstairs. I took an impression with clay. I tranced it on paper. I even took a photo of the key and inside the locking mechanism itself. When I got to work the next day, I got clean, untraceable blanks and made them in our shop. We have all the tools necessary to cut professional grade keys. I just had to measure the length on the notches and ridges. Input the numbers and let the key duplicator do the rest. Guys are working on stuff like that all the time for practice, so nobody even noticed. The measuring process is never perfect. That is why I gave you six slightly different variations on that chain."

"I am assuming then that you had no trouble departing the area unseen?"

"My route was solid. I went back the way I came and changed again in the woods. There is an industrial park nearby with no security. Their trash compactor took care of my clothes and gear for me. I mitigated the possibility of any trace elements from me to that residence in the event further action was warranted. I even had time for a beer at one of my cover stops heading home."

"Well, it certainly was a success. As I indicated earlier, we are developing several leads from Mr. Wells computer. His tech skills are good, but our guy is better."

"And what about old Myron? Do you require further assistance with him?"

"Thank you, but we do not. It seems Mr. Wells has a severe allergic reaction to peanuts. So severe in fact, he always keeps an EpiPen on him. Last night he must have accidently consumed something that triggered his allergy. Apparently, he did not take his phone or EpiPen to his bedroom. His brother found him in his bedroom near the door, dead from anaphylactic shock. He must have been crawling for help. Oh, and our man reported that the second key he tried from your set worked perfectly. He wanted me to pass on his compliments."

"Well, thank you. And that must have been agonizing for Myron," Dane smirked.

"I am sure it was. However, we do have another target that appears to be suitable to your skills."

"Before we get into a new target, I want to discuss Angela. Her case. My case."

"As I told you before Mr. Cooper, others are tasked with monitoring her case. May I remind you that it is unorthodox, and not to mention illogical to work your own child's case."

Dane could feel his frustration creeping to the surface, but he did his best to control it. *"Unorthodox. I would say everything this club is doing is a little bit unorthodox."* He took several deep breaths before continuing while Charles clearly was waiting him out. *"Can you at least provide me an update?"*

"I sympathize with you Mr. Cooper. I can assure you that her case will not be forgotten. Sadly, there are no updates or leads currently, but we are still looking."

Dane took the blow as best as he could. *"Ok, I understand. What is the next job?"*

"Have you ever heard of Henry Galfini? Florida resident but formally of New York City."

"Yeah. Some sort of mob guy, right? Working the family business in Miami. Supposedly killed his girlfriend and her daughter and then just disappeared. I am pretty sure he made it into the FBI's top ten most wanted. They have been looking for him for over a year now. Nothing."

"That is correct. Mr. Galfini was handling some low-level financial service operations on behalf of the family in the Little

Havana area. His father, Michael, the previous head of the family, passed on a few years back. There was a restructuring of sorts. Henry was considered too immature and volatile to lead the family business. At times he demonstrated very violent and very public outbursts, and there were rumors of underage prostitutes which the family disapproved of. His uncle was named the head of the family instead. Temporarily. He is acting as a sort of Regent to the throne. Henry was sent to Miami to prove he could lead and expand operations. He was to establish a foothold there to prove he was worthy someday of leadership. We are confident that those days are over for him."

"I guess even the mob has standards. How did he even come up on your radar?"

"I discussed his proclivity for underage prostitutes in New York. Apparently, he tried to change his ways with a fresh start in a new city but fell into his old routines and regularly raped his girlfriend's daughter. According to a police report filed by the girlfriend, this had been going on for nearly a year. The daughter was terrified of Henry but finally confided in her mother. Tragically, their apartment burned to the ground before formal charges could be brought. Both were burned alive."

"I remember that. I remember the news initially said it could have been faulty wiring but later changed the narrative claiming arson. Boyfriend Henry was wanted for questioning."

"Correct. It seems that in his younger days, Henry had quite the talent for torching businesses either for insurance claims or

retribution for failing to comply with family directives. The police did not have all this information at first. It wasn't until the FBI got involved that he was revealed as an arsonist."

"If the FBI hasn't been able to find him in over a year, this is going to be a little difficult. I am no magician. I at least need a starting point. I don't think that will be Miami. Pretty sure he has left there considering his notoriety."

"We have one for you, Mr. Cooper. And it is in the Bronx. It appears that Henry may have returned home. His family is understandably unhappy with his actions, but he is still family, and they may provide him assistance. We assess his surfacing will be brief. Probably to collect some assets and fade away underground again. We need you to take care of him before that happens. Can you do that?

"Yes, I can. How do you know he is in the Bronx?"

"Our analyst at the NSA has provided a general location. She has access to all National collection platforms and databases. We provide her names from time to time, and she can clandestinely monitor the network. Henry has been sitting in her queue for quite a while. His cell phone registered briefly yesterday on a cell tower in the Fordham neighborhood. She then notified me."

"You have someone in the NSA monitoring the cell phone network?"

"And the internet."

"Wow. Ok. I guess I shouldn't be surprised."

"As I told you before Mr. Cooper, we have many members, filing many roles."

"Hah, I bet. You mentioned that before."

"What I don't understand is if she can monitor his phone number, why wasn't the FBI doing the same thing? They should have those types of resources or at least some sort of access."

"They can receive assistance with monitoring, and they are at the moment. However, they are monitoring Mr. Galfini's last known cell phone when he was in Miami. The number we are monitoring is an old Bronx's cell phone. Actually numbers. We have several numbers that he used in his early days when he wanted discrete communication. He must have retrieved a stash from somewhere and fired up an old phone."

"Ah, makes sense. Ok, so, am I to assume this needs to be done quickly?"

"Yes. We would need you to leave right away. Is that going to be a problem?"

"No. I can come up with some emergency leave excuse and easily head up to New York tomorrow. I have plenty of gear and clothes at my storage unit for another several jobs. I am just confused about planning timelines. I need to plan to get up...."

"Transportation has been taken care of Mr. Cooper." Charles slid him a manila envelope. *"Inside, you will find an address and a hangar number for a private airfield. The key card will get you through the gate. The flight will land at a private airfield outside the city, and you will be dropped off at the place of your choosing. Completely untraceable to you. Also, you will find some cash for expenses while in New York along with a, I believe you call it a burner phone. My number has been saved in the contacts."*

"Ok. That's a good start. Private plane? Do I even want to ask? I am going to request leave. Local. The unit is pretty good about last minute requests. Especially since we are slow right now and I have days I have to use anyway, or they go away at the end of the fiscal year. At first glance, I would estimate that this is going to take me at least a week, if not longer. Public transportation will be limited for me due to all the cameras. I will need a motorbike. Something beat up and unremarkable but reliable."

"I can arrange for that."

"Can I rely on assistance from your contact at the NSA? I assume real-time monitoring is not possible, but maybe updates if he comes up on different towers. I can pull the cell phone tower mapping data from work. If she can tell me a tower and panel anytime he comes up on the network, I should be able to triangulate and narrow the search area."

"I will talk to her. I have already asked to be updated anytime the phone is active. I will provide you with time and locations."

"Great. My personal cell is going to be an issue. I can't take it with me since it could tie me to New York. However, I also can't be away from it for too long either. Work could call. My son, etc. A day or two is feasible, but a whole week? I'll have to figure that one out. Contingencies. If, for some reason, I came up on law enforcement's radar I need to have a solid alibi. I don't want my phone on the network in locations near Galfini or even in the city, for that matter. Murphy always gets a vote."

"We have a contingency. We had our IT specialist work out a solution." Charles handed Dane an index card. *"Go to that website on your burner phone. My IT specialist will remote into your phone, take over, and install an application. He has created a very special program for... he called it spoofing cell towers. He said he would need about twenty minutes to complete the installation. And he requested you have a strong internet connection while he is working."*

"How is he going to spoof it? The phone will connect to the towers in New York. It will constantly jump panels looking for the strongest service. It is a non-stop activity while your phone is turned on. That is how the network works."

"I am not very technical Mr. Cooper. All I know is that he creates custom programs based on each phone. Somehow, he can hide your number in a given city and simultaneously have it on a cell tower in another one."

"That would be an incredibly handy little trick if it works. Private planes. Coders. NSA Analysts. You seem to have more resources than most federal agencies."

"In some way we do. And less burdensome to coordinate. As I am sure you have seen by now, our members are extremely motivated, much like yourself."

Washington, D.C.

The next day, the Washington Monument's shadow encompassed nearly the entire Mall area as it made its' way west to the horizon. The download to his phone was nearly complete. Dane had opted to retrieve one of his Wi-Fi hotspot pucks from his storage unit for the mysterious program load on his phone. Even though Charles had ensured him that the IT tech was a trustworthy member of the club, Dane decided to keep him off his private home Wi-Fi network. Precautions.

The stop at the unit had been quick and painless. CSM Reynolds readily signed the last-minute leave form, barely listening to Dane's crafted reasoning.

"Dane, you don't have to explain desired time off to me. You earned the leave. Your shop is solid and will survive a week without you. They did just fine before you came aboard."

After that, he proceeded to his storage unit to gather his necessary equipment. He was selective in the gear he chose since one, he was going to have to carry it most of the time, and two, New York had some of the strictest laws when it came to the possession of weapons and/or burglary tools. Most states allowed up to five-point-five-inch blade knives. New York restricts it to four inches. Like that makes a difference in the lethality. Nevertheless, he reasoned that if he needed something unusual, the wad of cash in his backpack could convince proprietors of black-market venues to provide. The only difficult item to find would be a gun. However, he wasn't planning on using one anyway. Charles had requested an accidental death.

The Uber arrived at the World War II memorial that he had summoned on yet another untraceable phone once his personal cell was in the Faraday bag. It whisked him to a small private airfield in northwestern Maryland, a good distance from D.C. After being dropped off, the card key he had been given unlocked one of the passenger gates, admitting him to the airfield. Since there was only one visible hanger, it was reasonable to assume he would find his ride inside.

He could hear the Gulfstream plane before he saw it as he entered the building. The pilot was clearly conducting pre-flight procedures in anticipation of a pending departure. The hangar was void of people. Void of equipment. Void of everything except the twenty-six-ton aircraft in the center, its stairs deployed, awaiting its passenger. As he climbed the steps, a young man exiting the cockpit met him. Probably, the first officer. It takes two to pilot the aircraft. The senior pilot was working on the start-up.

"Please have a seat anywhere, sir. We will be departing momentarily." With that, he retrieved the staircase, ensuring the door was properly sealed, and returned to the cockpit. Moments later, Dane could feel the plane lurch slightly forward, taxiing for the runway. *Damn, these guys don't fool around.*

CHAPTER 18: THE URGENT JOB

New York City, NY

Dane put his short flight time to good use. The club had provided a robust file on Henry Galfini. It contained dossiers on family members, business associates, and confidants. *Confidants*, he thought. Just say other known criminals. Equally important were establishments he had frequented as a New Yorker. Dane wasn't looking for his favorite restaurant or the park where he learned how to throw a baseball but rather seedy places from his past where he could seek shelter. Henry had spent nearly thirty years of his life in the city, beginning work at fourteen years old as a Runner. Messenger. Running notes to and from different family rackets throughout the city. Mostly in West Bronx.

The mob caught on much quicker than other criminal enterprises when it came to wiretaps, which made complete sense since it seems to have been created just to catch them in illegal activities. Wiretapping is as old as the invention of the telephone. Upon the birth of the phone, ways to record it followed shortly. Although, wiretapping began in the eighteen-nineties, it was established as a tried-and-true law enforcement technique during the Prohibition era. Bootleggers were the target, the Al Capones of the country. Elliot Ness and his crew would track down those early mobsters, based on information they received over the wire. The technique of course, evolved as did the modern telephone system in the country. Wires connected the United States through switchboards in the early days. Operators then manually connected calls. That was eventually replaced by fiber optic and then augmented with the modern-day cell phone.

However, with each advancement in communication came a new way to intercept it. Dane was never particularly skilled at those techniques. He was familiar with how the networks worked and understood the intercept theory. Cell phones jumped from tower to tower, constantly looking for the best connection. One second, you could be on one tower, the next another. The user never knew. Dane was able to use some of the equipment and locate and lock phones. The equipment would act as a cell tower. The phone would attach and stay attached. It would not jump to another tower, hence locked. There was then a signal between the fake tower and the target's cell phone. Different pieces of equipment would then be used to follow that signal to the specific targeted cell phone. However, those days had passed. Dane had not been involved in the developing technology for several years, which may as well have been a lifetime. 4G, LTE, 5G. Advancements in technology moved so fast. He always overheard guys talking about new equipment and new techniques at the unit all the time. The Maze had a room where they would test all new sorts of gear and gadgets to find and lock a cell phone. In Henry's case, Dane had both an advantage and a disadvantage. Since Henry fired up an old phone, the technology was outdated. His phone was 3G. A dinosaur. Easy to find and locate. However, there was an expiration date. The big networks were slowly phasing out the service. 3G would be gone soon, and Henry's phone would no longer be of use to him. But Dane still had time.

His intent was never to utilize any specialized equipment. It would be too cumbersome to drag that gear all over New York. He would need a large vehicle with lots of power. It would stand out in the neighborhoods he would need to work. It would also be extremely difficult to navigate the reckless New York Drivers, the pot-holed streets, and the endless road construction while trying to use the equipment. It would take two to three people for that type of operation. Instead, the plan was to ascertain the general locations of the phone and then try to correlate locations from Henry's past.

The aging network provided several interesting data points about the phone attached to its network. The one that Dane was interested in was timing advance. It was not an exact science, but it was useful to determine a search area. Timing advance was basically the approximate time the cell phone signal took to reach the nearest tower to transmit a call. It is measured in steps of time. That could then be converted into an approximate distance based on the speed of radio waves. Dane trusted the math done by others. He had sat in several courses on radio wave theory. It made his head hurt. The bottom line was that he used the tower mapping data acquired at the unit for these measurements. The data was a little older since it was obtained for an exercise a few years ago in the city. However, since the 3G network had not changed as resources were put against 4G and 5G, he was confident in its accuracy. He could then identify what tower Henry had used, and what panel he had used and then input the timing advance. It would then give him an approximate distance Henry was from the tower. It provided a general location. A very general location. Standard cell phone towers have three panels. A, B, and C. They span one hundred and twenty degrees of coverage for that tower. Hence, the three panels combined provide a complete three-hundred-and-sixty-degree coverage, a circle around the tower in theory.

Dane knew that signals bounced around all the time. Buildings, hills, and anything obstructing the line of sight interrupted them. Signals were also pulled from tower to tower. Depending on the amount of phone traffic on one particular tower, a person could literally be standing fifty feet from a tower, yet their cell phone was connected to a tower eight-hundred feet away. It all had to do with timeslots, which made Dane's head hurt even more. He was going to use the information on Henry's phone as a starting point. Nothing more. He would start his search in the neighborhood area that, in theory, should connect to the tower and the specific panel provided by Charles' mysterious NSA analyst. If she provided additional tower data, he would triangulate and narrow the search area. Hopefully, he would find an establishment or person of interest from Henry's past in those locations. That would be his start point.

Dane planned to concentrate first on known confidants. His reasoning was that although Henry returned to his roots, he may not be entering the welcome arms of his family. Even though they are criminals, they have a livelihood to protect. They also would most likely not place themselves in the same criminal category as the black sheep of the family. Racketeering, money laundering, even murder of a rival is one thing. Henry sunk to a new level entirely when he raped and murdered a child. The Family would have thought, *Nope, we are out.* They might not turn him in, but Dane was fairly certain they would turn him away. Former business partners would react similarly. Businesses could not suffer by tainting their reputations associated with Henry. It would have to be confidants. Old friends. Real pieces of shit like Henry. Guys that couldn't care less what Henry had done and Dane had two promising prospects.

Dane woke to the noise from the streets outside. He had arrived late in the evening after departing the airfield and making his way to his current location at some crappy little hotel. He had enough money for a nicer location, but those types of places rarely took cash and always wanted identification. This was the type of place that you could rent for a day or an hour. Not that he cared. He just needed a place to sleep at night. He anticipated being on the streets all day, and he certainly wasn't going to leave any valuables in the room. The anonymity was more important than comfort. He had received a text last night from Charles for a second hit on Henry's phone. It had popped up again nearby the other tower. Exact triangulation was impossible, but it did help narrow his list of possible locations. He opened the mapping program on his laptop and found the section of Fordham in West Bronx where the two cell phone towers overlapped. A large area still but better than nothing. Dane had identified two people from Henry's past in that area, two dive bars he was known to frequent, and a pawnshop he had a relationship with. By relationship, that meant his former fence. The fence fell into the category of former business associates he was originally ruling out, but the man's business was in the area. Family business partners would be reluctant to be in contact with Henry, but a former fence may not care since it was a quick transaction of legally questionable items. The fence would move the merchandise without anyone knowing he received it from Henry. Might as well check it out. The two dive bars didn't open for another few hours.

Dane found the shop easily enough. The rundown storefront had seen better times. Garbage was strewn about the sidewalk and streets. The cinder block walls showed obvious cracks from wear and tear over time. Even a window was missing, a sheet of plywood filling in as a substitute. The neon sign signaling that the place was open for business was almost completely burnt out. A small bell jingled as he entered. His bag contained an old camera that he had purchased from another pawnshop several streets away. He removed it and presented it to the young man behind the counter. The young man's age told Dane that this wasn't the fence. *Maybe his son?*

"Good morning, sir. How can I help you?" the man asked Dane.

"Wanted to see if I could get anything for this camera. I found it cleaning out my mom's old place. I have no use for it, but it looks old. Figured it might be worth something to a collector or whatever."

"Let me take a look. Anything that isn't digital these days is considered old," the young man chuckled.

"Thanks. Where's George. I haven't been home in a few years, but he is normally here all the time."

"Oh yeah. That's my dad. He hasn't been doing so well for the last couple of months. The cancer came back. Had to set him up with hospice. I have to keep this place going for him to pay the bills. I am afraid he is not going to make it much longer."

"Hell, kid, really sorry to hear that. Tell your pops Mark said hello and I hope he rebounds."

Strike one, he thought.

Later that day, Dane identified the location of both bars from Henry's youth. He decided not to enter either of them initially. The more he showed his face, the more likely he could be remembered later if anyone asked around. These were local bars. New faces would stand out. Those new faces would also be challenged. This was a tough guy neighborhood, and tough guys had to make sure new faces understood the order of things. Fortunately, for him, the surrounding area was trashed. Garbage on the streets, run-down buildings. He felt like he was driving through a bombed Iraqi neighborhood at the height of the war. He wandered across the street from each bar, exploring the area. He was looking for items in which to conceal cameras. Loose brick, large pieces of trash, even cinder blocks if he could find them. He selected small items from each area. Things that blended in and would likely remain on the ground or a wall if left behind. Something people would not even notice. He wanted to have eyes on the buildings. He doubted the bars would gather many patrons until later in the day and evening, so he returned to the flophouse with his treasures. He removed several small but powerful cameras from his backpack and started working on his stay behind devices. These devices were intended to blend into the environment and conceal the cameras. He had glue, putty, and a few other items to help camouflage the cameras. He would place two of his creations covering each door of the bars. His plan was to film the locations each evening and then review the four tapes overnight and into the early morning hours. After resting, he would replace the cameras and repeat the cycle.

Dane was betting on the fact that nobody would move his carefully placed debris. The cameras would work in the day as well as the night, just not as well at night. He hoped the lights he spotted over each door worked in the evenings. He would need some level of light if he was to recognize Tony Mazzo. He was a lowlife like Henry. They had grown up together on the streets of Fordham. Both scrapping by with their knuckles and wits, trying to prove their worth. Petty theft. A little breaking and entering. Even some grand larceny when they were fifteen. They stole a neighbor's Cadillac for a joy ride, ending after only a few blocks by crashing the beast into a bus stop shelter. After high school, Tony joined the Army. He didn't have the family connections afforded Henry and, therefore, no guarantee of work and protection. He was treated like family, but he was not family. He had to earn that kind of respect and inclusion. He had told people that he was joining for combat training. He boasted to anyone who would listen that he would gain skills desperately wanted by the family and prove his merit.

He did gain the skills of an infantryman. He also nurtured and intensified already apparent characteristics of cruelty and sadism. He and the Army parted ways after four short years. The packet provided on Tony was a little thin due to the haste this job required. The mysterious Colonel was light on the details. But Dane could read between the lines about Tony's combat service. There had been several investigations of wartime atrocities. And although he was never charged, Tony was barred from re-enlistment and sent back to the Bronx. Moreover, just six months later, the Army vet found himself on Ryker's Island. The charges of home invasion and assault and battery were later joined by Felony murder when his elderly victim died a week after the beating he received from Tony. That charge would be reduced to Involuntary manslaughter. He would go on to serve fifteen years.

From there, Tony was molded by the system. The violent and unstable combat veteran returned a hardened Nazi. Another feather in his cap. A party affiliation initially chosen for survival turned into a way of life. With his long black coat and combat boots, a fad worn by many people, Tony added to his style and brought it to another level completely. He had a bald head with silver metal piercings covering his ears and nose. The coup de grace or finishing stroke was full sleeve neck tattoos along with a swastika behind each ear. Altogether, it will make him easily identifiable. The nighttime camera footage will probably pick him up. *War criminal. Thief. Murderer. And Nazi. I have no problem removing this oxygen thief from the planet if necessary.*

The next five days were grueling. Dane's internal clock began to re-set like it had done so many times in the past. The combat operations of his youth mirrored this cycle. The motto that Special Operations owned the night was the standard. Rest and refit were done during the day. The night was for the hunt, but this hunt was different. Since he was a one-man operation, he found himself with very little sleep. In combat, during the day, analysts would pour over the intelligence found on target from the previous evening while the hunters slept. At dark, the mantle would be passed as the analysts briefed the new targets and then often sought their own refuge, knowing that fresh information would be waiting for them to sift through in the morning.

As the wars progressed and the military learned, many analysts adopted the same cycle as the hunters for various reasons. The first was that intelligence taken from capturing one individual could very lead to another person of interest. Command often worried that the second target might get spooked if they knew their compatriot was captured. These were called time sensitive targets, which meant a reloading of ammunition and often a second helicopter flight of the evening courtesy of the government. Those nights were brutal. Dane had never gone out a third time in one night but was sure some of the direct-action specialized teams did. Analysts also often stayed up during nighttime operations to provide real-time intelligence. They would advise commanders, analyze changing environments, and, most importantly, monitor video feeds that came from UAVs or unmanned aerial vehicles. These drones would be used to clear routes for teams that were driving, keep eyes on the objective to ensure things hadn't changed, or identify any squirters after a hit. Squirters were enemy combatants that fled the objective rather than fight. They often fled to re-group and then counterattack. The eyes in the sky reported on them. However, Dane was now analyzing his own intelligence collection. He didn't have drone footage, but hours upon hours of video covering the front doors of the seedy bars which required viewing, along with the task of triangulating various cell phone tower locations sporadically provided to him by Charles. His big break came on the fifth day.

Unbeknownst to him, the NSA analyst was conducting research of her own. As Charles explained, she had to be careful to leave no trace in the system. However, her delicate probing had paid off. She acquired not one, but two locations for a cell phone that Henry had called to, on several occasions. The location was in the coverage area servicing Rosy's bar. It was the second of two bars Dan had selected. He just had to find the owner of the phone. He was hoping that he had guessed correctly, and that owner was Tony Mazzo.

Cop: *There are several cases that I feel may be interconnected.*

President: *Interconnected kidnappings? That would not be the first time, but rare.*

Cop: *Three kids almost exact same MO. Fourth case also very similar.*

President: *Send over the jackets. We will review with a fresh set of eyes.*

CHAPTER 19: THE INVESTIGATION

New York City

Pupil: *This one is working out.*

Keeper: *Glad to hear it.*

Pupil: *I am going to start looking for a third.*

Keeper: *Just make sure you are ready for that responsibility before you grow your collection.*

God, I hate this city. He had been posted to the New York office in the late eighties through the early nineties. It was right before Mayor Giuliani was elected and began his steady crackdown on crime. The streets were dirty. The people were dirty. He felt dirty. And despite all the efforts over the last three decades, it was becoming that way again. Lawlessness and crime were exploding across the country. New York was not immune to this cancer. The city could not disguise its disease from a thousand feet. *It is a disease,* he thought. And we seem to have no cure. Politicians spout out at the mouth. They rant about guns. They rant about corrupt police and most vocally, they rant about each other being the cause of the problem. But none of that is the problem. It is our culture. Its rot. Our apathy. Our lack of decency. Our lack of humility. Our loss of morals. *It is us.*

The pilot informed Carl that they were two minutes out. Their destination was a railyard along the Harlem River. Two idiots had wandered into the yard sometime early this morning. They were either drunk morons stumbling through the area after overindulging at a Yankee game or criminals hoping to score something of value. All that didn't matter at the moment. Both men were in pieces all over the yard, apparently struck by one of the trains early this morning. An express train, *yuck*. Normally, this would not concern Carl or the FBI. However, it was believed one of those scattered pieces belonged to Henry Galfini, heir to the Galfini empire, currently on the run for double homicide and rape of a minor.

What the hell was Galfini doing in New York? Over a year on the run, and he shows up here. What made him re-surface? And was this really an accident? All these thoughts went through Carl's mind as the helicopter began its final approach. He knew the crime scene would be a circus. NYPD, transit cops, FBI and the U.S. Marshalls, to name a few. Nobody could pass up the investigation of a highly prolific fugitive. However, Carl didn't travel all this way because of Henry's crimes both as a New Yorker and a Floridian. Others at the Bureau would be looking at mob connections. He had convinced his superiors to let him fly up because of his theories about pedophiles and child rapists, of which Henry was both. Carl believed someone else may have hunted Henry as prey.

"You sure you don't want to use the fast ropes?" Carl heard the pilot say in his headphones. *"You would make one hell of a grand entrance sliding down out of a helicopter."*

"You're a real comedian. I prefer to be set down on the ground rather than descend at a high rate of speed."

The helicopter belonged to the FBI's fabled Hostage Rescue Team or HRT. Headquarters was currently short on rides, so Carl had called in a few favors down at Quantico. He sat among several of the operators. They planned on conducting some urban warfare training while Carl was down at the scene. They were awash in enough combat gear to take over a small nation. Rifles slung, packs at their feet, and even a few working dogs made the trip. Their long tongues hung loose as they panted in anticipation of a good day's work. He was lucky they had a planned flight up here today. The proverbial two birds with one stone. Carl had arranged for them to conduct some mock drills on Governors Island near Fort Jay as bonus training in exchange for the free ride.

New Yorkers were used to helicopters buzzing around the area as tourists sought the views of the metropolis from above. The shot out from tall skyscrapers in lower Manhattan crossing the East River by the Brooklyn Bridge before flying a lazy southwestern loop over to the Statue of Liberty and then up the Hudson River. The FBI bird would fit right in. It also provided the pilots with good training in communicating with air traffic control in the crowded airspace, should they need to enter a similar place during future executions of their mission. The military conducted similar training. The air traffic control in combat is normally some orbiting beast flying well above the battlefield tracking, all aerial platforms, both enemy and friendly. Here, as in most cities, was probably an overworked and underpaid civilian controller on their sixth cup of coffee after only a few hours on shift, wishing to God they had more people to help track the aircraft over the city.

The pilot set down a good distance away from the flashing lights of all the responder vehicles. The rotor wash from the spinning blades would play havoc with the crime scene. The pilot knew better than to scatter possible evidence literally into the wind. Carl gave them a quick thanks as he unbuckled and exited the side door. He hustled away from the aircraft so it could quickly depart the area and cease covering everything in dirt and filth. As he made his way over to the large grouping of officers, he scanned the railyard. It had been shut down temporarily, which he figured must be tormenting the train company.

This part of the country relied heavily on rail for everything from goods shipments to commuters both in and out of the city. New York was a major East Coast hub. He took in the scene to also get a sense of what may have happened if this was not an accident. Chain link fences with crowns of razor wire appeared to encompass the entire area. Tracks crisscrossed the yard, but it was devoid of much else. There were a few railcars scattered about, but the terrain was generally flat. The cameras he saw mounted on tall poles throughout should have captured the sequence of events culminating with the death of Galfini. Lights appeared to be mounted on every available pole in the yard as well. This place should have been brightly lit, and video surveilled.

Carl recognized one of the lead FBI agents upon entering the crime scene. The two men shook hands.

"Hey, Dan. Want to walk me through this mess?"

"Good to see you, Carl. I heard you were coming up to see us New York boys. The scene is still pretty fresh. NYPD and Transit did a thorough job roping the area off and preserving the scene. But this is not going to be easy."

"What a nightmare." Carl peered south along the tracks where officers were placing yellow, numbered placards in an area that seemed at least equal to a football field. The entirety of the tracks was covered in a sea of yellow. It appears that various parts of the two criminals traveled quite a distance.

"It stretches for quite a ways." Dan pointed about twenty meters north along the track near some sort of switching box about five to six feet tall. *"That is where the blood pattern starts. Give or take a few feet, of course. We must assume initial contact caused some blood splash in both directions, but we believe they were struck by the switching box over there. The conductor didn't see a thing until some blood got on the window. He hit the wipers, and he quickly hit the emergency all-stop when it smeared a dark color. Keep in mind it was pitch black, so he couldn't immediately*

tell what it was. He wouldn't have even been able to tell if it was a human or a large animal. The procedure is to stop regardless in case the train is damaged. Not sure how any living thing could damage a beast like that, but rules are rules, I guess."

"How did he not see them? It looks like this place is lit up like a Christmas tree with all these light poles. Plus, the trains have headlights, don't they?"

"True on both accounts, but not every light in the railyard is working. A lot are burned out. Quite a few to maintain. Along this stretch alone, about ten or so are out. The ones along the adjacent tracks have the same problem. The whole area is quite dark at night. The train lights should have caught the two victims, but if they had passed out on the tracks or fallen over near that switch box, there is a very good chance they wouldn't have been seen by the crew. And then, even if the conductor saw them, these things don't exactly stop on a dime."

"I would assume they travel relatively slowly through this yard, Dan. With all the various tracks and switching lines that must occur, they should have been able to stop if they see something."

"You are right when it comes to local trains. But this was the express, hence its location on the far edge of the yard, away from the other lines. This one runs from Boston all the way to D.C. A lot of commuters head out on a Monday to the big cities and then stay for a week and commute back on Fridays. Very common. And these trains start running early. There was a complete lack of visibility at four- thirty in the morning when the conductor called the

emergency stop. They were moving fast. Hence, the phrase expresses. Going between sixty and seventy. Gotta get those important people to D.C."

Carl pointed around at the various cameras in the area. *"Have we started going through footage yet?"*

"We are compiling all of it now. But just like the lights, many don't work. Cameras aren't really a priority anymore for these railyards. Nothing to steal, so there is nothing to protect. Their stance is, why spend the money? They adhere to Federal Railroad Administration guidelines regarding safety, and that is really it. They maintain the fences and barriers to keep the public from wandering in and hurting themselves. Their position is that if you somehow happen to stumble into the yard, you should still be able to avoid the big shiny things moving on a single line."

"Hah, well, that clearly didn't work."

"Thanks, Carl. I wouldn't have figured that out if I didn't have a hotshot from D.C. advising me," Dan smirked.

"You're welcome. Maybe toxicology will give us some indication of what happened. Alcohol. Drugs?"

"The coroner will do his best, but you can see he has his work cut out for him with getting clean samples." Dan cast his arm about the area, demonstrating the scope of the crime scene. To Carl, it looked all too familiar regarding long forgotten battlefields, spotted in dark, red stains. Body parts were everywhere. *Would*

the coroner be able to even test the parts that were intact for alcohol or drugs?

"Alright, Dan. So, what's up here? What happened, and why was Henry here? I assume the Miami guys are already on their way, if not here yet. You guys must have a working theory. After all this time, why did he surface? And why did he surface here, of all places? This is the one town where he could be easily recognized"

"We think he may have been desperate for funds and that is why he surfaced. He was working some loan shark operations for the family out of little Havana before he went on the run. He must have had funds to sustain himself for a little while but not indefinitely. Being a fugitive isn't cheap. All his accounts were frozen in Miami once he became the main suspect in the rape and murder. He quickly bolted. He got a little out before then, but still not enough."

"So, he comes back to his roots for some financial aid? I can see him coming back to the familiar for some comfort, but I can't see the family touching this guy with a ten-foot pole. He may be family but, contact with him could hurt business."

"That is our theory. As far as we can tell, he had no contact with anyone from the family. We are going to have to pull some strings with a judge even to obtain cell phone records."

"Can't you just look at his pho..." Carl stopped himself right there. *"Let me guess. It is in little pieces of telephones all over these tracks."*

"Exactly. Not much for our guys to work with. But we did identify them from two wallets. The other hero here is Tony Mazzo. Real scum. Murderer. White Supremacist. You would have liked him. He was a childhood friend of Henry. He has been implicated in some armed robberies as of late, but nothing has stuck. We think Henry reached out to him to score some work. Tony is just as big a piece of shit as Henry. He wouldn't have cared about his reputation. We think he was going to cut Henry in on a few big scores. Put some money in his pocket and then send Henry on his way. Henry would be free to crawl back under whatever rock he was hiding under."

"But the express train ruined their plans. Therefore, that still leaves the cause of death. Drunken mishap or murder?"

"As strange as it sounds Carl, I think these two idiots got hit by a train on accident, making the world just a little bit better. If it was a hit, it was a strange way to do it. It would be a pain in the ass. Just shoot them and drop them in the bottom of the river. NYPD shares this theory. And it is their backyard. They have to deal with the Galfini family on a full-time basis. Unless one of these cameras tells a different story or some miracle lead falls into our lap, I think Amtrak just took two very bad man off the streets."

Fairfax, VA

"Well, the dog died. That really sucks." Patricia placed a folder in front of Roger as she took a seat at her desk. *"That is from the animal hospital out in Dale City. That's where they took Jon Parker's dog. Amazing that it survived as long as it did. Even more incredible that it crawled after the boy."*

Roger was looking at side by side photos of both the crime scene and the location of the now-deceased dog. *"What was the dog's name?"*

Patricia looked up a little perplexed but then confronted her notes. *"Shelly."*

"Shelly. Thanks. Just like to be accurate. Am I reading this right? Eight stab and slash wounds to the torso, front legs and the head and neck area?"

"It is horrible. She lost her left ear and eye, a good portion of her jaw and a partial amputation of the right foot. I can't believe she was able to give pursuit for nearly a block."

Roger nodded his head. He was looking at the trail of blood the Pitbull had created trying to save a member of her pack. *"The loyalty of a dog will never cease to amaze me. Anything from the medical examiner or the canvas of the area from the other officers?"* Roger asked, knowing that he and Pat had come up empty regarding the people in the neighborhood they had spoken with.

"Nothing so far. The medical examiner went to the animal hospital to evaluate the dog as it relates to the crime scene. He will have a report later, but he was not optimistic that there would be any helpful evidence. Mostly looking for human blood in the event the dog got in a bit or two." Once again consulting her notes, she continued. *"No strange vehicles were reported. Nobody was drawing attention like they should not have been there. It is a small,*

local park. Used mostly by the surrounding community, but outsiders stop in or pass through occasionally. One lady I talked to said cyclists will pass through often as well as joggers. She has even seen a businessman sit at one of the park tables, eating lunch and talking on the phone. But nothing on that day."

"Damn. Can this be related to Cooper, Chase, and Jones? It is so similar."

"It is Roger. But the race thing is throwing me off. Most serial criminals victimize their own race. Not a one hundred percent hard and fast rule. Jeffrey Dahmer never seemed to care, but he was an anomaly."

"And let's not forget gender. Three girls and then a boy? If it is the same guy, he is an extreme anomaly. Dahmer killed black, white, and Hispanic men but not women."

"Maybe, and maybe not."

Roger looked at his partner and indicated toward the board, encouraging her to work out her thoughts out on paper. Or rather dry, erase board.

"Ok. So, let's say it is the same guy. The order is Cooper, Chase, Jones, and now Parker. Chase is the only one killed. That we know of anyway, but let's assume the others are still alive. So, he still has Cooper, and he had Jones from Pennsylvania along with Chase for a short period of time before he killed her."

"Correct. Time of death on Chase is after Jones was taken."

"So now he has three again. He doesn't seem to care about race. Chase was not violated in any way, so if we assume the others are not sexually harmed, what have we got?" She asked.

"We have a psychopath abducting children around ten to twelve years old. And not for sexual purposes," Roger answered.

"Exactly," she added. *"But maybe we should be replacing the verb here. Is he abducting? He seems to be collecting."*

Cop: *Blanchard arrived on scene asking questions.*

President: *Does he have anything to go on? What is the agency's working theory?*

Cop: *Nope. Your boy was clean. Nothing is pointing at homicide right now. Accidental death is the working theory.*

President: *Thank you. Please keep me informed if the circumstance change.*

CHAPTER 20: THE CASES

Arlington, VA

Charles blew gently across the top of his coffee mug as he listened to Dane recount the details of the New York job. The roaring fire flickered before the two men. They were comfortably settled in their leather chairs, chairs seemly designed for the telling of wild exploits.

"Once the phone was tied to Roxy's bar, I had a good starting point. I was hoping that Tony was on the receiving end of Henry's call, but I couldn't know for sure. I had pictures of some of Henry's other old buddies, but Mazzo just felt right. I kept video surveillance on the other bar but concentrated my personal efforts on Roxy's. I also kept the cameras on Roxy's in case I missed him any night I wasn't there."

"You mentioned before that you were hesitant to enter any of the establishments since they were local bars, and you would, how did you say it, stand out like a sore thumb and possibly be remembered if something happened to any of the patrons or the authorities came around asking questions. What made you change your mind, or what changed in the environment where you believed that the risk of recognition was worth entering the bar? Not that I am second-guessing your choices. You have a unique background,

and I admit I enjoy learning about the detail that goes into these types of operations."

"Not at all. I am happy to discuss techniques. Keeping a low profile was true for the initial narrowing of the target. I didn't want to keep showing up at these bars for no reason other than to sit there and wait on one of Henry's idiot friends. However, I knew I would need to get closer at some point. I waited until the time was right, and we had narrowed the target. Now, I just needed an angle so that I wouldn't be easily remembered."

"And what angle was that?" Charles asked.

"Smoking." When Charles gave him a questioning look, Dane continued. *"No smoking inside bars in New York anymore. Hell, nowhere in most bars across the country and the world anymore, really. Therefore, people must go outside to smoke. I had scouted the area a few times and noticed a huge construction site about six blocks down the road. So, I decided to become a construction worker, take up smoking, and make a friend. The smoking area was outside the front door and along the side of the building. That is where people would congregate to indulge their habits."*

"I still don't follow."

"I dressed the part and played a role. I went to the local thrift shop and picked up some well-used clothing. Rugged, construction worker type. I waited in the vicinity of the bar until a small group came outside to smoke that I thought would be receptive to me. Then, I simply approached. John and Rick. Turned out to be decent

enough guys. I had my smokes out as I approached the smoking area, which centered around one of those outside ashtrays that they make look like little cactus trees. I fumbled around, searching for a lighter. Came up short. One of them offered a light and I struck up a conversation. Two smokes later, I was inside chatting with them at a small table over a couple of beers. I fed them a story about being from Philly but up here on a short stint doing some framing on the new construction site up the road. Day labor type stuff. They were mechanics at a small shop a couple of blocks over. Blue collar meets blue collar. They were regulars at Roxy's, so nobody paid them any attention. I knew a dive like that may have a shitty camera around the door, but the only decent camera would be at the bar. And that camera would not be aimed at patrons. It would cover the register and the bartenders. So, I wasn't worried about any video footage of me."

"How long until you identified Mr. Mazzo?"

"Actually, he came in that night. He was with another guy. I didn't recognize him at first. I couldn't see his face and he was wearing one of those beanie caps. It was one of the guys I was with that alerted me to him. Rick said something about why do they allow that Nazi in here anyway. And now he is bringing more. So, I watched Tony that evening. He seemed calm. In his element, which told me if he was in contact with or was meeting Henry, it certainly wasn't tonight. I came back for the next five nights. He normally came in with a skinhead buddy or two. Drank a few beers. Sometimes some pool or darts. He normally stayed no more than

ninety minutes. It was on the last night when he looked twitchy. On edge."

"The night I provided you with an updated call to the same area from Henry?"

"Exactly but let me back up. He came in those other few nights as well. The second night I was outside with the guys smoking. Tony didn't even give us a second look. He was walking so I assumed he lived close. I watched that night and he went back the way he came so I guessed that home was in that direction. Each following night I would meet the guys but about twenty minutes after Tony arrived, I would call it a night and leave. The first night I headed north from the direction Tony had originally came from and waited a few blocks up. Sure enough he came that way about thirty minutes later and turned west on one of the blocks. So, the next night I went to that block and then headed a little west and waited again. I was doing a modified picket surveillance. By the fourth night I had found where he was staying. It was a rundown motel where you can pay by the hour or the month. Real shithole."

"I have never heard of picket surveillance."

"It is useful if you have a start point on someone and you want to know a place they go daily, such as a job or their home. We call their home a bed down location. You wait at the known location outside of work or something and wait to see the direction they take. Left or right. No matter what, you don't follow. You stay put. The next day, you go as far as you were able to see them the previous day and wait again. Left, Right, or straight, and so, on-and-on until you

find their final destination. It can be very time-consuming. But it is the least alerting technique if you want to follow someone. Especially someone who may be trained to detect foot or vehicular surveillance. It is very common overseas as well. Hostile countries will use hundreds of informers to tell them where Westerners go. They will pay locals who may be sitting outside a shop or operating an outdoor booth to record the comings and goings of anybody who does not look like them."

Dane continued, *"The Chinese, Russians, us, everyone gets followed in some places. The local government keeps tabs on foreigners, lest they incite some sort of unrest. Develop patterns of life. Find their homes. Everything. Most of those types of countries are holding onto power by a thread and removal from office normally means death. I used picket surveillance because following Tony with just me would be very alerting. Especially at night in that neighborhood. Empty streets with very poor lighting. Don't need to be trained when someone follows you several blocks home from the bar. Tony is a criminal. He would have noticed."*

"I agree. That is a logical conclusion. What I am most curious about was your selection for disposal of these two and how you were able to complete the task. I am hearing from my sources in law enforcement circles that they have no idea what happened. Presently they are calling them both accidental deaths."

"Nothing accidental about it. That night I found Tony's apartment. I also found his car. He retrieved something from it before he went into the apartment. I did a hasty tag and threw a tracker up underneath his car. Old shitty Firebird from the eighties.

Plenty of metal underneath. I wasn't sure if they would meet here or someplace else. I was hoping for somewhere else. Someplace a little more secluded and Tony obliged. He took a call about thirty minutes later while smoking by his car. He jumped in and took off. I had the motorcycle close in the event he drove to the meeting. Following was easy since I could stay back and use the program on my phone to check on his location. Thank your tech guy for me. I appreciate him helping me get the program on a phone. Way easier than using a computer and a lot less alerting if someone saw me. People don't normally check their computers while driving or walking but they sure do check their phones every few seconds."

"I will pass on the praise."

"A short time later he stopped on a street bordering a park along the Hudson River. He was near a sidewalk that ran perpendicular to the street. The sidewalk disappeared into the woods so I figured this would be the entrance he used. I think we had crossed into Yonkers."

Dane paused as Jack entered the room to refill their coffees. He then surprised Dane by pouring one for himself and selecting a chair near the two men. It was the change in pattern that threw him off.

"I asked Jack to sit in with us, Mr. Cooper. He is also an active member of our club and although in recent years he has taken on less of a, how shall I say, hands-on roll, but I believe we have an emerging situation that may require the pooling of resources. But first, please continue with Mr. Galfini and Mr. Mazzo."

"Sorry I am late sir. There was another matter I had to attend to," Jack said.

Dane was intrigued by this turn of events and was anxious to discuss a new project. He hurriedly described the meeting between the two men in the park. Total seclusion. Not a soul in sight. Dane had parked farther up the road and entered the park silently. Locating the meeting location was easy. The two men were clearly amateurs when it came to clandestine meetings and security. They were so busy talking that they didn't notice Dane until two tasers had put each of them on the ground. One fired from each of his hands. After a light tap on the head with a ball bat, Dane had plenty of time and privacy to complete the assignment. Both men were unconscious and out of the fight.

The petty cash he was provided for the mission was more than enough for the heroin he purchased. He gave each man a hefty does before dragging them one-by-one to Tony's car. From there, he proceeded to an access point for the railyard that he had scouted when he first arrived in the city and was debating on disposal methods. On continuous evenings, he had disabled lights and cameras in preparation for the final night. The final touch was the prepositioned furniture dolly. He strapped both men to the dolly with two large lengths of tubular nylon, ensuring he had a quick release pull tabs for each. It was like moving a refrigerator. Train came right on time, and boom, Dane flung the bodies in front of the engine car from behind a tall switching terminal. He had plenty of time to leave the area, rid himself of any equipment, and make his way home. He knew the crime scene would be a complete nightmare, and any taser marks or lumps on the head would be concealed among the chaos of body parts. If they were somehow noticed, the injuries would be attributed to the impact of the locomotive. And all that the body parts would tell investigators is that both men had a wild night on heroin.

Both Charles and Jack sat in silence at the conclusion of Dane's brief. It was Jack who spoke first. *"Where did you get the furniture dolly?"*

"I liberated it from behind a large trucking company. It was just left there overnight with several others. The company is fenced and secure so they must not have any issues with people borrowing their equipment. I bleached it down after I left the railyard and returned it in case they keep an accurate count. But I doubt it."

"And Tony's car?"

"I drove it a few blocks away from the scene. Made sure it was between the railyard and the bars around Yankee Stadium. I wiped it down and left all the drug paraphernalia in the front seat. Help strengthen the drug induced accident story."

"What did you..."

Dane cut him off. *"Not to be rude Jack, but I am clean. No trance evidence. No camera footage. No record of travel. And if your IT guy came through as promised with my phone, my digital footprint should never have left the D.C. area. Why do I feel like I am being interrogated?"*

This time, it was Charles who answered. "*Please do not perceive that this is an interrogation. I invited Jack to the de-brief to get to know you a little better and observe how you work. We think we have a bigger problem on our hands, and it will take some collaboration. A more hands-on team effort. Jack will lead that team and coordinate efforts among you and another man on the streets. The other member is one of our more successful members.*"

"*I was not questioning your techniques Dane,*" Jack said. "*I was trying to get a feel for how you operate versus my experience. Maybe I should formally present you with my background. I entered the British Army at sixteen years old straight from a little village south of Cork in Ireland. The British Army is one of the few remaining forces that actually recruit solders under the age of eighteen. They will enlist men as young as sixteen years old. I entered the Parachute Regiment or the Paras as we like to call it. I did my mandatory three years and busted my ass to get a recommendation to attend the selection course for the Special Air Services or SAS. My recommendation was approved. I completed the selection process, and the year-long course. All that landed me in the Falklands in the spring of eighty-two. Short but nasty little conflict. It was my introduction to warfare. I then spent time in the Persian Gulf with your chaps as well as Bosnia and Afghanistan. Even supported Task Force Black and Knight in Iraq in the early two-thousands. I read your military file. We fought on some of the same ground. I liked working with the Kurds. I saw that you assisted them on two separate occasions against Al-Qaeda and then later ISIS.*"

"Impressive," Dane replied. *"I always liked working with you guys. But one question I always had was why you would put a Scotsman as your radio operator? All your teams had Scots on the radio, and nobody could understand a word that was being said. One team even gave him the call sign of mush mouth or something."*

Jack chuckled, breaking the stoic look he always seemed to wear. *"It was to confuse the enemy if they ever intercepted our communication but more importantly it was fun to watch you chaps thoroughly confused on the radio."*

This time it was Dane's turn to laugh.

"If you two are quite done telling war stories, I suggest we talk about these cases," Charles interjected. *"First, we have a little problem with an FBI agent. A Mr. Carl Blanchard. He is investigating unusual deaths involving child predators. He was on the scene at Fort Hunt Park, the home of the late Myron Wells, and I was recently informed that he flew up to New York to visit the railyard scene. He is looking into not just high-profile cases, but other accidental deaths and he is maintaining a close relationship with the Virginia State Police. He probably also has contacts with Maryland and Pennsylvania but most of the current cases are in Virginia and that seems to be where he is concentrating his efforts. He is comparing both abductions and the demise of predators."*

"I have so many questions that I will ask them one at a time," Dane replied. *"First, what happened at Fort Hunt Park?"*

"A well-known pedophile and child molester committed suicide. He ran the exhaust into his own car while he was parked there."

"Right. Ok. Special Agent Blanchard. I have met him."

This time, it was Charles that was surprised. *"When? Under what circumstances?"*

"One of my meetings with the State Police about Angela. The two investigators were providing me an update. He was there as some sort of courtesy. It was all bullshit. They had nothing. But that FBI guy was an ass. Seemed like he was interrogating me. But I had nothing to do with you guys at that point."

Charles and Jack stared at one another for a moment. Upon a nod from Charles, Jack cleared his throat. *"Special agent Blanchard is a danger to our club. He has created his own little task force to investigate predators as Mr. Thornton explained. However, it goes deeper. Blanchard believes there is a group conducting these killings and his superiors obviously pay credence to his theories since he can investigate as he sees fit. It was only a matter of time that he would begin to profile possible members of this group. He may not have suspected you when you met, but rest assured he knows your military background. He may not know your specialty like we do but you are certainly on his radar."*

"And not to mention, he is a federal officer," said Charles. *"He can move freely from state to state regarding his suspicions. Jurisdiction is not an issue for him. He can move like us. He has been moving with us. I do not believe his meeting with you was random."*

"How so?" Dane asked.

Jack stood and crossed the room to a large ornate desk at the far end. He removed four thick files and returned to his seat. *"These files contain all the available evidence on four unique kidnappings in the last year and a half. The circumstances are nearly identical. The Virginia State Police believe they are connected but just can find the thread to break the cases open. Blanchard has consulted with them and received the same briefing. We think he believes our club will go after this mystery man. His logic is to follow the cases to find us. We ourselves have poured over these files many times but are just as baffled as the authorities. If this is the same guy, we have no leads. But if we figure this out and this is one perpetrator , we will need a team to bring him down. I would like you on the team."*

Dane stood to retrieve the files from Jack. But before he could, Jack had one last thing to say. *"I think a fresh set of eyes from you might find what we are missing. Your analytical and intelligence background may see things differently. I cannot stress how important this is."*

Jack paused.

"I am sorry Dane. One of these files is your daughter's. Angela."

CHAPTER 21: THE SUSPECT

Washington, D.C.

Pupil: *I found someone like us.*

Keeper: *Can he be trusted?*

Pupil: *Completely. He is totally devoted to me.*

Keeper: *Pass me his information and I will vet him.*

Carl's coffee sat untouched as he poured over his notes from New York. The final wisp of steam disappeared; his attention laser focused on the information in front of him instead of the caffeine booster set to the side. He had not only his notes and observations but also complete jackets from the NYPD and the FBI New York field office. Galfini and Mazzo. Accidental deaths. Bullshit.

The digital forensics work was impressive but not very helpful due to the damage each man's cellphone had sustained. Investigators found pieces strewn along the track, presumably residing earlier in front or back pockets before impact. They could only pull limited data. The phones had communicated with each other. That portion of the report, Carl could understand. The remaining technical jargon and description of the forensic process might as well have been written in Latin. It wasn't until the last paragraph that he once again comprehended the words on the report. The phone believed to have been Henry Galfini's was old. It also wasn't a number that had been associated with Galfini from previous investigations. So, it was clearly a burner. Except that it was an old burner. Henry hadn't just bought and activated the phone. The number and selectors associated with the phone had a history of connecting to the cell network nearly five years ago. *However, it is not any of his known numbers we had been searching for. Did someone else have this old number and the means to track it?*

Death by train. This was definitely one of the more bizarre cases he had ever seen. It is completely plausible that they wandered into that railyard. With all the heroin found in their car and in a few small body parts they were able to test, the two men were obviously zooted. Transit police did find an open gate near the far end of the track. The lock was missing, and the chains holding the small gate closed had fallen in the dirt. They certainly didn't open it in their state of mind. *Did a vagrant* leave it open? Was it done by their killers? Or was this all just one big cluster? Carl needed more to go on. The evidence was there. He knew it. They just had to find it and find out who was committing these murders. Whoever they were, they had great support, both technical and financial. Operations like these were not cheap. He had analysts scouring flight records, train logs, anything.

With a short tap on the open door, Ken popped his head in. *"You got a second boss?"*

Carl waved the young man in. He rose from behind his desk and found a seat at his small conference table, big and round. He knew Ken had something to discuss, as indicated by the files tucked under his arm. Carl hated collaborating on projects from behind a desk. It is easier and more efficient to slide documents back and forth around a table than to reach over computer monitors and files on his desk. He also discerned over the years that subordinates were often more hesitant to share thoughts and theories when sitting in a visitor chair in front of the boss. It made them feel like a child sitting before the principal, afraid to speak out for fear of further repercussions.

Everyone seated at the table implied equal participation. Equal input. Equal consideration. He jokingly called his colleagues the Knights of the Round Table when working on a big project. That was the type of collaboration necessary at the FBI. Sadly though, a type that Carl rarely witnessed anymore. Executives were often more interested in perceived or actual accumulation of power. Carl had no interest in the pecking order of participants when it came to an investigation. If he thought the janitor may have some useful insight, Carl would hold the chair for him. Maybe that was why he was on this floor and not the seventh. *"What do you have Ken?"*

"I did some research and cross-referenced the parents of child predator victims, along with their home of residency, current occupation, and previous work history going back ten years. Ten years was also the timeframe I used for the date of the crimes. I believe you originally asked for fifteen, but there was only one set of

parents on that list. The father was killed overseas in Iraq and the mother remarried and moved to California. I ruled them out."

"Ok. Fair enough. Good work. How many do we have?"

"Fifteen names came up on my list. Twelve men and three women. I won't bore you with my analysis and how I ranked the probability of them being involved in these deaths unless you would like to discuss. Oh, and I forgot to mention that none of these people on my list have any connections to the dead predators. I checked both personal and work relationships. Nothing. These people are all complete strangers to our victims."

"No. I trust your methods Ken, or I wouldn't have asked you to do this."

"Great. What I brought today is three jackets. My top three most likely, most able, and the most capable of exacting revenge on behalf of their children. It seemed reasonable to research these suspects in small batches."

Carl nodded for Ken to continue.

"Ok. Number three is John Ferguson. His daughter Lucy was taken six years ago from the suburbs of Richmond. One moment she was playing outside in the yard and woods, the next she was gone. The story was a major headline back in the day. Huge media campaign. Posters everywhere. Tip lines, etc. The whole nine yards. Little girl was found in a field about four miles from her home a week after her abduction. Her father went ballistic."

"I remember that story. He was the retired cop from Miami, right? He took out ads, made public statement in news conferences about how he was going to hunt Lucy's killers to the end of the earth."

"That's him. He is still in the area. Lives just outside of Fredericksburg. Southside. Became a private investigator. He still hounds the police to this day about the case. Not that I can blame him. But he is still actively looking for revenge. Does that mean he would avenge other parents in his search for closure? I don't know. But he is in the area, was a highly decorated officer in Miami, and now conducts investigations on his own."

"Before we go any further, did you happen to establish any loose locations for these suspects during the commission of the mysterious deaths recently?"

"Not yet boss. It is hard to track them digitally without a warrant or physically without a dedicated team. I think we would need a solid case to take before a judge before we can acquire cell phone records."

"So, they made the list based on their current residency and proximity to the crimes?" Ken nodded. *"Ok. So, Ferguson is in the running."*

"Number two is Dane Cooper. I think you are familiar with that case. Daughter Angela was taken almost a year and a half ago while he was deployed overseas."

"Yeah. I met him a few months ago when some Virginia Special Agents were providing him an update on the case. He came up on my radar as someone with the means to take revenge. I didn't mention him to you since I didn't want to contaminate your research. Guy was a hothead and kinda an asshole, so I am glad you came up with him on your own."

"I bet. Well, he has a unique history and was a contender for the number one spot. Career military. Graduated college yet joined the service as an enlisted soldier. Infantry, basic training, Airborne school, and then straight into the Ranger Regiment. He saw serious action in Afghanistan and Iraq. And he kept going back, so violence doesn't seem to faze him. He then was stationed here in Washington D.C. but here the trail goes relatively cold. Some Special Operations unit up on Fort Meyer. At least that is where this unit is supposedly stationed. They do Red Cell stuff against other military entities. Test security at bases. Try to get aboard naval vessels. Infiltrate secure areas to test protocols. That kinda stuff. I think there is more to what he does. I have some contacts and could dig further but I didn't want to possibly alert him that we were investigating. Especially if this happens to be our guy. Our one of them, right? Could be more than one guy doing these things."

"Good call. We can call in favors if we need to in the future. Moreover, you are correct. It could be multiple suspects. So, Cooper, intelligent and associated with Special Operations. Where does he live now?"

"Washington D.C. Divorced and has a son living with the ex. He lives in a basement of one of those downtown D.C. brownstones."

"And he is still on active duty, right? Ken nodded. *"Well, now I really want to see number one."*

Ken opened the third folder. *"Sam Turner. His daughter, Rachel, was kidnapped four years ago and has never been found. His wife died when Rachel was about five years old. Turner left the military to become a single dad. He had settled in Winchester. He got himself a large piece of land and turned it into a state-of-the-art range facility. He has been a small arms trainer ever since. All interviews with neighbors during the investigation of his daughter's disappearance, stated that he adored that little girl. He was never a suspect."*

"What did he do in the service?"

"Fifth Special Forces out of Fort Campbell, Kentucky. Early involvement in Afghanistan and Iraq before he got out. Guy saw a lot of action and got a bunch of awards for his efforts. He also did a stint with the Army Marksmanship team. He won a lot of contests. Also competed in his free time in three-gun competitions."

"What is that?"

"Shooting events. Sometime called multi-gun. Shooters compete in multiple events with three different firearms. A pistol of some sort. A rifle that is normally an AR frame and then a shotgun. He still competes and even holds events at his facility. Oh, and he also passed the Army Sniper School. This guy knows guns."

"He is a strong candidate, but what makes him stand out over Cooper? They both have experience in the service and are immune if not resistant to violent behavior. Turner may have more experience with firearms, but our recent batch of victims have not been shot that I am aware of."

"Turner has a record. Well, all of them have had some run-ins with the law. Even the ex-cop but the encounters were minor. Turner was charged with stalking. Charged on three different accounts."

"Do I even need to ask who he was stalking?"

"Registered child sex offenders. He became obsessed with offenders in his area and began stalking them looking for his daughter. But he was smart about it. He didn't trespass. He didn't physically threaten anyone. He just observed. He followed several of around for months. He didn't even try to be sneaky and hide from them. He would loiter around their work and homes. One complainant even cited an example of Turner following them every week into their local grocery store. Enough complaints eventually reached the authorities. He was charged on three counts. However, the judge was extremely lenient in lieu of his military service, plus the loss of his wife and child. He was given two years' probation with monthly check-ins with his parole officer along with community service. And obviously restraining orders regarding the three registered sex offenders."

"Good work Ken. These are solid but I agree we don't have enough for a judge to give us a peak at their phone records. Yet. So, Turner is your number one?"

"Yessir."

"Ok. Please leave these packets with me. Continue to develop the other twelve until these three are deemed clean. We'll start with Turner. I think there is enough with his past to take a hard look at him. I will see if the Virginia State police are interested in playing."

Fairfax, VA

Roger knocked on Captain Ivers' door and was motioned inside. Patricia was already seated. *"Sorry, had to take that call."*

"Its fine, Special Agents Stills was updating me on the Chase and Parker cases."

Roger took a seat and opened his notebook. "*Well the call I took was a very interesting one and may be related to other cases we have here in the section.*"

"Well you certainly know how to grab the attention Roger," Captain Ivers responded. *"Please share."*

"Well, Sir, we have a request from the FBI. A request for assistance to surveil a person of interest that may or may not be involved with recent deaths in northern Virginia. Deaths of suspected or convicted child predators."

It was Patricia who responded. *"Wait what?"*

"I'm with her. What?"

"Let me start at the beginning and give you both a little background. Do you remember when we were providing an update to the Coopers a few months ago about their daughter? The FBI agent that attended the meeting was the one on the phone requesting assistance or rather a joint operation. Apparently, he has the juice but not the manpower."

"I do remember him. He was at the crime scene for Chase also, wasn't he. The one that flew in on the helicopter while the rest of us peasants drove."

"That's right Captain. He was also at Fort Hunt Park. He arrived on scene where Arthur Camp committed suicide in the car."

"I remember him. We thought it was odd that he was at the park, right Roger?"

"It was odd at the time Pat but makes a little more sense now. Special Agent Blanchard has a theory that a person, or group of persons are targeting child predators. He is focusing on people who have lost a child and have the 'occupational specialty', his words, necessary to carry out these crimes. He came to the Camp scene

because he knew that Camp was a convicted molester and he wanted to see for himself if there was any possibility of foul play. He believes there was."

"Why did he come to the Chase scene?" She asked.

"He believes that this person(s), are righting any and all perceived wrongs. That is to say, they are looking for revenge for their own children but also to avenge parents incapable of that kind of violence. Doing it for them and to keep other children safe. He thinks that these people will also keep tabs on all child abductions. He feels that they may insert themselves into investigations or conduct their own. He felt that they could not pass up the Chase murder. That was why a request was sent a few days after we found her for all the logs at scene. We figured that he wanted all the contact information for the investigators. Not the case. He was looking for one of his suspects in the crowd. I talked to guys over in Alexandria as well. FBI office also requested the photo logs. The request came from Blanchard's office. He was looking for evidence that one of these 'hunters', again his words not mine, was at the scene."

"Is Cooper on his list? Is that why he came to the briefing with them?" Pat asked.

"Yes, Cooper is on his short list. As well as some ex-cop down in Fredericksburg." Roger looked at his notes. *"John Ferguson. But his top priority is a guy named Sam Turner. Lives out in Winchester but is in this area a lot for business. He runs a shooting range out there but also has an office in Fairfax. He does some security consulting on the side."*

Captain Ivers sat back in his chair and expelled the breath he had been holding. *"Ok, this is getting a little complicated. So, this fed has a suspect who obviously lives in Virginia since he is reaching out to us. I am going to assume he has other suspects in other states. Other jurisdictions. If I remember correctly, Cooper lives in D.C."*

"Correct sir. Cooper is D.C. so nothing we can do there. Blanchard was frank with me about his theories and the cases, but I don't think for one minute he is disclosing everything to us. He just needs help with Turner."

"What does he need us for?" asked Captain Ivers. *"He has a whole federal agency at his beck and call. Plus, why aren't they putting the screws to this guy. Digging into his personal life. Work life, Digital life for that manner."*

"They are in the preliminary phase. He conceded that he did not have enough evidence for a warrant. But he wants to start somewhere. Apparently, Turner has a record of criminal stalking for several years ago. He was tracking and stalking registered child sex offenders. That is why he is looking at him first. With that criminal history, it is a smart move. He wants to watch him for a week or so. Develop a pattern of life and see where it leads us. He is asking for me, Stills, and two other agents. Ten days."

"That is a lot of manpower for me to commit."

"I understand that Captain. But if his theory is correct, we may be able to re-open and resolve some cases. Hell, maybe Myron Wells wasn't an accident."

"You mean the guy that died of a peanut butter allergy in his bedroom because he forgot his Epi-pen? How is that not an accident?"

"You never know Captain. Stranger things have happened."

Shadow: *We need to meet tonight. Urgent. I found something.*

President: *Tonight. 7pm. Use alternate location.*

Shadow: *Understood. Everything alright?*

President: *Take precautions.*

CHAPTER 22: THE LAST JOB

Alexandria, VA

Pupil: *I think I have found a good place to get another one.*

Keeper: *Just be careful. With all this activity, the police are on high alert.*

Pupil: *I will. If it doesn't look good, I will walk away.*

Keeper: *Happy hunting.*

The door of the southbound yellow line hissed open. Dane exited the metro car at the Braddock Road stop in Alexandria. He had chosen the front car for this portion of his surveillance detection route. The President was clearly worried about something so, Dane was going to ensure he did not compromise this meeting by being followed. From the front car of the train, he had to turn left back into the station toward the stairs at the center of the platform. Walking alongside the train heading to the ground level exit would give him a good look at everyone else exiting the remaining metro cars. This was not usually a popular or crowded train stop, which was exactly why he chose it. The four individuals with him on the platform were not familiar faces. He was clean. He still had thirty minutes until the meeting, and although anxious to share his findings regarding the recent kidnappings with the group, he knew patience was required. Thirty minutes, plenty of time to conduct a provocative zone route.

Dane knew that he really should run two provocative zone routes or legs with his overall detection route. It was textbook standard to run two, but it was often overkill. The provocative routes were the final legs taken when someone was ninety-nine-point-nine percent certain they were free of surveillance. The provocative part was a non-sensical route, taking multiple turns for no reason, walking in the least efficient direction to reach your final destination, and even stopping for nothing other than to look around. This was a route no reasonable human would take from point A to point B. A last safety check. Nobody should follow him during this walk. If someone took the same route as him during a provocative zone, he may as well just sit down and have a chat with them.

Thirty minutes later, Dane entered the front of the posh restaurant in downtown Alexandria right on time. As he approached the hostess stand, he presented his orange RFID key card. Very similar to a hotel key, this card would not only open rooms upstairs, but also activate the elevator located in the back of the restaurant. The hostess gestured toward the back hallway where the elevator was tucked away despite Dane's knowledge of its location from a previous visit. The President had met him here once before, after his recruitment into the club. This location was to be an alternate meeting site in the event their normal location was compromised. Dane was curious as to why the alternate was selected. The elevator lifted occupants to a private club on the second and third floors of the building. The setting offered multiple lounge areas, a private dining room, and even its own walk-in humidor with smoking areas. The glass walls with glass shelves of the humidor offered a selection of the finest cigars from around the world. However, Dane headed toward one of the private meeting rooms. The expansive selection of cigars and upscale bourbons found at the lounges would have to wait for another time.

He was met by Charles and Jack, along with a third unknown man. He was a little shorter than Dane. Lean build. Wiry. Dane guessed that he was around the same age as himself. This guy is a fighter, Dane thought. He holds himself like ex-military. I bet this guy has some sort of Special Operations background. Are you the guy who took care of Myron Wells.?

"This is one of newer members, the Shadow," Charles told the man while introducing Dane. *"And this is the Closer. We will need to update our naming convention as more of you join the team."*

Dane extended his hand to the man. *"Dane Cooper."*

"Sam Turner."

"Well, I guess trying for some anonymity was pointless gentlemen. The intent was for names to be left out in the event of a compromise."

"It's ok sir," Dane replied. *"I have been extremely impressed with the talent of this organization. I am hardly concerned that Sam knows my name."*

"Ditto," Sam replied. *"And I trust in Jack's abilities should any of us stray."*

"Well, I will explain the necessity of meeting at this location later, but first I believe Mr. Cooper has some urgent news we are all anxiously waiting to hear. Please have a seat." The room was set up for impromptu meetings and had all the necessities. A table dominated the center of the room. A small area along the back wall was used as a kitchen with a refrigerator and sink. Large steel framed windows offered a view of King Street below. It seemed the sidewalks were perpetually in motion with the crowds that always found themselves in the heart of Alexandria. They were in the busiest portion of the district, the two blocks of King Street below, hosting several pubs, restaurants, and unique eateries.

The four men sat at a large round table. Dane removed several stacks of paperwork from his leather satchel. In the center of the table, he placed the original police files he had been given to examine. He then slid each man a slim folder, cleared his throat and said the following, *"Wilson Simmons. I believe this man is responsible for the kidnapping of Angela Cooper, Dana Chase, Holly Jones, and Jon Parker and the murder of at least Dana Chase."* The last part was difficult for him. Just knowing Angela's name was on this list terrified him. He knew that the evidence he found tied the other three together, but Angela's case was simply similar. He didn't know what was worse, solving her case only to find out she had been murdered or not linking hers to the others and remaining clueless as to her whereabouts. *Keep it together, man.*

All three men looked stunned as they opened their individual folders. Each was a carefully crafted target package on Wilson Simmons containing a brief history of the man, previous encounters with the law, and whatever other useful information Dane was able to obtain. Dane was not expecting the presence of Sam Turner. He had only brought three target packages, so he slid his copy to Sam. He had memorized the contents.

"I must say, this is impressive Mr. Cooper. The amount of research you have conducted in a short amount of time is appreciated. May I ask how you have ascertained Mr. Simmons involvement in these crimes?"

"Yes. Never pee at a crime scene."

"Ok, I have got to hear this," said Sam. *"Good advice of course."* Jack nodded in agreeance, having yet spoken while maintaining his normally stoic state.

"I reviewed the four cases you gave me. I came to the same conclusion as the police that it is very likely the same guy conducting these abductions. The way he executes these crimes are meticulously planned. He has targeted a similar age group, but I will admit, selecting a boy would throw a lot of investigators off the scent. And the boy is black. I am surprised the authorities even included Jon Parker's jacket. They must have less leads that I thought. Any sort of serial criminal whether murderer or in this case child abductor

almost exclusively stay inside their race. Except of course sex traffickers, but they are in a category of their own and I don't see them fitting in here. This is one guy. I still have no idea what the motive it, but one guy. Everything points in that direction, but nothing has linked them until this. Well, I linked three of the fours. But I think that may not matter. I will explain."

He slid another sheet of paper to Charles, Jack, and Sam. *"I can hypothetically tie Simmons to three of the four scenes. You can see from the reports that U-40 Porcine Insulin Zinc Suspension was found near the Chase, Jones, and Parker scenes. Chase and Jones were near dog parks and Parker was in a field where a lot of people run their pets off leash for exercise. Several other chemicals and evidence were also found which should be expected at those locations."*

"I am assuming this U-40 is for diabetic dogs. Were any of the animals diabetic?" asked Sam. "Were any of them on this type of medication?"

"No," Dane replied. *"It's a pretty rare disease for dogs. Probably exacerbated by the fact that many people don't utilize regular check-ups for their pets so undiagnosed dogs could be higher. However, the generally accepted number is one percent of dogs in the United States have diabetes. The odds are slim that all three locations would contain this chemical combination. That bet would be a high payout in Vegas."*

"I am still not clear how this leads to Mr. Simmons. Are you saying he has a diabetic animal and he left behind trance evidence

at the scene from his home? Is that even possible? I guess if the dog's urine finds its' way onto Mr. Simmons clothing, it could be left behind at a crime scene?"

"Nope," Jack answered, breaking his silence. *"Wilson is the diabetic. He urinated at some point waiting for his victims. With Dane's daughter, he either didn't have to go or went somewhere the crime scene didn't canvass. Wilson left behind the Porcine insulin."*

"Wait, you said this stuff was for dogs." Sam looked confused.

"It is now in the country, but it wasn't always that way," Dane explained. *"This type of insulin was used on humans up into the eighties. Two kinds were developed, I think sometime in the sixties. Animal insulin was taken from the pancreases of animals and then purified to lessen the chance of negative reactions in human patients. Porcine come from pigs. Bovine from cows. Humans typically reacted better to porcine insulin. But as I said, in the eighties synthetic human insulin was created and the use of animal products was phased out over time."*

"So, you believe our suspect is still using this porcine product. Why?" Charles asked.

"Like I said, it was an anomaly at the scene. A thread, so I pulled it. I figured that our guy must be a little older. He was probably diagnosed with diabetes before human insulin was created. His treatment began with pork insulin. And remember, it took a while to phase out the animal products for human use. Maybe Simmons didn't react well to the synthetic stuff. Maybe it was too expensive.

The porcine is a lot cheaper. So, for a while he is still able to get the stuff here in the States. But eventually, even the porcine use on animals began to phase out as well as more synthetics for animals began hitting the market. Eventually, production of UH-40 ceased in the United States."

"Let me guess. It is still made somewhere but it is rare. Does it have to go through customs, perhaps?"

Dane nodded to Jack. *"You sir are correct. There is one remaining company that makes what is called a Protamine Zinc insulin, and it is made in the United Kingdom. Veterinary clinics will still stock the item, but human pharmacies have long removed them from their shelves. But nonetheless, small quantities are still imported into the United States."*

Charles nodded slowly as the pieces came together. *"So, you then queried imports of this insulin eliminating veterinarians?"*

"Yes, and I further filtered by age and criminal record. I was looking for someone most likely between fifty and sixty, who was a known or suspected child predator. I have a friend at Homeland Security that provides me access to their database now and then for some off-the-book inquires at work. I scrubbed the list, discarding anyone with a severe disability and those over seventy. Out popped Wilson. Just shy of sixty-five, and he has two convictions for Crimes against Children. He dropped off the radar nearly a decade ago after his last stint behind bars. He never registered his new location nor followed the terms of his parole. The case became so old he was

forgotten about. His name didn't even alert Homeland when he was ordering a product from overseas."

"This is impressive Mr. Cooper. However, I am not sure how to proceed. We have considerable resources, but I am at a loss at how much further we can pursue these cases. I am assuming since you didn't mention an address, that remains unknown. We may need to pass this information to the authorities for them to find Mr. Simmons if he is holding multiple children. Multiple hostages."

Dane smirked. *"Or we can follow him when he picks up his next shipment. The FDA admits the stuff into the country, and it remains in customs for up to fourteen days before release. It ships to a post office box in Falls Church in two days."*

"Are you enjoying yourself Mr. Cooper?" Charles frowned.

"A little bit."

"Very funny. But there is another matter we need to consider, and it pertains to the reason we are meeting here this evening. We have come to the attention of the FBI."

"Shit. It's me, isn't it?" Sam asked. *"I knew this could have happened, especially with my history."*

"Your history?" Dane inquired. Dane smiled. He knew the feeling.

"Actually, it is both of you," Jack interjected. "There is a special agent named Blanchard who is running his own little task force

regarding the mysterious demises of certain predators. We have known about him for some time now, but we do not believe he has the whole picture."

"That guy is an asshole."

"Be that as it may Mr. Cooper, he is in fact a very intelligent and determined asshole. He has enlisted the assistance of the Virginia State Police. There is a third suspect with whom we are unfamiliar with but, we need to prepare ourselves in the event they decide to focus on either of you."

"I have been on high alert since New York. I don't have any eyes on me. My phone is clean, as well as my truck and motorcycle. I haven't swept my apartment for listening devices in a while, but I can do that quickly, if only to rule it out."

"Forgot to mention New York. Nice touch with the train thing. I like your style. I am clean as well. Nobody around the ranch in Winchester. I would see them coming a mile away. And my dogs bite. Office here in Alexandria is clean also. I have it swept monthly. I do have a long commute from home to the office so they could monitor my travel along I-66, but it wouldn't provide them with any information and when I work protection details or security consults, me and the team would notice surveillance."

"I am not privy to the timeline only that if an investigation has not yet begun, it will shortly. This is where tracking Mr. Simmons may become an issue. Hence my offer of presenting Mr. Cooper's findings to the authorities."

"Why are they targeting us? I know they can't have any hard evidence." Dane asked.

"Because you are both men capable of violence. You each suffered a great loss. We had hoped to operate under the radar with our activities, but this was bound to happen eventually. We could pull in another team and let you two cool off for a while."

"Absolutely not. We can handle this." There was no way Dane was letting this guy slip through his fingers. *"I have not been able to link him with Angela's disappearance but, he looks good for it. This will be a delicate operation and I don't want him getting way."*

"Concur. We can still do this. First sign of trouble with the authorities and we regroup and reassess."

It was Jack that steered the group to the operation itself. *"You are both professionals and it will be your necks on the line. If you are both in, so am I. I will direct the operation via communications you both feel is best. Will two of you be enough on the street?"*

"I think so. I did a map reconnaissance of the post office box. It is a small, little urban area. There are plenty of shops or places to hang out and wait. It opens at nine am. Deliveries probably start arriving by ten. I would expect our guy to come late morning or early afternoon to pick up his stuff. We can take turns. Tuesday is the delivery day. I will take first watch. Which days are you normally in town Sam? At the office?"

"Tuesday through Thursday is my normal routine. I like to be back at the ranch Thursday night. I like Friday to set up the range for

any shoots I have over the weekend. But I am free next weekend, so I could stay in town longer."

"The most important part for us is know our status before we begin surveilling Simmons. How much training have you had? Any real world experiences?" Dane asked.

"I did some training in special forces. They sent us through a three-week course. I understand the basics and should be able to determine my status."

"Ok. What we need to do is coordinate our routes. Make sure we are not crossing paths or at the very worst using the same cover stop. Jack, I assume you are trained to run a team? Jack nodded. *"Excellent. Probably wouldn't do any of us any good to be seen together at all. I recommend that this is the last time we meet until all of this is over. They would swoop right in and probably arrest us on the spot and spend all their time trying to pin us to those accidents. Jack, we will need some items. If you can procure the phones with wireless earbuds that would be helpful. We will leave our phones at our respective offices. If someone engages us and ask, we simply tell them we forgot our phones at work. Not the greatest of lies, but better than having a digital footprint anywhere near Simmons."*

"Sounds good. I can get the phones. Sir, I do believe now is the time we discuss what we are going to do with Mr. Simmons if he truly is involved in these crimes. We need to discuss the children and we need to ascertain his fate."

CHAPTER 23 THE STALK

Washington D.C.

"The car is ready boss."

"Thanks Ken. Who's driving?"

"Bob Shultz from the Special Surveillance Group. He and his team just finished up a four-week stint against the Russian embassy. The Rezident was doing his change over and supposedly the new guy is some bigwig spy from the Motherland. Apparently, the FBI followed these two all over Washington D.C. and Northern Virginia to see what they were up too. Meetings, contacts, spy stuff. I don't follow all that but, Bob is supposed to be one of the best in the bureau."

"Excellent. I am going to head down now. Meeting the Virginia guys at six and I don't want to be late. Call me if it is urgent, but just take care of it, if it is routine. I am going to be all over the radio coordinating this surveillance and will be busy. I suspect this will be a long day. Hah, probably should let Bob coordinate and I drive."

"Funny. Got it Boss. Oh, and by the way, Bob was also able to get foot surveillants in the event Turner goes walking around anywhere. They are also from the Group. Husband and wife team. Also good from what I hear. They sure brought a lot of outfit changes. They followed the Russians all over Alexandria and

Arlington. Metro cars, buses, even a boat. Apparently, the Russians took one of those D.C. dinner cruises on the Potomac. Bureau thought it may be a cover to meet with someone, so this couple got dressed up all fancy and had fine dining on the river curtesy of the American taxpayer."

"Excellent, thanks Ken. Appreciate you staying on top of all this." Carl said as he exited the office. A quick elevator ride to the basement he found Bob and the crew ready to go. The plain-looking sedan had seen better days. But it looked functional and non-descript. Best type of car for surveillance. After introductions were made all around, the group loaded the vehicle and departed the garage. Carl began briefing them enroute.

Fairfax, VA

"Roger, Winchester PD called and said Turner is not at his house. An undercover went by, and his vehicle wasn't there. Looks like he left Monday later afternoon or early evening like normal to come to his Fairfax office."

Roger was followed into the team space by two other plainclothes detectives. Shedding their normal professional clothing of suits and highly shined shoes, they were dressed casually in jeans and sweatshirts. Everyone had a small bag in tow. They were full of clothes in the off chance anyone has a close encounter with the suspect. If he sees you in a blue shirt, make sure you are wearing a red hoody next time.

Roger briefed the team as radios were passed around and call signs were confirmed. The FBI was sending a four-man team with one car. The Virginia Special Agents were also a four-man team, but they were utilizing four vehicles courtesy of the impound lot. The plan was for five vehicles to follow Sam Turner. Carl would be in the fifth car coordinating the surveillance operation. He was also bringing two special agents specifically trained to follow people on foot. If Turner entered an area inaccessible by cars or he tried to use public transportation, they would follow. They were experts at it and extremely proficient at navigating the maze of Northern Virginia trains and buses.

"Let's head out. We are meeting the Feds at six."

Falls Church, VA

Dane sipped his coffee while staring absentmindedly out the window. He was watching the front door to the small postal store for any sight of Wilson but was only keeping that part of his brain focused and alert. He allowed the rest of his mind to drift. He thought of it as stretching his brain waves before a major operation. That way his brain was ready when called upon.

"Would you like a refill, sir? Sir..."

"Oh, sorry. Yes please." Dane moved his cup within reach of the young waitress. *"Thank you."* He was grateful that he had not returned to work after the New York job. For one, he had been exhausted when he returned home. The job had taken a lot out of him. Secondly, it would have been difficult to return to work and request more time off after two days back. Extensions, for some reason, were always more welcome. Dane told his boss he just needed a little more time.

He had spent the entire morning making sure he was clean. He started with a five a.m. run. He moved freely around his neighborhood looking for anything out of the ordinary. People out of place, cars running for long periods without moving; and even new faces with new dogs. Surveillants used all sorts of tricks to get close to and observe their targets. He had witnessed a real world follow during a training event in California several years ago. He had passed a mailman who appeared nothing but, sitting in his vehicle near a small community park. He was just cutting through the area when he felt a strange vibe in the air. The mailman looked the part down to the pressed blue shorts and knee length socks. It was the earpiece tucked into his shirt and running to the obvious bulge of a radio on his lower back that uncovered the ruse. Mailman did not need that type of communication gear for dropping off mail and packages. Dane had then broadened his view and picked out other anomalies. Why were two grown men in overalls and work jackets sitting at a picnic table having coffee? Why were there suddenly three joggers in the same area in the early afternoon? It also looked like a lot of dogs suddenly needed walking in the neighborhood. Dane could not leave quickly enough.

Once he was satisfied that the apartment was not under observation, he ate, showered, and changed. The motorcycle had been stashed in a parking garage near the postal store the evening prior. That had been an ordeal as well, but Dane knew for certainty that its whereabouts were unknown to any possible surveillance. He then walked to the unit to get the truck. He knew that vehicle was clean and there was no way someone could tamper with it in the unit's parking lot. Old faithful started up quickly. From there he headed over to the Metro Center Station. There was a nearby garage that offered long term parking. Dane purchased a three-day pass which met his needs perfectly. He did not intend on being out on the streets for three days, but he wanted to make sure he had that option if necessary. His route continued, transitioning from metro to bus to foot, and then an old-fashioned cab to his final destination. He moved the motorcycle from its parking place for easier access and then posted up in the crappy little diner to act as the trigger. He would be the one to spot the target and alert the rest of the team.

He checked in with both Jack and Sam. It was nearly two hours since he took up residence in the diner and he would have to move on shortly. Sam had completed the final leg of his route when Dane took his static position, having left his place early that morning. His business had a small apartment above, on the second level. Instead of renting the place, Sam used it for times he was in town for business or hunting. He reported clean when he entered his final leg of his surveillance detection route with no issues. It did not appear that he was followed. He reported his final status when he arrived in the area and proceeded to loiter to provide Dane with assistance when needed. The initial plan was for Dane to follow on foot if necessary and call in Sam if Simmons went mobile. Once Sam had eyes on him, Dane would retrieve his motorcycle and join up in the chase as soon as possible. Jack was at a nearby hotel parking lot ready to join when called upon. The plan wasn't the best one but for three men, it was the best possible solution. They did not have enough people to cover every direction Simmons may travel. That was why Dane had selected to stay in a fixed location and provide directional information to his two partners in vehicles. Those positions were referred to as mobiles. Dane had tags ready to slap underneath Simmons' vehicle the first chance he got. If he was able to get the GPS tracker on the car, following him would be much simpler with a smaller team.

Good luck prevailed however, and it looked like he wouldn't have to re-locate after all. A banged up red, Dodge minivan pulled up in front of the store. A man exited the vehicle matching Wilson Simmons' description. He was in his mid-sixties and stood around six feet tall. He looked fit to Dane, and despite the poor condition of the vehicle, he was dressed neatly as well. *What were you* expecting dummy? What does a child sexual predator even dress like? Dane quickly alerted the team about the possible sighting. He turned to his phone opening an application courtesy of Charles's mysterious IT associate. The app was already connected to the security cameras inside the store. Dane was even able to move the camera and had previously focused in on Simmons' mailbox. Sure enough, not even twenty seconds later Dane watched the man, open the box, remove a slip, and then head to the counter to receive a package. *Gottcha.*

"Standby, standby. Sixty to sixty-five-year-old white man. Five feet nine inches to six feet tall. Grey hair cut short. Medium build. Athletic gait. Brown hiking style boots. Blue Jeans. Light grey hoodie sweatshirt. Entering red Dodge minivan with faded grey spots all over. Virginia plate Victor, Charlie, Hotel, niner, niner, zero. Intending west on Lee Highway from postal store."

"This is Charlie. I can quick join west on Lee Highway."

"Roger Charlie. Inform when you have control."

Fairfax, VA

"Looks like he isn't here," Carl said to Roger as he walked over. *"One of my guys did a close look. Business is obviously closed and there doesn't appear to be anyone in the apartment. His truck is not in his spot around back. He must have left early. No idea when he will be back. He could be at the gym somewhere or he may have left town."*

"Damnit." The group was huddled around the FBI agent's car sipping on coffee and finishing up smokes. *"I really thought six was early enough. We know he is in town, and this is the only place he stays. Pat, can you hit up the Winchester PD again? Ask them if they can keep a patrol unit in the area around Turner's home or along the route he would take to return from this area. I would hate to waste our time setting up here while he pulls into his driveway back in Winchester."*

"On it."

"What do you think?" Carl asked.

Roger thought about it for a minute. *"We have a lot of information on this guy, but no pattern of life. We assumed six a.m. would be early enough, but we really don't know his daily routine. He could be swimming in the river for exercise. Or he could be at breakfast and pull in any minute."*

"The reason we are doing this is to establish a pattern of life in the first place. Are you recommending we leave?"

"No. I think we should set up the box and wait. We are already here. Might as well put in some work. If he does come back, we will be ready."

A short time later the team was set. Carl had set up the box for the surveillance team. He had his team covering the four major avenues to approach or depart Sam's office. The box was set that so whatever direction the target departed, a team member could follow quickly without any radical turns or maneuvers that would alert a suspect. Carl's vehicle was in a parking structure around the corner from the office building. Carl and team could watch the back door where Sam parked his vehicle. They would be able to alert the team when he arrived home.

Roger and Pat each had a position in the box but since they were close by one another Patricia walked over to his vehicle so they could continue talking about the cases.

"I have a hunch."

"What is it Pat?"

"I just called the office before I headed over. I had Andrew grab the photos we had of Turner, Cooper, and Ferguson and fax them over to the office handling the Camp case."

"Why?"

"David Bell. Remember him?"

"Camp was the suicide in the park. Bell was the other janitor that did not show up to work and disappeared around the same time as Camp?"

"Yes." Patricia flipped through her notebook. *"Here it is. The comment from the assistance principal about Bell stuck with me for some reason. She said Bell was a good worker, caused no problems, and kept to himself. But she also said that he just didn't seem like the janitor type."*

"I do remember that. I think I see where you are going with this."

"It has been bugging me for a while, and it took a hot minute for me to work it out in my brain. But, if Carl's theory is correct, what if this Bell guy is a member of this group? So, if these three men are his top picks, then it would make sense one of them is Bell. I am waiting to hear back from the lead detective after he gets those pictures in front of the assistant principal."

"Good call partner. Very good call."

Falls Church, VA

"Do you have control, Charlie?"

"Affirmative Bravo. You are clear to retrieve your ride. Intending East on Lee Highway."

"Charlie has control. Alpha is parallel left. Bravo is no longer backing. Inform when moving."

The three men had selected simple call signs for the operation. Their cell phone communication should have been secure, but any additional risk was unnecessary, especially since two of the three were already persons of interest with both State and Federal authorities. Jack would be Alpha, Dane Bravo, and Sam was Charlie. Dane had watched Simmons exit the postal store and climb into his red minivan. Sam had been nearby and actually turned onto Lee Hwy at the same moment that Simmons pulled from the curb. He would take up the eye, or eyes-on until Dane could catch up by motorcycle. Jack, just a block away also began heading west on a parallel street about two blocks south. He would be in a favorable position to assume the eye when necessary.

"Alpha checking in parallel south."

"Roger Alpha. Target west on Lee. Crossed Tinner Hill Road. Intending to Hillwood Avenue."

Dane listened as Sam gave the update on movement. He listened while he fastened his helmet, started the bike, and exited the parking garage one block north of Lee Hwy also heading West. He heard that Simmons was still on Lee Highway traveling West. Simmons had already crossed Tinner Hill Road and was intending or rather heading toward Hillwood Avenue where the highway would start head northeast. Dane had three blocks until he would be able to take up the position of eye if needed. He used the Bluetooth function in the helmet to connect to the phone. When he depressed a button installed on his handlebars the microphone activated and allowed him to communicate.

"Bravo just turned west on Lee Hwy. Intending Cameron Road." His cell phone was open on the map function and stored securely in the motorcycle's gas tank bag. The clear plastic cover allowed him to navigate the streets, hands free from his phone. Surveillance was always more difficult on something

like a motorcycle, but Dane had found the vehicle so versatile that the extra effort was worth the flexibility.

"Heads up team. Target northwest on Lee Hwy. Maintaining speed in the left lane. No indication of turns or stops. Possibly intending interstate sixty-six. Recommend Alpha post one block behind me on Lee, Bravo behind him. Upcoming interchange gets fast and loose. Recommend tightening up the follow."

Fairfax, VA

"Carl, Roger here. We have new information about Turner. Recommend meeting at our original location to discuss options. This is urgent."

"On my way."

Moments later the team was converging around the hood of Roger's vehicle. *"I can't take credit for this, so I will let Special Agent Stills explain."*

"Thanks Roger. Special Agent Blanchard is aware of a previous case but many of you may not be. The Cliff note version is that we had a convicted pedophile commit suicide in an Alexandria parks several months back. Guy by the name of Arthur Camp. Currently, the death has been ruled a suicide but there have been many theories floated that he was instead murdered. One of those people is Special Agent Blanchard. As we have already discussed we are trying to develop a pattern of life for Mr. Turner because it is

suspected he is in some sort of group violently targeting child predators."

"We have not been able to find any connection between Camp and either Turner, Cooper, or Ferguson. Are you telling me you have found one?" Carl asked.

"Yes. While conducting interviews at the school, the lead detective discovered that Camp was not the only janitor who was absent that day and never showed up again. A janitor by the name of David Bell was never identified. His records were clean. Almost too clean, like he didn't exist. It was a statement from one of the staff members that has really stuck with me. She said that Bell didn't cause any trouble, did a thorough job, but just didn't seem the janitor type."

"I never delved deep into that case but that would strike me as odd as well. We just thought the suicide seemed a little elaborate and that is why I came out to the scene."

"I sent the lead detective pictures of Turner, Cooper, and Ferguson. He got them in front of the same staff member, and she picked out Turner. She claimed he looked like Bell. Now again, we don't have anything on Turner/Bell for the death of Arthur Camp. No evidence that he was involved so, we didn't chase down that angle very hard. But given light of your theories, I think now may be the time."

"So, what is your suggestion?" Carl asked.

"We send out a BOLO, be on the lookout for Turner's truck. We get every cruiser on the street looking for him. Once found, we bring him in for questioning about Camp. It will serve two purposes. One, we can sweat him a little bit about Camp. See if something does come loose, and ."

"Two, if he is working with a group, it may shake them up, and force a mistake on their part," answered Carl.

CHAPTER 24: THE HUNT

Northern Virginia

"I have him north on highway six, niner, four at Lincoln Avenue. Intending North west Street. Approaching Interstate six, six but no freeway entrances. Continue as eye."

Dane keyed his mike. *"Good copy Alpha. Bravo and Charlie are backing."*

Dane monitored the team's progress on his phone. Although Alpha, Jack, was the team lead and overall coordinator of the surveillance, when he took up a follow position, it was agreed that Dane would take over temporarily. He and Sam were in the backing, or support positions which meant it was easier for them to see the big picture while Jack concentrated on the target. Coordinating a team was difficult enough, but to do so while taking a turn as the eye made it even harder. With only three vehicles, precision was key. Dane doubted that Simmons had any professional training in surveillance detection but that didn't always matter. He was a criminal with a criminal's heightened sense of awareness due to a fear of being caught. They certainly did not want to spook him. Seeing the same vehicle twice may just do that. All Dane wanted was for Simmons to stop long enough for him to slap a tracker on his minivan. The team would still keep eyes on him though. This was too important to blindly trust technology. Trackers do fail or fall off. Sometimes, even their signals bounced erratically off buildings and other structures failing to provide an accurate location. The tracker was simply a back-up. An insurance policy giving the surveillants' a little piece of mind. *We will follow this piece of shit to the end of the earth if we have to.*

"Target is still traveling north toward highway one, two, tree. Intending Interstate four, niner, fife, underpass. Be advised no freeway entrance. If he takes a turn down an obscure road, I will be a little warm"

Where are you going Simmons? Dane knew the area well. Simmons appeared to be heading up to the southern bank of the Potomac. Unless he changed course, he couldn't get on I-495 so he wasn't crossing over into Maryland. At least not here. He may be going further west. Dane had a hunch.

"Alpha. Bravo is moving up. Will be within range in one mike."

"Roger Bravo. Good Copy. Standby, standby, standby. Target intending right, right, right, on Swinks Mill Road."

That is what I thought. *"Standby Alpha. I am caught up. I have the eye. Turning right, right, right."*

"Roger Bravo. Alpha no longer has control. I will back, parallel left on Spring Hill Road. Alpha has control. Charlie back Bravo, north on Swinks."

"Roger Alpha. Charlie is backing."

The loose convoy continued up the winding road heading north toward the Potomac. The river was a natural barrier between Virginia and Maryland. Neighborhoods became sparser. What didn't become sparser were the parks. The shoreline was dotted with them. If he was right, Simmons was heading to one of those parks. It is his MO after all. Some were small community parks accessible only by foot. Some ran along the Great Falls, cascading waterfalls that bordered parks on both the Virginia and Maryland shorelines. The Virginia side had only one way in and one way out. Not a smart place to abduct a child. My bet is Scott's run. Parking at several different locations. Easy access by car, bike, or foot. Great place to walk a dog and feel safe.

Fairfax, VA

The group had taken over one of the small conference rooms to await word on Turner's location. Carl had dismissed his driver and the other two surveillants from the Group. This was a Virginia case now and didn't require Federal involvement. No sense in tying up their time. But he of course would stay. There was no way he was missing this.

Roger entered the room with Captain Ivers and the two men took places at the table. Roger had already cleared the BOLO through the Captain. The desk officer had published it to all active patrol units about an hour ago. The BOLO was also ready for the next shift's briefing which would be in about two hours if they still hadn't found Turner.

Captain Ivers turned toward Carl. *"I have no problem coordinating with the FBI. Roger has thoroughly briefed me and although I support this operation, I really do think the evidence is slim connecting Turner with any of this."*

"I understand your apprehension, Captain. I really do. And the evidence is not as solid as I would like. Absolutely. But the circumstances are surreal. If this janitor Bell was really Turner? What would be his excuse? I just took three weeks off from my lucrative shooting facility and security consultant business so I could see if I would enjoy a different career in the custodial arts? Makes no sense."

"Oh, I agree. If you can connect him to that school, that would be huge. But it is my understanding that the witness thinks Turner looks like Bell but not exactly. Same height, same build, but Bell had a receding hairline and a mustache. She also thought the eyes looked a little different. About the only thing she is sure of is that of the three pictures she saw, Turner was the only one that looked familiar."

"All those changes can all be done with a talented makeup artist. Wigs, makeup, and even prosthetics. If... when we bring Bell in, the witness can see him in person. That will be a much more honest look."

"Plus, Captain, I found this." Roger slide him several printouts. The first was a printout from Turner's webpage. It said that the range was closed for a month for repairs during his possible time posing as a janitor.

"Ok. Not abnormal. He may have been refurbishing. Putting in new shooting lanes. Who knows? He also might have put a month on his website in case the project ran long."

"Agreed sir. But he also wasn't taking clients at his security consultant office either. I called over there on a hunch. Got ahold of the receptionist. I told her there was a billing problem from last month. I made up the name of a company that supposedly used Turner's services during the timeframe Bell was working at the school. Guess what she said? Told me that there couldn't have been a billing problem. Turner wasn't taking any new clients for that month in order to work out at his shooting facility."

"Again, it is logical and makes sense."

Roger directed his attention to the other sheets of paper. *"Those are country records for construction permits in Frederick County. Some counties are lax when it comes to construction permits but they don't cut any corners with shooting ranges and there are several around the Winchester area. They are super strict with those guys and go over their paperwork with a fine-tooth comb. As you can see from these reports, Turner always followed the letter of the law. Those are the permits from the last four years on his property. He filed four permits in that time for everything from range construction to range cleanup. The last one is followed even closer than the others since it involves cleaning up all the expended ammunition. There are a lot of EPA regulations for digging up the ground and disposing of bullets, especially lead. As you can see, there were no permits for the time period in question. If he was doing range maintenance, certainly he would have filed it with the county."*

"Again, I agree that the whole thing looks strange. I am simply requesting caution. This is all very circumstantial. Sam Turner has broken no laws that we know of. This is a delicate matter and needs to be handled as such."

"Captain, I fully understand. I realize that I am a guest at this point. Nevertheless, let me make myself crystal clear. Whatever animosity some people believe exists between federal and state authorities is crap. I will take full responsibility and go to the mat for this operation. My gut tells me that we are close, and that Turner is a key piece. And if he provides that critical missing piece, I will have the full weight of the FBI along with their resources to help solve all these deaths."

Roger noticed that Patricia was absent from the conversation. He looked over at his partner's side of the desk. There she sat, phone to her ear, furiously scribbling in the ever-present notepad. He could hear bits of her conversation.

"Are you sure? Uh, huh? Both doors. Did you run it twice through the database?"

Blanchard and the Captain suspended their conversation also noticing Special Agent Stills on the phone. All three men stood in anticipation of whatever news she was gathering.

"You are the best. I will keep you in the loop. Yes, yes, you will be the first to know. Stop giving me shit, us Staties are not going to try and steal your case. Thanks, Andrew."

Pat hung up the phone and finalized realized that all eyes were on her like she was going to announce the winning lottery numbers for Powerball. She grinned and Roger knew his partner well enough to know that a break-through was coming.

"That was Andrew. Lead on the Camp case. He was the one I asked to show that assistant principal the photos of Turner and she thought he looked like our missing janitor Bell. Then I asked Andrew for another favor on a hunch. They had prints from some of the places Camp may have used to spy on children. They concentrated heavily on the various utility closets throughout the school. Especially those near the bathrooms and the gym locker rooms. They checked all the mops, brooms, etc. The sheer volume of prints in a place like that is daunting. Too many people touching things to count. Not to mention prints can get smudged by other prints."

"The hunch Stills," Roger reminded his partner impatiently.

"I am getting there. The faculty at the school park out back in their own lot. There are two doors for them. Visitors park in the front of the school and use the main entrance. But there is a fourth entrance. It leads to a small parking lot on the west side of the school.

It is where they get deliveries and load trash in the commercial dumpster. There is also a small space for the janitors to park. I had the outside door handle and inside crash or touch bar, whatever you call it, dusted for prints even though the scene is in no way preserved. A long shot. And it paid off. Sam Turner's fingerprints were found on the crash bar. He was at that school."

At that moment a young officer burst into the room. *"Special Agent Patterson. Your vehicle has been spotted. A McLean patrol unit just reported in. The suspect vehicle has entered Scott's Run Nature Preserve Park."*

McLean, VA

The west side of the park contained two parking lots. At least that is what the website listed when Jack looked up the park. Dane followed Simmons north into the first driveway after Jack let him know that he had two choices to park if Simmons decided to stop. That was the benefit of having a controller not in an active follow state and doing some serious map reconnaissance. Dane's plan was to stop in the first lot if Simmons passed it or continue to the northern spot if Simmons chose the southern lot. As expected, Wilson stopped in the southern lot. The fastest way to leave if anything went bad. Dane continued past and quickly found a parking spot for his bike, which was easy since the lot was nearly deserted. There was no actual second parking lot. Just spaces on either side of huge wooden steps leading into the park. He and Sam had talked briefly on the way to the final stop. Sam also had a tracker with him and the experience to emplace it under Simmons' vehicle. He was about five minutes behind Dane, which would be plenty of time for Wilson to exit his vehicle and begin whatever adventure he was up to in this place. Dane would follow on foot and update Sam regarding locations so that he would have relative privacy tagging the vehicle.

"Foxtrot. I have the eye."

Dane stood by one of the park entrance billboards that provided hiker details for the numerous trails and pathways. The park ran along the southern shore of the Potomac right up to the river's edge. Although sparse, residential areas bordered it to the east, west, and south. Plenty of park patrons. How many were young children walking dogs? He studied the glass encased map determining the fastest route to catch up with Wilson. Dane had parked in the Nature Preserve parking lot which was not connected to all the trails as were its two sister lots located off Georgetown Pike Road. The problem was only one single path led to the interior of the preserve from their current location. Simmons was already at the base of the steps. Dane was going to have to move cross country to keep Simmons in site without literally following him down the trail That might be a little noticeable.

Luckily, Dane had brought one of his backpacks to carry items he may need during surveillance. He removed it from the rear seat of the motorcycle, cinched the straps over his shoulders, and moved directly into the woods, approximately fifty meters parallel to Simmons. He moved quickly and with ease keeping slightly back and out of Simmons' peripheral view. The path wound eastward and saw very little foot traffic. Dane was wondering why Simmons would choose this place. It wasn't packed with hikers, but there were enough people on the trails and in the parking lot to make an abduction very difficult. Serious hikers took the back country like he was currently doing, but he saw countless families pushing strollers along the path enjoying the outdoors. Certainly, someone would see a child in distress. Maybe Simmons was realizing this place wouldn't work either.

After a short time, Dane could see Simmons slowing along one of the paths that headed into a neighborhood. Dane paused nearby as he watched the man emerge upon the residential street and kill time while looking around. Simmons had pulled out a cell phone acting as though he was trying to get service. Bullshit. He is checking to see if this is a good place to leave and depart without being seen. He is not planning to use the parking lot at all. He is looking for a good ambush site.

At that moment his headset squawked. *"Alpha, Bravo, this is Charlie. I am at the target vehicle. Cursory search complete."*

"Any problems?" Alpha asked.

"None. Fairly deserted. Doors locked. Be advised Subject may not live alone. Could be an innocent bystander at his final bed-down location."

"How do you figure? Innocent bystander or accomplice?"

"I hardly doubt this belongs to an accomplice. I didn't notice before, but the van is modified. Rear door, driver's side. There is some sort of wheelchair lift. It looks like a ramp descends to the ground for easy loading. And there is a wheelchair on its side in the back seat. Plus, as a final touch, he has a handicap placard hanging from his rearview mirror. But his license plates do not indicate handicapped."

Dane spoke up. *"That is how he is doing it. He is drugging the kids. He uses the wheelchair for transport. He somehow paralyzes them, and they can't move much or speak. Maybe just erratic movement and slurred speech. All anybody would see is a dedicated father or grandfather taking a special needs child into the woods for some fresh air. People would literally be ashamed to look too closely. He makes himself invisible by drawing attention to a disability that people avoid out of pity."*

"If you are right, that is sick. I am heading back to the vehicle for the tag. I can do it quickly on the passenger side. Plenty of metal for the magnet. Not the best but it will do for now until he stops for the night."

"Charlie. You are clear to tag. Bravo has the eye. Will provide updates on target movement."

Dane watched Simmons re-enter the path along which he previously traveled. He was heading back toward the parking lot but turned abruptly south after a couple hundred yards. Another subdivision. This one looked much larger and had a pedestrian crossing path with a flashing yellow light and white stripes painted on the asphalt. Georgetown Pike was a winding road along the southern part of the park and seemed too dangerous to cross. But sure enough, there was a straightaway section of road with all the safety measures in place for pedestrians. Pedestrians such as hikers, jogger, and children walking their pets. Simmons was checking multiple locations. Dane studied the map on his phone. If Simmons held to pattern, next he would head back to the parking lot and then move north along the park ranger trail. Multiple neighborhoods were situated along that route just off the wood-line. It was then that the earpiece once again broke his attention.

"Break. Break. Break. We have a problem guys. Virginia's finest just pulled into the lot and they are clearly not here for our target. Lights, sirens, the whole works. Two cruisers in the lot, and one temporarily blocking the entrance."

"How do you know they aren't onto Simmons?"

"Because I am surrounded and being ordered to show my hands. Consider my phone compromised. I have to go now boys."

Both Alpha and Charlie could hear the commotion from the arresting officer. The officers were ordering Sam to raise his hands, turn around, stand with feet shoulder length apart, and lean across the hood of his truck. Sam was able to provide one final transmission before the cell phone was extinguished.

Shit, Shit, Shit.

Aide-De-Camp: *Sir. We have mission compromise. One of the men was arrested.*

President: *What happened? Which one?*

Aide-De-Camp: *It was the Closer. Virginia State police and Blanchard.*

President: *Keep me informed. I will make the necessary arrangements. Does our other friend still have the target?*

Aide-De-Camp: *I hope so, sir. All communications are dead for now.*

CHAPTER 25: THE FIND

Scott's Run Nature Preserve, VA

"Shit. Shit. Shit."

Dane crushed the cell phone beneath his boot. Alpha had put the call out that the net was compromised once the authorities had swarmed Charlie. It was redundant since Sam had provided one last transmission before he was arrested.

"Happy hunting boys. Looks like my part to play is over. Charlie out."

The cops would find Sam's phone and it could lead to the rest of the group. Better to get rid of it now. Dane casually picked up the pieces while taking in the scene down the road. This was a real shitshow.

Sam had already been searched and cuffed and was now sitting idle in the rear of a state cruiser. Dane was sure the gun they pulled from his back belt did not help in any small way. Several officers meticulously searched his vehicle announcing each find to be bagged and tagged as evidence. Dane could only imagine the treasure trove of circumstantial evidence that was being retrieved from Sam's truck. As a weapons instructor and security specialist, his equipment most certainly danced in the gray area between labeling him a law-abiding citizen or inmate.

Sam, however, was not his immediate concern. Simmons was the target and the priority. Sam was on his own for the time being, fully knowing the risks of membership in the club. He was a professional. He would remain calm and keep his mouth shut. Dane was certain the President already had the wheels of justice turning once Jack informed him of the roust. But how did this happen? Dane pushed those thoughts from his mind for the moment. He still had eyes on Simmons. The only eyes on Simmons. What would he do?

As if to answer his question, Wilson Simmons began to casually walk into the parking lot. Sam had parked on the opposite side of the lot containing the target vehicle, so Simmons' path did not bring him into direct or even close contact with the authorities. He gave the scene the normal curiosity it warranted from any citizen, but then he moved on quickly as if to declare his lack of involvement and therefore innocence. The police didn't give him a second glance as he entered the beat up mini-van and turned over the engine.

Dane would have to play it just as cool. He was in the northern parking lot, his route south passing the chaotic scene. He would have to hope the authorities would provide him with the same safe passage as Simmons. He could not lose the target. He was the last eye before Simmons was gone and there was no way to immediately call for help. Thankfully the bike started with ease. Dane wasted no time in his pursuit. Not only was Simmons getting away, but if the cops were targeting Sam because of suspected involvement with the club, how long before they realized that an accomplish could be close by? Face shield down, Dane was virtually unrecognizable. The choice of the motorcycle may have just salvaged this operation. As he passed by the law enforcement swarm, familiar faces stood out in the crowd. Patterson and Stills. The agents from Angela's case. And that asshole Blanchard. He was behind this, Dane thought, as he casually glided past and took up pursuit of Simmons.

"Good luck, Sam."

Roger and Patricia watched as the scene unfolded before them. After racing over to this park, the following turn of events felt anti-climactic. Carl had hitched a ride with the pair and observed as the uniformed officers systematically searched the truck. They seemed pleased upon each weapon found or surveillance camera discovered. They even found what some would consider burglary tools. Lock pits and other tools for security defeats. However, they didn't know the bigger picture. The three expected these items from a weapons instructor and security specialist. Each would be thoroughly scrutinized but Roger had no doubt they would be identified as properly registered and thereby legal. It was other items he was anxious to get his hands on. Phones, notes, personal items, and even trash could tell a completely different story. Roger knew that the FBI agent's agenda was to link Turner to some mysterious band of vigilantes intent on circumventing the judicial system and ridding society of child predators. As a law enforcement agent, this was of interest to him as well. But only secondary.

His primary focus was the children. If Turner was part of some group, and if he had somehow tracked down a predator, Roger intended to ensure that information was put to good use.

The patrols waived the group over, indicating that their initial search was complete. The scene was safe and ready for the investigator. As if choreographed, all three donned latex gloves to preserve the scene in as pristine a manner as possible. Vehicles outside the immediate area were allowed to depart having seemingly nothing to do with the task at hand. The local police were clearing the lot of cars to make room for more cruisers. Roger didn't know why, but a motorcycle heading out from the northern lot caught his attention. He couldn't quite nudge the information from his brain into a tangible thought.

"You coming partner?"

Northern Virginia

Simmons was definitely spooked by the affair in the parking lot of Scott's Run. He played it cool and calm in front of the police, but he was anything but, as Dane watched him weave in and out of traffic. Simmons was skirting the law regarding reckless driving. It actually made it easier to conduct a follow. Dane was able to stay several cars back, easily identifying the mini-van's erratic movements.

Simmons' first stop was a Walmart just off the highway. The parking lot was full, forcing him to select a space quite a distance from the store entrance. It was perfect for Dane, parked a couple of rows over. As soon as Simmons began the long trek to the store, Dane went into action. A quick glance at the light poles confirmed the absence of security cameras. He wasn't expecting any. Upon reaching the passenger side of the van and after another glance for observers, he took a knee to tie an already laced boot. From his right pocket, he smoothly retrieved the tracker he had brought and slapped it under the vehicle. Hasty. Sloppy. And not at all to be relied upon but considering the circumstances it was all he had time for at the moment. The device would at least give him some piece of mind. Back on his feet, his next focus was the vehicle's interior. He tried each door hoping that luck would provide him with easy access. Locked tight. He didn't have the time or the tools to open one of the doors. Even if he did, broad daylight in the middle of a busy parking lot was not the ideal setting. A glance through the windows would have to suffice for now.

The glance told him nothing. The battered minivan was surprisingly neat on the inside. No trash. No personal effects. Nothing really. A coffee cup and an air freshener hanging from the rear-view mirror as well as the wheelchair that Sam had noted earlier. That was it. *What were you expecting*? Not like he was going to have a bucket of candy to lure children into his vehicle. Learning virtually nothing, Dane turned toward the store entrance. Time to find out what he is up to in there.

Dane found Simmons easily enough in the back corner of the store. Simmons had not bothered with a cart for any of his purchases. He was examining some items in the tool section. He was carrying one of those large painters' buckets and would occasionally drop a purchase into the container. It was his makeshift shopping basket. And as far as Dane could tell from his vantage point there was nothing particularly alerting about Simmons' intended purchases. He had some shop rags, some cutting blades that appeared to be for a jigsaw and an assortment of files. Just a regular guy re-stocking his garage. But Simmons was no regular guy and Dane didn't like the look of these purchases. He followed Simmons to the front and watched him avoid self-check-out and use a regular shopping lane. He is avoiding the camera at the self-check kiosk. Simmons also paid cash for his items, although he did accept a receipt, he shredded the paper once outside and deposited it in the nearest trashcan. The trashcan most likely to be used by patrons and therefore the one likely to be changed the most. To Dane, the whole picture started to take shape. Wilson was shopping. He was avoiding cameras and using cash to sever any trail back to him. He took the receipts and destroyed them to ensure no trace was left behind. The park must have really spooked him. *Am I seeing him assemble items he needs to get rid of any remaining children?*

Scott's Run Nature Preserve, VA

Roger, Pat, and Carl stood outside of Turner's truck going through the list of items found by the officers and themselves. *The sheer number of weapons in the truck was quite impressive,*

Roger thought to himself. Along with a pistol found in a back-waistband holster on his person, two additional pistols were found mounted in the truck. One to the lower right of the steering wheel for quick driver access and the other in a mount inside the middle console of the truck. Turner obviously wasn't planning on ever being car-jacked. The back bed of the pickup also included a built-in safe. In there was an additional handgun on a tactical belt with multiple magazines, first aid pouches, and a dump bag with loose ammunition. He also had several long guns with impressive and expensive scopes. The find was not that surprising due to the nature of his work, but still quite a few to carry around on a normal day. The serial numbers would all be run through the national database, and Roger had no doubt regarding their legality.

Other items found included police batons, several knives, and even an old-fashioned sap like the police in the sixties and seventies used to carry to dish out street justice. Roger was certain those were no longer legal to own but he doubted the possession of a sap would land Turner behind bars. In addition to the arsenal, the team also found gear for surveillance and security. Again, to be expected. Roger was certain that one case containing camera lenses of all sizes was probably worth more than his monthly salary. Maybe two months. What they didn't find was anything that screamed I am part of a secret club that kills people. No scraps of paper. No little black book with a list of names partially crossed off. Not even a decent cell phone to exploit. Turner only had what appeared to be a burner phone. It was a cheap, off the shelf kind that could be purchased at any store for cash. Anonymously. *But wait.*

"Pat? Has he said anything about why he was here?" Roger asked his partner. She had done the initial interview with Turner in the backseat of the cruiser.

"Nothing. Said he likes nature and then clammed up. Why?"

"You got a thought Roger?" Carl asked.

Roger stood lost in thought for a minute. Carl looked ready to ask if he heard the question when he noticed Pat slowly shaking her head indicating that now was not the time to interrupt her partner's chain of thoughts. As if to answer them both, Roger began walking toward the northern end of the parking lot along the road that led to the upper lot. He stopped and turned around.

"Both of you guys were at the office a few months ago when Cooper came in, right?"

Pat and Carl both nodded.

"Wasn't he carrying a motorcycle helmet?"

It was Pat that spoke up. *"You're right, he did. Where are you going with this?"*

Roger walked over to a group of patrolmen that were directing traffic away from the parking lot. They had already placed cones on either side of the driveway connecting them with yellow crime scene tape.

"Guys, have you kept track of the vehicles that were in this lot? The vehicles that left?"

"I am sorry sir, we did not. We were not told it was a crime scene, only an arrest scene, so our instructions were to let everyone out of the area and prevent others from entering. We were specifically instructed to cause as little disruption as possible. Sorry."

Roger walked back to Carl and Pat who both had remained in place while Roger worked out his thoughts. *"Ok, what was Turner doing here? It certainly wasn't a nature walk. What if he was following someone? He has no reason to be here, an arsenal in his truck, and no cell phone."*

"We found a phone boss."

"Not one that can be tracked or traced to him." Carl opened the flip phone they had found. *"Only two numbers in here. This is not his everyday phone by a long shot. This was for surveillance."*

"Exactly," Roger exclaimed as he pointed to the phone. *"And whoever else is behind those phone numbers may very well have been here as well. Shit."*

"Motorcycle?" Carl asked.

"When the patrols were initially searching Turner's truck, I noticed a motorcycle rolling down from the northern part of the lot

and then out of the park. It stuck with me for the moment, but I couldn't figure out why. Cooper rides a damn motorcycle. I don't have any proof whatsoever that it was him, but if you think he may be involved with Turner, we may have just missed him and others. Turner was conducting a coordinated surveillance operation with others. That is what my gut is telling me. And we missed them."

"Uh boss? If that is true, then we also missed the monster they were following."

Northern Virginia

Dane followed as Simmons made several more stops along his seemingly non-stop journey. He pulled into multiple hardware stores, thrift shops, and even a West Marine store. Dane could not enter every store with Simmons to observe the purchases he made. Some of the stores were too small and Dane was not certain if Simmons had seen him already. He certainly did not want to spook him further. Simmons appeared to calm down as his driving certainly became more stable. But he was a man on a mission and Dane was more certain than ever that this was preparations to dispose of bodies. Each time Simmons exited an establishment, the receipts would be shredded and disposed of in the trash. And each time it was unnerving. Bags were placed in the backseat of the vehicle. One stop even included the purchase of a new shovel.

Dane was all alone. The cell phone had been destroyed out of precaution. Sam was most likely in jail. Jack was probably trying frantically to locate his missing surveillants. In addition, here he was with no way to signal for help. His cell phone was sitting on his kitchen counter so as not to tie him to any possible scene. I should have put it in a Faraday bag. Traffic had surged earlier, making the follow even more difficult. Simmons had certainly not made it easy choosing to stop randomly. He did not follow a normal flow or pace. He seemed to erratically select places to shop as they caught his eye. He would stomp on his brakes at the last moment affecting traffic and the lone surveillant behind him. However, Dane had hung in there. He was a nervous wreck but still in the game. He prayed that Simmons would finally find his way home. But then what? Rush the house? Or try and go for help? Simmons could very well go home, make a sandwich, and then murder those children only to leave later to dispose of the bodies. Dane could not leave. He had to stop him by whatever means necessary. Simmons exited the thrift store and seemed pleased with himself. Dane watched through binoculars from a corner lot across the street. The fading light was going to render the glasses useless in the next few minutes. However, that look of satisfaction was telling. Dane saw it on his face. I bet he is done. He looks ready to go home after accomplishing something important.

A short while later Dane had gotten his wish. Simmons had driven around in circles for nearly another hour before finally heading home. Dane was thankful that the motorcycle got such good gas mileage. If he had used the truck, he would have gassed up at least twice. The final stop was in a small neighborhood between the freeway and Route One.

The city of Woodbridge did not have the best of reputations, even though Dane knew certain sections were actually quite nice. This was not one of those sections. The homes were mostly rundown, with at least one junk car on each property. Property lines were defined by stark chain linked fences, which gave the neighborhood a prison penitentiary feel to it. All the houses seemed similar in design. Single story, ranch style homes probably built in the fifties and sixties. They were perfect for the standard American family; husband, wife, and two point two children. Since those times, the neighborhood had drastically changed. It got older, more worn down, and was left to mother nature and father time to control the aging process. But the homes had survived thus far. Built to practically withstand a nuclear blast, the cement foundations and brick walls looked ready to stand another half century. Architects and home builders would refer to these types of homes as those with good bones. Dream homes to renovate and upgrade, but Dane saw something else. He saw a solid brick building that would contain noise. Suppress the sound of gunfire. Even muffled screams. Dan saw an objective that would contain the noise from the violence he was about to bring upon this man.

CHAPTER 26: THE FIX

Woodbridge, VA

Pupil: *I may be in trouble. The police swarmed a park I was stalking.*

Keeper: *Did they question you? Follow you?*

Pupil: *I left quickly. They arrested another man. I think they may be close. What should I do?*

Keeper: *Eliminate your collection. Destroy any evidence. Disappear. Reach out to me once you have started over in another location.*

Dane retrieved several items from one of the motorcycle saddlebags. He didn't have much to work with and no time to waste. He was going to have to execute this mission on the fly. He had gloves, a balaclava for riding in the cold weather, a hunting knife, and a baton. I can work with that. The motorcycle was parked on Route One behind a rundown strip mall. He had found a torn-up tarp near one of the dumpsters and covered the bike. He wasn't worried about cameras since there clearly weren't any here nor anything of value to protect. The storefronts didn't even appear to be open during normal business hours or functioning. He just didn't need some bum or drunk stumbling across his ride.

Once he donned his gloves and mask and stowed his weapons in his pockets, Dane moved into the shadows of some trees near the target. He took a knee and studied the back of Simmons' home. It appeared to be a single-story dwelling with four entrances. There was no indication of a basement, so he would only have one level to clear. He squinted his eyes, waiting for them to adjust to the darkness. He allowed his mind to relax and push out all other thoughts except for this very moment. This ritual had served him well over the years, allowing him to hone his entire focus on the mission at hand. Dane pictured himself moving swiftly through the house, clearing each and every room until he found the children and eliminated the threat. Angela.

He pushed that thought away as quickly as it popped into his brain. He knew that he may finally get closure on his little girl tonight, but he could not let that cloud his mind. He could not afford a misstep or to take an unnecessary risk. If he failed, he would also be failing her and the other children. Focus on the threat. Focus on Simmons and ensure he could not hurt anyone ever again. Save all the victims. Slow is smooth. Smooth is fast.

Dane exploded from his concealed position toward the rear of Simmons' house. He had noticed a rear exit from the garage into the backyard, which would be the ideal entry point under the circumstance. He didn't have picks or other entry tools. Blunt force was all he had. The garage was dark, indicating that Simmons was somewhere in the interior of the house. Dane was hoping that the confined garage space would contain the noise. He jammed the knife into the doorframe, level with the doorknob. With one powerful kick to the handle, the knife smashed into the frame insert, slicing open the wood. The box in the frame that holds the lock retention was destroyed and the locking mechanism released. The door sprang open, with Dane following close behind into the garage.

He remained in a low crouch, gently pushing the door shut. He listened. The garage was nearly pitch black, but as his eyes adjusted further, he could make out certain shapes. The minivan was the main fixture, occupying the garage and over half the space. He had seen it enter earlier when Simmons arrived home. A few shelves lined the far wall with nothing but the normal items found in such a place. Some tools, an old welding machine with a generator, and several cans of gasoline. A refrigerator and deep freezer along the back wall were the last items. With his eyes focused on the door leading into the house, he listened. His knife was stowed in his sheath but ready at a moment's notice. The baton not yet fully extended in his right hand, ready to expand to its full length and deal destruction when called upon.

After a few moments, it was clear that the entry had gone unnoticed. Or worse, Simmons had heard the noise and was poised inside the house to ambush the intruder. "*Try to think positively*," Dane took some solace in the fact he may have still retained some element of surprise. With his left hand, he slowly turned the knob on the door leading into the house praying that it was unlocked thereby removing the need for another dynamic entry that would certainly not go unnoticed this time. It was a solid door, shielding any light from within the house. Dane had no idea if he was stepping into a dark, unoccupied room or the crosshairs of a gun. The knob turned soundlessly with ease.

No pistol awaited him, only a dark laundry room with the barest of furnishing. Besides the machines, a small wooden bench was the only furnishing. A simple bench for donning or removing footwear. A single pair of boots were tucked beneath it on the floor. The next door was open and led to a small dining space and a gallery kitchen beyond. To the right was a small living room with a hallway presumably leading to the bedrooms. His eyes scanned the spaces he could see from the doorway. Moonlight was able to enter these spaces, improving his vision slightly. He listened.

The furnishing here was also meager. Impersonal, as if placed as an afterthought to keep up some sort of illusion of normalcy. The dining area had a small wooden table. Two chairs tucked alongside. Something found cheap at a Goodwill or thrift store. Used merely for function. Nobody to impress. The living room was equally bare. One small, well-worn loveseat sat against the wall beside a brick fireplace. The TV on the table opposite the couch was the only visible item of any value, and even it was small and worn. The rooms were empty. Simmons was nowhere to be seen. Dane began to question everything he had done so far. He had watched the home and only took his eyes off for a few moments while he retrieved the necessary items from his motorcycle. *Had Simmons left on foot? Possible, but unlikely.* The hallway had three doors. All shut. Presumably two bedrooms and a bath. *Was he hiding in one of those rooms? And if he was the abductor, where were the children.* Dane was thoroughly puzzled.

He moved quickly down the hall. The immediate door to his left opened easily into a full bathroom. It was neat and clean. The counters were void of anything except a single bar of soap. The shower curtain was partially drawn, and Dane easily cleared it of any ambush. Just another bar of soap and a shampoo bottle stared back at him. Simmons was not hiding in here.

He turned and cautiously reentered the hallway. Left or right? He only had two more doors. He choose the one on the right since it was closer. Not by much. The doorframe was less than a foot closer at most, but Dane did not want to pass up a room and possibly have an assailant behind him. He eased it open as he had all the others. And it was empty, just like all the others. A single bed sat in the center of the room. The closet at the far end was empty. This room felt like a mausoleum. It was dusty and stale. Dane was certain that he was the first person in a long time to step in here. The room was an afterthought. Simmons probably forgot it even existed. That left one more room. This was bizarre.

Back in the hall, Dane settled his gaze on the final door. This was it. He had cleared the entire house and found no sign of the man he had hunted. Simmons had to be in this room. Dane debated on his entry technique. The slow, casual opening of the door would be unwise. Simmons was trapped and could be poised to strike. Lash out at whoever invaded his home. The gig was up either way. Dane knew that the next few seconds would end with a violent struggle or the complete absence of the man he hunted. Normally, Dane would enter with a boot to the door, just parallel to the knob, with his pistol or rifle ready. But since he had neither and couldn't be sure of his opponent's arsenal, he needed to enter the room quickly and bring with him as much chaos as possible to disrupt Simmons' plans. With one final breath, he switched the baton to his left, lowered his right shoulder about a foot from the door, and after a powerful explosion from his legs, Dane crashed through the final bedroom door with all the energy he could bring to bear.

Fairfax, VA

Patricia entered the small interrogation room. She placed a cup of coffee in front of both Sam and Roger and then took her seat next to her partner. The room had a simple table with three chairs. Two occupied by Pat and Roger and the third hosting Sam Turner directly across from them. Roger had his case files open and was studying his notes. Turner sat casually, seemingly without a care in the world. He was not cuffed or restrained in any manner. This could have easily been a job interview or staff meeting rather than an interrogation. Carl glared at him from behind the one-way mirror on the opposite wall. He and Captain Ivers were listening and recording the entire interview. Sam accepted the cup from Patricia.

"Thank you. Appreciate it."

Roger cleared his throat. *"Mr. Turner. We have some questions about your recent activities."*

"Well, my cooperation depends solely on the situation here. I do not believe I have been formally arrested. You have certainly not cuffed me to this table, but you have taken personal items from me and made it quite clear that I am not free to leave this room of my own volition."

"You have not been formally arrested Mr. Turner, nor charged with any crime. Yet. You have been lawfully detained for questioning pertaining to a possible crime or crimes."

Sam nodded, indicating he was more than willingly to discuss. *"Well, that certainly clears things up. Please proceed."*

"Please state again why you were in the park."

"As I told the other officers, I was planning on going for a hike. I had heard the place was beautiful. I also was checking the place out for one of my survival courses. I teach them out in Winchester, but I often have clients in this area."

"Survival courses?"

"Don't think trapping game and wearing animal skins for warmth. I teach the basics. How to collect and purify water. Land navigation. Which plants are edible, and which will cause you serious problems. Mostly for people unfamiliar with the woods who might be planning a hiking or camping trip with family or friends and want to learn the basics in case they have any emergencies. I

also do first aid. How to make splints with tree limbs, etc. Things like that."

"I see. Do you have a current client list in this area that require your services?"

"Like I said, I often have clients in this area. I don't currently, but never hurts to be prepared with an outdoor classroom if necessary."

"I see. So, you are telling me that you were not following someone to that park?"

"I don't know anything about following someone."

Roger slid a picture across the table to Sam and looked for his reaction. *"Do you know this man?"*

Sam was staring at a picture of Arthur Camp. *"Can't say that I do."*

"How about this man?" Roger slid another photo across the table. This time a picture of Dane Cooper.

Sam studied the photo for a moment. *"I can't say that I know him, but he does look familiar. Maybe I met him one time. I just can't place my finger on it. What is the interest in these two men?"*

Roger ignored the question and hit Turner with another. *"Mr. Turner, why were your fingerprints found at Hill Elementary School?"*

"I have no idea what you are talking about."

"Where is your cell phone, Mr. Turner?"

"I assume it is still with the nice man that took my keys, belt, and wallet and put them in a little box for me. Even gave me a receipt." Sam smirked.

"No, Mr. Turner, your real cell phone. Not the burner we found."

"I don't know anything about a burner. I keep a spare phone in all my vehicles. Safety precaution. Plus, I forget mine all the time. My regular phone is probably on the kitchen counter at home."

"Have you ever worked with this man?" Roger slid another photo of Camp in front a Sam. The picture was much older.

Sam shook his head.

"Any of your friends drive a black motorcycle?"

"I am sure some do. I have lots of friends with motorcycles. I just can't remember the color each one has."

"Why is your gun range currently closed?"

"Maintenance."

"You didn't apply for any permits, though."

"Didn't need to. Grating and filling gravel on existing roads around the property. County doesn't require a permit for that."

Roger nodded to Patricia and they both stood. Without a word to Turner, they left the room to confer with Carl and the Captain.

"He is not giving us much." Roger said, upon entering the viewing room.

"Agreed. He is playing it cool. He is answering your questions, but not directly. He knows his answers are weak, and I am pretty sure the fingerprint question rattled him."

"Maybe Carl. I suggest we let him sit for a little bit. Hit him with some softball questions again in about an hour and then dig into the fingerprints again. What do you think?" The last question had been directed at Captain Ivers.

"No objection here. I wouldn't wait that long. Pretty sure his lawyer will be here soon and put an end to further discussions. We also need to tread lightly here regarding his guilt or innocence. We cannot hold him too long without a formal arrest. A magistrate would not look too kindly on us holding him and then he is found innocent. I would also recommend pulling the thread on Cooper a little more also. He practically admitted to knowing him. I want to know why."

Carl answered before Roger could speak. *"It is because he is smart. He knows we are onto him and now Cooper. An outright lie about not knowing Cooper could put him in a bind later. He left that door open. He was simply stringing us along to see if we would show our cards. He is not innocent. He is biding his time."*

Arlington, VA

Jack entered the mansion and headed straight back to the library. That was where he expected to find Charles, but the room was empty. So, he went to the second place he would be and found him on the back deck, packing his pipe. This was his thinking space.

Jack took a seat opposite the man and waited until the pipe was lit with Charles puffing away. *"I was unable to reacquire the target or find Cooper. There was not much I could do there. Returning here seemed the logical course of action. Do you have any news?"*

"Mr. Turner was indeed detained and taken in for questioning. His vehicle was towed to the nearest impound yard. My sources tell me he is being interrogated by the Virginia State Police. Not the FBI. Mr. Blanchard however, is present as an observer. He has not yet been formally arrested or charged with a crime. However, if they went through all this trouble to follow him and bring him in for questioning, it is only a matter of time. It doesn't help that he was detained while conducting an operation. I am not sure how much the authorities know."

"Do we have anything to worry about?"

"There is no immediate concern yet. Nothing we could do if there was. Legal representation is on the way and will be able to provide us with an update. Mr. Turner is a professional, and I have no doubt about his loyalty to us. He will not involve us or the club. He knew the risk. We all do. But this has to remain on the back burner for now. Our priority is Mr. Cooper. If Wilson Simmons is indeed our child predator, aiding Mr. Cooper and stopping this monster is what we need to focus on."

"I will have all police nets monitored along with Fire and Rescue. I have our analyst helping as well. She is doing some probing of the route Simmons was taking and possible search areas. It isn't much, but it is something. She is also canvassing the net to see if Cooper pops up anyway on the network. I am not sure how else he could reach out. If he found Wilson's bed down location, he will not take his eyes off knowing the children may be inside. And remember, he thinks Simmons may be the one responsible for his daughter. He will go after him. Cooper will complete the mission, even if he has to do it alone."

"That is precisely what I am afraid of."

Later that evening.

Shadow: *I need a pickup for two Angels. They do not require immediate medical attention.*

Aide-De-Camp: *Thank God. Where?*

Shadow: *Alley behind strip mall. Oak and Route One in Woodbridge. North end.*

Aide-De-Camp: *Enroute. Twenty mikes.*

Shadow: *Two gets you one.*

Aide-De-Camp: *Roger.*

Aide-De-Camp: *He made contact. I am picking up two Angels.*

President: *That is good news. Make sure the drop-off is far enough away to not connect any actions the Shadow may have taken, with that of the found children.*

Aide-De-Camp: *Will advise when complete.*

President: *Thank you.*

CHAPTER 27: THE FINISH

Woodbridge, VA

Dane smashed through the door into a dark and seemingly empty bedroom. He ripped open the closet and kicked in the bathroom door. No reason for any further subtlety. Both empty. He even looked under the bed. What did I miss? Where is Simmons? Where are the kids?

He moved swiftly back into the hallway, scanning every inch. I couldn't have missed an entire door. He checked the ceiling in every room, looking for some sort of attic entrance. There were none. He then made his way back to the front of the house. The living room and kitchen were exactly as he left them. Empty. He re-checked the hall closet. Empty. Back into the garage. Empty. Did Simmons have another place where he kept his captives? Did he sneak past me? A million thoughts ran through his head, but he pushed them away. He needed to focus. Dane cleared his mind just as he had minutes before when he began the dash from the woods to the back of the garage. And he listened.

A draft. He couldn't so much as hear the movement of air, but he could feel it. Ever so slightly. Dane was slowly pacing, covering every square inch of real estate to see what he missed. The draft was in the kitchen. But not a single window was open.

His mind analyzed every possible cause or connection. It was a tiny kitchen warranting a tiny pantry. He hadn't opened it since it was much too small to hide a man. It was then, that his brain made the connection. The laundry room was nestled behind the kitchen, but it did not extend the full length. There was dead space behind the wall that the machines were aligned against. That meant there was dead space behind the pantry.

The door opened at a different angle than the final bedroom, so he was able to transition his weapon back to his right hand. And this time, due to what appeared to be a small space, Dane retrieved his hunting knife and stowed the baton. The knife would be better in tight quarters. He slowly opened the door to find a built-in, floor to ceiling wall unit lined with several shelves holding very little in the way of contents. There were a few cans of soup, a box or two of crackers, and some mysterious looking glass jars of what appeared to be pickled vegetables. At the top right corner of the wall panel, he found a razor thin cord connected to the pantry door. That was how he made sure the door was closed. Close the false wall and it pulls the pantry door shut. Dane ran the finger of his left hand along the edges of the pantry and found the hinges. A small cutout on the side attached to the wire, allowed his fingers to take hold and gently pull the wall open. He gently pulled it open.

The space behind the pantry was about four to five feet long, with a slanted ceiling like those found underneath a staircase storage space. At the other end was another door. This one looked to be a lot more solid than anything he had seen in the house so far. A large, opened padlock hung from the hinge clasp. The door could be secured from the outside, meaning it was a place to refrain people from leaving. Dane hoped that there was not a locking mechanism on the opposite side allowing Simmons to keep out intruders when he was inside. It was then that he noticed the door was slightly cracked. That was where the slight breeze was coming from. There must be some sort of circulation system down there. *I bet it vents out through the fireplace.* As Dane pulled the handle toward him, all his senses were struck at once.

Beyond the door was a narrow staircase with an incredibly steep pitch. His eyes were met with a surreal light show of blazing red and white strobes. They pulsated on and off creating a visible distortion when descending. Music blared from below in a series of rhythmic thuds and thumps. It could hardly be considered music but rather a series of various sounds meant to throw off someone's equilibrium. It was the type of music Dane and others had used overseas in the cells of terrorist detainees. The noise was meant to keep the prisoners off-balance in-between interrogation sessions so they could not gather their thoughts and compile a convincing lie. Worse than the sights and sounds was the smell. It assaulted Dane's nose as he tried to focus on the navigation of the stairwell. A combination of sweat, vomit, and feces mixed in with fear. Another memory from his deployments overseas that he would rather forget.

The stairs were definitely homemade. No respectable builder would have devised such a dangerous addition to the home. It was probably some amateur bomb shelter built back during the Cold War when armed conflict with the Soviets seemed imminent. Dane descended slowly focusing as far ahead as he was able. At the bottom, the stairs turned sharply right into a long tunnel. Dane envisioned the layout of the home and determined that he was entering an underground bunker that extended into the backyard instead of under the house. That would explain its design. It was clearly dug out by hand over time. Wooden posts were set every five to six feet and held up loose boards to create a makeshift ceiling. He doubted that they were providing any real support but rather keeping loose dirt from falling and from which to string the strobe light. Random speakers were mounted haphazardly to every third or fourth support post. The power cords for all of them were stapled to the ceiling. The hallway had no access to rooms until the very end. It forked left and right, with wires for power taking each turn. It was decision time. After a quick glance around the corners he spotted a room at either end with closed doors. He had to choose. And both choices meant his back would be to a closed door. Not a popular technique when clearing a building unless you want to be shot in the back.

Without hesitation, He moved quickly down the hallway to his left. He made the decision rapidly solely based on the position of the doorknob, which indicated he could open it easily with his left hand while keeping his fighting hand free to attack or defend. The element of surprise might still be in my favor, he thought as he pushed his way into the room. He was unprepared for what he found. The room was the size of a small bedroom. Each wall of the room was designed for a specific purpose. To his right were the settings for a child's room. A small rug was up against the wall. A dusty table sat in the center with long forgotten puzzle pieces strewn about. Plastic bins lined the wall with toys that time had clearly not been kind to. To his left was a small wooden stage covered in the same black drapery that adorned the wall. A single rocking horse sat upon the platform with a camera and tripod aimed at framing the scene. He made a makeshift photography studio. But it was the backwall that was the most horrific. It was a built-in cage. A series of eight cages, four on four stacked floor to ceiling, covered the entire wall. As he moved closer, Dane could see movement in two of them. This is where he kept the kids. Dane crossed the remaining distance in a sprint. Only two cages appeared to be occupied. Listless bodies lay on the floor. Their tiny bodies were draped in rags. Movement. He could see the faintest movement of their strained breathing. They were drugged. The first occupant was a little boy. He knew right away that it was Jon Parker. The face of the second was covered. Dane opened the door and gently pulled back a thin, stained blanket. It was not Angela. It was Holly Jones.

He pushed the cage door back shut and latched it. He still had not found Simmons, and he didn't want the children to get hurt in any struggle or crossfire. Or inadvertently hurt themselves. He remembered the stories of prisoners found in the concentration camps during the Second World War. It pained them to do so, but the soldiers kept them locked in the camps until they had a plan and the resources to properly care for them. Dane couldn't even fathom the level of trauma these kids had been put through. He gave another quick glance over his shoulder to ensure Simmons hadn't come up behind him and then searched the other six cages. They were clearly empty. Dane felt the lump in his throat. He was holding back the panic as he frantically searched for any evidence of Angela. A scrap of clothing. A message. Any clue to indicate whether she had been here or was taken somewhere else. Maybe Simmons had her in the other room at this very moment.

As Dane turned, the whirl of movement alerted him in the primal part of his mind. The part where survival often lay dormant waiting for when it was needed. Instinct took over and he was barely able to raise his forearms to his front to protect his head. His left arm took the entire force of the blow, and he knew immediately that his Ulna was broken, or at least severely cracked. As he fell back against the cages, he slashed across the space with his right hand, the knife offering some resistance as it cut across Simmons' abdomen.

It wasn't a deep wound, but it did cause Simmons pain enough to hesitate, and that split second was all Dane needed to go on the offense. He squared up to Simmons as the man pulled back his right arm, preparing to strike Dane again. A strike that never happened. Simmons' first blow was the only one he would land. Dane became unstoppable. The rage he was feeling fueled his power, but his mind controlled it. Only letting it out where needed and with precision.

He kicked out at Simmons with a powerful front kick. He could feel the satisfying crunch of the knee as Simmons' leg bent backwards in an unnatural manner. As the man was falling to the ground, Dane slashed Simmons' weapon hand, the pipe and several parts of his fingers falling to the ground. Simmons was unarmed and crippled. Perfect. Dane intended to show no quarter. He watched his prey squirm. The adrenaline flowed through his body, numbing the pain of the broken arm. Simmons struggled to his feet and attempted to hobble out into the hall, back toward the last room where he must have been hiding.

Dane replaced the knife in its sheath and exchanged it for the baton. He did not want to cause excessive blood loss. He still had a lot of questions for the man. He smashed the baton against Simmons' opposite knee causing full collapse to the floor for the last time. Simmons continued to crawl toward the hall, but much slower now, moaning as his legs dragged helplessly across the concrete. It gave Dane the opportunity to splint his left arm with some scraps of wood and a handful of rags. It would do for now. The arm would be of little use to him, but he wanted to prevent further damage. Damage caused by bone, possibly cutting muscle and skin. He only needed one arm for Simmons at this point.

Finished with the splint, he followed the path of blood left from Simmons' sliced hand. Dane found him in front of the door pawing at a doorknob he just couldn't reach. Dane helped him out. He stomped hard on the small of his back, Simmons assuming the fetal position in the dirt. Dane opened the door and dragged the man inside by the collar of his sweatshirt. The room was similar in size to the previous room but with an entirely different set-up. No photography studio or makeshift playroom for children. The backwall was a large array of computer monitors and towers crowded on and under a crude wooden table. But that wasn't his immediate focus.

The center of the room was arranged like a scene from a morgue. A large metal table, complete with straps and tie-downs sat in some sort of cement drainage pool that was clearly homemade. There was a large industrial kitchen vent above the table; the kind found in large restaurant kitchens. A long row of instruments sat along one wall. Some on a table, others mounted on the wall. A hose was on the other wall, curled up and lying in a pool of dripping water. This was a place to dissect and dismember a body for easy disposal. A renewed sense of rage gave Dane the strength to haul Simmons onto the table and lash him down. The man groaned in agony but still hadn't spoken. Dane would change that, but first he needed to care for the children and get them to safety. For that, he was going to need help. The computer was on, but the screen was locked. When he wiggled the mouse, the computer asked for a biometric identifier. The keyboard had a space for the imprint of a finger or a thumb. He went back down the hallway into the children's room and removed two of Simons' digits from the floor that had been lost in the struggle. He hoped it was one of these since he didn't want to risk more blood loss. He wanted Simmons conscious. Fortunately, the bloody thumb worked and since

Dane had memorized the dark web protocol server address, he was able to contact the club. He needed Jack.

Shadow: *I need a pickup for two Angels. They do not require immediate medical attention.*

Aide-De-Camp: *Thank God. Where?*

A short time later, Dane was once again crouched in the wood line. This time with three precious items. Both children, and a duffle bag full of all the computer hardware along with any paper notes he found. Charles should have someone to crack decipher all of this. The kids were still knocked out. He had wrapped them in blankets he found upstairs.

Just then a sedan pulled slowly around the corner of the shopping mall. As is stopped, two short bursts of light shown from the driver's side, shot in the general direction of his hiding place. He immediately returned one blast from his flashlight and began moving toward the vehicle with both children in his arms. Jack already had the back doors open and assisted with securing each one in the backseat. Dante retrieved the bag of evidence and secured it in the trunk.

"Are you ok, Dane?" Jack asked, looking at the splint on his arm.

"Better than Simmons."

"What else do you need?"

"Nothing, I am good. I can clean this up. Just get them somewhere safe and get that box to one of those tech wizards. I have

a few more questions for Mr. Simmons. I will let you know what else I find."

Back in Simmons' underground lair, Dane dumped a bucket of water on the man's face to wake him up.

"Morning sunshine. Time for you and I to have a little chat."

Simmons rolled his eyes. Dane could see that he was groggy from the pain. He let the man come to his sense slowly while he perused the set of implements along the wall. He didn't believe that this area was used to torture any of the children. Jon and Holly didn't have a scratch on them. The other girl they found dead had her limbs broken, but that was postmortem and done out of necessity to transport the body. No, these were not torturing devices in Simmons' hands, but they were in his.

"I am not going to tell you shit!"

"Ok. I have all the time in the world." Dane turned back towards the prone man, and without hesitation, smashed a metal mallet down on his left clavicle. Simmons' screamed and bucked against the restraints. Once his body settled, Dane struck the other side.

"Stop! Stop! Stop! I will talk!"

Dane ignored the man's pleas. He had his chance. The knees were already smashed, so Dane had to decide on another location. He wasn't going to strike anywhere on the head or the torso. He wanted the man to be conscience and alive. Internal bleeding would be too difficult to treat. The limbs would have to do for now. Dane found additional tie-down straps on the table and cut them into several long strips. He tied them above both of Simmons' knees and elbows. Tightening down, the two-inch, polyester material made an excellent tourniquet. He used a screwdriver on each strap as a windlass device to tighten it ever further. Dane finally spoke. *"Fingers or toes?"*

"What? Are you insane? Neither! Take me to the police! I will confess everything! You have to take me in!"

Dane moved very close to Simmons' face and growled. *"I don't have to take you anywhere."* Since the man had not chosen, Dane picked for him. He decided to be fair. He moved around the table with a pair of metal snips, removing the pinkies from each hand and foot as if pruning a troublesome bush. Simmons bucked and screamed, but Dane couldn't have cared less. Another bucket of water shocked Simmons into the moment. *"Ok. Now let's see if you can answer some of my questions. First, did you take this girl, or do you know who did?"* Dane had removed a picture of Angela from his breast pocket and thrust it in Simmons's face.

Simmons just sobbed. *"I don't, I don't.... nothing...I did nothing."*

Dane remained cool and calm. *"Ok. What is up with your little chat group I saw on your computer?"* Dane asked as he gestured to the now empty workstation. *"Who is the Keeper? Is he some kind of cult leader for you and other sickos? Did he take this girl?"*

"He's, he's just, guy, just this guy. I don't know man." Simmons continued to cry.

"You are not doing so good buddy. You are batting zero for two. Let's see if you can redeem yourself on number three. I know you killed and dumped the Chase girl. How many others have you killed? Where are their bodies?"

"None! None! She was my first! The only one! She was broken! I didn't want to hurt her! I just started collecting! I never wanted to hurt them!"

"Collecting. Is that what you call it? Rot in hell, bastard."

Dane retrieved the can of gas he had brought down from the garage. He began to pour it over the table as Simmons screamed. Dane didn't even hesitate as he lit the match and tossed it on the table engulfing Simmons in flames. Ensuring the kitchen vent was working properly to slowly vent the smoke through the chimney, he turned and entered the room where the children were held. He torched the cages, anything he had touched, and the trail of blood across the room and down the hall. He wanted to make sure that no trace evidence from him remained. Once everything was thoroughly burned, including Simmons, Dane put out the flames with the hose as if simply extinguishing a bonfire. He felt numb. He felt nothing. No remorse. He returned to the pantry entrance and sealed and locked the metal door. He then removed the pantry cutout from the hinges and nailed it into the wall, completely covering the door. He looked back with satisfaction. Nobody will even find that entrance unless they rip this section out. He smiled to himself. The new owner has a much bigger pantry.

After one last sweep through the house, Dane exited the way he had entered. He had already constructed a makeshift patch of the exterior door he damaged, which would pass a cursory inspection. Considering the type of life Simmons had lived, he doubted that his social calendar was full. *Who knows if anyone will notice him gone? Well, probably the bank will eventually.*

CHAPTER 28: THE AFTERMATH

Washington, D.C.

"Thanks for spending your morning with us. We are bringing you all the news you need for the greater Washington D.C metropolitan area. If you are just waking up, then you may not have heard the amazing developments overnight in the case of Jon Parker from Dale City, Virginia. Little Jon Parker has been found and is recovering at a local hospital. Let's go to Andrew Newton outside D.C. Metro Hospital for this incredible story, over to you Andrew."

"Good morning, Eric and Joyce. I am here this morning outside D.C. Metro Hospital, where overnight an astonishing turn of events occurred. Authorities were contacted in the early morning by Reverend John Anderson of the Humane Hands of D.C. on Pennsylvania Avenue. The Reverend reported that two children were found in the church alcove, claiming they had been kidnapped and wanted to go home. The details are unclear about their escape or how they found their way to this D.C parish. As you may recall, little Jon Parker was abducted a few weeks ago while playing with his dog in Cloverdale Park in Dale City. The boy's heroic dog had tried to fend off the kidnapper but was unsuccessful and later tragically died from its wounds. The Virginia police have had no leads up to this point and hopefully Jon can fill in some details. The boy is recovering in the hospital with his family. What many viewers may not know is the second child, Holly Jones went missing from Glenmoore, Pennsylvania, nearly a month ago. Holly was jogging with her dog at Marsh Creek State Park. The park hosts a

myriad of biking and running trails around the reservoir of the same name. Holly and her dog vanished without a trace. We are told both children are being treated for minor injuries along with dehydration and malnutrition. The Captain of The Virginia State Major Crime Bureau that has been involved in the case, assisting local authorities from the beginning, gave a brief statement this morning. Let's listen in."

"Good morning. I am Captain John Ivers from the Virginia State Police, Major Crimes Bureau. Our department houses the Crimes Against Children Special Victim Unit. I am happy to report that local authorities were contacted early this morning by Reverend John Anderson about two missing children, Jon Parker and Holly Jones. The families have been reunited while the children undergo medical evaluation in the hospital. The Virginia State Police will provide their full support to local agencies to bring the abductor to justice. We are asking for the public's help. The hotline for Jon Parker is still active and monitored. If you have any information about either child that might help us catch this person, please use that number. One, eight hundred, five, five, five, seventeen hundred. That is all I have for now. I will provide an update when we know more."

"As you can see, Eric and Joyce, the authorities are doing everything possible to capture this monster, but at least there were two good news stories for the Parker and Jones' families. I will keep you guys updated. Back to you in the studio."

"Thanks, Andrew. Wow, that is a good news story Joyce."

"I can't imagine the depth of joy in those family's hearts. I hope they find this monster."

"All I could find was this shitty hospital coffee. The Starbucks isn't open yet." Patricia said as she handed one each to Roger and Carl.

"That's ok. I prefer Dunkin anyway." The standing rivalry between the two partners was the quality of the two major brands.

"This is great, thanks," Carl said as he accepted the lukewarm Styrofoam cup.

The three had gathered in one of the large hospital conference rooms that the Metro D.C. police were using as a temporary operations center. The initial case was being handled by them since the kids were found in the district. Nevertheless, Roger knew it was only a matter of time before Virginia took the case back. Captain Ivers had released the official police statement and was in one corner conversing with the D.C. boys. He didn't think there would be any territorial fights. D.C. Metro had enough of its own problems with the growing violence and chaos in the capital. Gangs patrolled the nighttime streets of the city and provided the police with plenty of business. Not a single night passed without a violent incident. They didn't need to add a kidnapping case to their overloaded portfolio. He had also heard from the Pennsylvania State Police. Their detectives were enroute.

Carl had just recently arrived. He received the call around the same time as the two detectives, but he managed to dress immaculately, whereas Roger and Patricia had chosen the blue jeans and windbreaker route. His three-piece suit sharply contrasted with their casual street clothes, but regardless of fashion sense, they all looked exhausted. *"So, what the hell happened here?"* Carl asked. *"You can't tell me two kids just wandered into a church after escaping from their kidnapper."*

"Well, we know for sure that they did not make it to that church on their own. They are recovering, but they were heavily sedated. Trace doses of fentanyl were found in both their systems. That information was not released to the press, obviously. We think the guy used it to keep them manageable. The same was found in Dana Chase."

"So, you think this guy had all three and was the one responsible for Chase's death?"

Patricia answered. *"That is our preliminary theory, Carl. We have a long way to go to connect all the dots. We briefly spoke with the children this morning, but nothing was invasive. They have been through a hell of a traumatic event, and we don't want to make it worse. Counselors are being brought who that specialize in this. We have to tread lightly."*

"The FBI has folks also. Just let me know what you need."

"Thanks. We will."

The conversation was briefly interrupted by Captain Ivers, who joined the group. *"D.C. Metro is not going to fight us on this one. They are going to assist, but Virginia will take the lead. I have asked them to take a few of our guys over to Humane Hands to talk with the Reverend. The church needs to be treated like a crime scene. D.C. has it roped off for now, and crime scene techs are on their way. You two will need to get over there sometime today."*

"I think we need to talk about the elephant in the room, Captain."

"What's that, Carl?"

"How the hell did the kids get to that church? Somebody brought them there."

"So far, we have no leads. The good Reverend said the doors were locked. He heard a noise and came down from the rectory. He found the children in the front pews, wrapped in blankets. He has no idea how they got there. He said they were groggy and confused. He immediately called nine, one, one."

"Well, we know where Turner is. We need to look deeper into Cooper and Ferguson."

"One thing at a time. You don't even know for certain if either of them was involved. You had a decent set of circumstance for Turner, but I haven't seen anything regarding the other two. If you want to dig into them with your resources, I won't stand in your way. But Roger and Pat, I need you both on the here and now. I need substantive statements from the children. The child psychologist is on her way now. She will help you. I also have a team pulling camera footage from nearby the church and the surrounding intersections. Maybe we will get lucky and we can backtrack on the route our

delivery person took. However, priority one is the abductor. He is still out there. Number two is our good Samaritan."

"I get it, Captain. I fully understand your priorities. But if I am right about whoever did this, there are other criminals out there that deserve equal attention. We can't just have vigilantes running around. The FBI will assist with the abductor, but our priority is this rescuer or rescuers."

"I get it, Carl. And we will work that angle. But for all we know, the kids did escape after being drugged. They wandered around and saw the church as a safe place. The Reverend may have forgotten to lock one of the doors. Hell, the kidnapper could be close by, primed for us to pounce."

"I doubt it."

"Why is that, Carl?"

"I'm pretty sure your kidnapper is dead."

Arlington, VA

Charles walked into the study to find Jack and Dane seated in front of the fireplace. Jack was wrapping Dane's arm with proper splinting material and several ace bandages. *"I don't think it is too serious. It is not an open fracture. But I am sure it still hurts like hell."*

"It does." Dane grimaced as Jack finished the final tie. *"I will go into the clinic at work later today. I will tell them I got hit on the motorcycle. Put it down pretty hard on my arm."*

"I am relieved Mr. Cooper, that you have only minor injuries. May I presume that? How do you say it? You should see the other guy."

Dane laughed. *"You will never see the other guy. Well, at least I hope you won't. There was nothing I could do about the house. We are in the clear in the short term, but something will have to be done eventually. I don't know about relatives, acquaintances, anybody else who may notice him missing and go looking. I would prefer that the police don't receive a health and welfare request about that location and begin investigating. But we should have a little time."*

"Leave it to me, Mr. Cooper. I have someone who will take care of it."

"Why am I not surprised. Enough about my little scratch. How is Sam doing? What has been going on there? Why was he even arrested in the first place?"

"The issue will be resolved later this morning. My attorney has informed me that he is confident that Mr. Turner will be released and cleared of all charges. The attorney general is in for a surprise with respect to the circumstantial evidence he possesses. Mr. Turner will not be indicted."

"Once again, I'm not surprised. I heard the news on the way over here about the kids. Humane Hands. Nice touch. Am I to assume the good Reverend is part of our little club here?"

Jack spoke up. *"Actually no. I don't know the man. But he comes highly recommended from another of our associates. She engages with him in the community. We knew the children would be properly cared for by him."*

Dane stood up and snapped his finger. *"That woman. I remember that woman. Jill! I should have realized she showed too much interest in me. She was testing me. Asking me questions about morality. I was in such a funk at the time that I didn't see it. Damn"*

"That Mr. Cooper would be the Scout. She is good at spotting talent. She has come through on several occasions for us. She is a trusted member of that church. Even trusted with a key."

Fairfax, VA

"Wanna hear this shit, Roger?" Patricia literally stormed into their office. Roger was reading through the case files for Jon, Holly, and Dana. The interviews with Jon and Holly had gone as well as expected. They were careful not to press too hard since the kids had been through so much. The psychologists were helpful but moved at a much slower speed than necessary for this type of investigation. They had also stopped by the church and spoke with the Reverend. The crime scene technicians had nothing promising. The sheer volume of human traffic through

the area made collecting of any useable evidence insurmountable at best. It is virtually impossible to process that much information. And the traffic cameras had provided nothing yet. They were heading over shortly to the hospital for another round of discussions with the children, hoping to get a break somewhere.

"Turner walked." That got Roger's attention. He looked up from his notes.

"It turns out our eyewitness was right and wrong. She did see Turner at that school. Just not as Bell. Turner's security consultant company did an assessment for the school a few weeks prior to all this crap with Camp. The district spent some money on evaluating security at schools with all these mass shootings across the country lately. Turner got a small portion of that contract. The assistant principal recognized him, but the magistrate determined that she was unduly influenced in believing he had committed some sort of crime when in fact she met him as a legitimate businessman. And of course, he touched doors and locks. Why wouldn't his fingerprints be there?"

"May I assume every single item found in his truck was legal?"

"Correct. Not a single item is unaccounted for or not legally registered. The prosecutor tried to make up some stuff about how those types of weapons registered for his work should be at the range in Winchester, not in his vehicle here in Fairfax country. The judge wasn't having any of that. The guns were properly stored and locked. And anyone is free to explore state parks. All evidence was

circumstantial, and he warned the prosecutor that he better not see shoddy evidence like this presented in his court again."

Roger had buried his head back in the case files. He pulled the Angela Cooper file from his drawer and set it next to the other three.

"Are you listening to me, Roger?"

"I am Pat."

"You don't seem surprised at all."

"I knew the case was weak, but I also completely believe Turner is involved in something. Carl's instincts are spot-on, but the evidence isn't there in the eyes of the law. I have no doubt he will keep digging into all these guys. He must be fuming."

Patricia nodded toward the case jackets on Roger's side of the desk. *"So, any new insights? I heard that a canvass of the church members and surrounding neighborhood turned up nothing. The was no video footage around the church. No mysterious superhero dropping off two children in the night. Where does that leave us? And are Turner and Cooper part of this also? And if so, where is Angela Cooper?"*

"That is what I am trying to figure out. I don't think this guy is involved with Angela Cooper. If he was, she would be in that hospital with the other children."

"Maybe she couldn't escape. Or she might already be dead, and our vigilante wasn't able to retrieve the body. There are tons of possibilities. Once we find this guy, we will get some answers."

Roger just slowly shook his head. *"Pretty sure that is not going to happen. I think Carl was right at the hospital. I bet this monster is dead."*

Washington, D.C.

Carl swiveled his leather chair towards the window. This was one of those perks that other agents would kill for. They complained that most of the offices were like living in a prison, and they just wanted time in the yard. Time in the sunshine instead of stuck in a cubicle cell with only a glaring computer monitor to stare at. But that is not entirely the way Carl utilized this perk. He didn't mind the grind of investigative work. And he did get out of the office more than most agents. No, this view was for thinking. It was for letting his mind wander. Letting it expand and break free from any and all constraints. Allowing it to put the pieces of a puzzle together always lies solely in the subconscious.

He pressed the intercom button. *"Ken, could you come in here please?"* Moments later the younger agent arrived at the foot of the desk. He stood silently watching his boss, really his mentor, work through his next steps.

"You heard about Turner, Ken?"

"I did boss."

"I also called in a favor with a friend of mine in Richmond. Retired agent. Ferguson is clean in any of this. My friend had a small team on him while we worked Turner. I want you to start compiling the next three possible suspects based on the list you previously put together. Please put together target packages similar to the first three you provided. Then we will plan to confirm or deny their involvement in all of this. In the meantime," Carl paused.

"In the meantime, boss?"

"I want everything we can find. I want to know what sports he played as a kid. I want to know who his first girlfriend in high school was. I want to know his favorite movie. Everything. I want to know everything. We go all in on Dane Cooper!"

Benefactor: ***I heard about your recent victories.***

President: ***Yes, sir. We have had some success. Tying up loose ends now.***

Benefactor: ***Let's discuss tomorrow. I want to hear the details and talk about the future.***

President: ***I will be available any time.***

CHAPTER 29: THE REVIEW

Arlington, VA.

The fire in the great room was roaring. Charles and Jack waited for the call, both lost in thought. The sweet smell of tobacco from Charles' pipe filled the air. The last few weeks have been busy. They had several victories under their belt, but it had come at a cost. They had discussed the arrest of Sam Turner at length. It was a close call. Or, as Jack had put it, a wake-up call. They were going to have to be more careful in the future. Charles had acknowledged the man's concern. Mr. Turner will have to spend a little time on the bench. The ringing of the satellite phone on the side table broke the silence.

Jack answered the phone after entering the nine-digit code. He listened momentarily, and the person covering the mouthpiece said, *"The Benefactor for you."*

Charles accepted the phone as Jack rose to leave. Again, mouthpiece covered, he asked Jack to stay.

"Good evening, sir. Or at least it is here."

"Good morning, Charles. I am a little ahead of Eastern Standard Time. I just finished up breakfast."

"I trust my report was in order, sir?"

"It was. I appreciate the details. I am glad to hear your Closer was cleared of all charges. However, it sounds like you have a problem with investigators getting a little too close. How did he become a suspect in the first place?"

"Yes sir. As we previously discussed, it was bound to happen sooner or later. Unfortunately, it came sooner than anticipated. That is primarily due to the high interest targets we have removed from the board. I have not yet ascertained how Mr. Turner became a person of interest. I have asked our Cop to investigate the matter. In the meantime, we are taking steps to mitigate the risk."

"Good, good. I have faith in you, Charles. You and your team. The new man, the Shadow, seems like quite the addition. I was impressed with New York. I was surprised as hell when he pulled off another one the other day. You have kept him busy. You need to work on more names though as we grow."

"Yes sir, he is an excellent addition. The name is fitting. He has proven more than capable. He can bring about controlled violence when needed, but more importantly, he has the mind of an investigator. After all, it was he who found the connection between these abductions. His military file noted his investigative skills. I will continue to put them to good use."

"Yes, exactly. And that is why I think he would be perfect to lead a new investigation into a sex trafficking ring out of Miami and Savannah. My intel informs me that those two ports are both being used as hubs for moving underage women. It appears certain terrorist organizations are realizing the profit from this venture. They are hard strapped for funding. Traditional banking methods are closed to them. The drug trade from the Middle East has taken quite the hit as well. The cash from this trafficking helps keep them afloat. I guess terrorism isn't cheap. Especially when the third-world governments you are fighting against are often financially backed by one superpower or another. There is one group out of Somalia in particular, Al-Shabab. They have learned from their neighbors in Nigeria. Groups like Boko Haram."

"With all due respect sir, we have uncovered a possible kidnapping network in this region. It is unprecedented. It appears that several of these child predators are working together. Providing advice. Assistance when warranted. They are taking multiple victims. They claim they are collecting."

"I understand Charles. And please continue to focus on this ring. But I need people in Miami and Savannah to unravel the trafficking."

"Our resources are spread fairly thin."

"Then step up the recruiting Charles."

"We are doing our best, but we need to be precise. It is simple to recruit and train our supporting assets on how to acquire a car or

deliver a weapon. It is quite another for our operatives on the street. They must come with the skillset already and they must have the right temperament. I can't have rogue killers working on our behalf. That is why the Closer's unfortunate arrest was mitigated. He is a professional accustomed to working under extreme pressure and scrutiny. The wrong person would have handled that poorly and exposed the whole club."

"I understand Charles. Do the best that you can. But the sex trafficking has priority. I will be pushing funds today. I need your recruiters to hit the streets. I understand your desire to have the best of the best. But as the old adage goes, too many Chiefs and not enough Indians will sink your team. Not PC to say, but I am sure the phrase has been updated on some social media platform. Regardless, you have good Chiefs like your Aide-De-Camp and now this Shadow. Hit the streets and find some Indians for them to lead. Anything else you need?"

"Would it be possible for you to acquire a modest home in Woodbridge, Virginia? It needs to remain off the books for the foreseeable future. Maybe we will use it as a safehouse in the future."

"Done. I won't even ask. Send my man the details and he will work the shell companies. Thank you, Charles, for all you and your team are doing. I know I am pushing hard, but I hope you see that it is for the right reason. Take care."

The phone disconnected and Charles handed it back to Jack, who powered it down and returned it to the safe from which it came.

"I see his point, sir. I still have a few contacts from the old days. Several terrorist groups have found safe haven in Africa. Al-Shabab is one of the worst. U.S. Special Operations has been putting the screws to them for years, but them and other similar groups are not out of the fight. An influx of funding would put them back in the game."

"I completely understand Jack, and I am inclined to agree. However, this club may not be the best tool to bring to bear. We are a scalpel, and I am afraid our Benefactor is trying to turn us into a hammer."

Hòn Tẫm, Vietnam

The Benefactor handed the satellite phone to his aid. *"Philip, please secure this in the car and have it brought around. I need to head into town. Please arrange for Henry at the bank to receive me within the hour. I would also like Mr. Keith Miller there to discuss an investment property."*

"Right away, Mr. Lentz."

CHAPTER 30: THE BENEFACTOR

Monday September 7th, 1992

The Daily
Serving Silicon Valley

Palo Alto, California

Jessica and Sarah Lentz were the latest victims of a string of car jackings erupting across the valley this year.

Weekend Violence in the Valley
Prominent Family Car-Jacked and Killed

Greta Shayne

Federal investigators joined California law enforcement officials this weekend after another violent carjacking in the valley that left a mother and daughter dead. Jessica and Sarah Lentz were the latest victims or these horrific string of attacks this year.

Jessica and Sarah Lentz, wife and daughter of Silicon Valley mogul Jackson Lentz were violently attacked this weekend. The two were returning home from San Jose around 4pm on Saturday, September 5th. According to witnesses, while stopped at a light on Santa Clara St., mother and daughter were approached by two masked men. The assailants surround the vehicle with raised firearms. They dragged Jessica Lentz from the driver's seat and shot her in what can only be called an "execution."

The two unidentified men then sped off in the family Mercedes possibly not realizing that young Sarah was seated in the rear of the vehicle. Police responded and EMS rushed Jessica Lentz to the hospital where she was pronounced deceased, cause of death gunshot wounds.

The incident kicked off a state-wide manhunt for the assailants and baby Sarah. A vehicle description was in the hands of every California law enforcement official within the hour. However, any efforts at locating the vehicle appeared fruitless. That is until early Sunday morning.

There has yet to be any official statement, but it has been confirmed that the vehicle was found deserted west in the mountains off Highway 130. One officer that wished to remain anonymous described the scene as horrific. "These animals just drove the car off the highway and down the side of the mountain into a clearing of trees. Then they burnt the car with the poor little girl inside."

"We need the publics' help if we are going to find these criminals."

- San Jose Chief of Police Theresa Yang

An official statement concerning the location of the vehicle and the status of baby Sarah has not been released. Blanket statements from both the Chief of Police and the local FBI Field Office have acknowledged the incident and are asking the public for help but have provided no further details.

Jackson Lentz has remained out of the public spotlight. A spokesman for the mogul's company, Cibola, stated that the family is cooperating with authorities and requests that the media respects their privacy during this difficult and tragic ordeal.

AFTERWORD

Unknown

Acolyte: *I think I found one I want.*

Keeper: *Is it a safe hunting ground?*

Acolyte: *I have checked the area. Far from my home. No cameras.*

Keeper: *Check, check, and then re-check. Make sure it is clean.*

Protégé: *My third one is acting up.*

Keeper: *Did you break him yet?*

Protégé: *Not yet. Still has outbursts.*

Keeper: *Remember the carrot and the stick. Be patient. It takes time.*

Disciple: *I think I am being followed.*

Keeper: *Do you have any packages right now.*

Disciple: *I don't. Have been looking though.*

Keeper: *Stop for now. I will contact you later about determining if you under investigation.*

Votary: *I found the chemicals you needed.*

Keeper: *Can you meet at our usual place tomorrow night?*

Votary: *Yes.*

Keeper: *I will see you at 9pm.*

Zealot: *I need a place to dump.*

Keeper: *What happened? I thought you had a solid plan.*

Zealot: *Things got out of hand. Good Samaritan jumped in. Got the package. Need to dump him quickly.*

Keeper: *Stash for now. I have a place. Will contact later.*

: I want to start collecting. Is this the right place?

Keeper: *Maybe. Who sent you?*

: The PUPIL. A few weeks ago.

Keeper: *He is missing. Contact me if you hear from him again. I will contact you in the future. You will be DEVOTEE.*

Keeper: *Where are you? What happened?*

Pupil: *I am here. And I happened.*

Keeper: *This is not Pupil. Who is this?*

Pupil: *You're right. I am coming for you next!*

About the Author

Sean Hagerty is a retired Special Operations Soldier with over 25 years of experience. He spent his younger years training and conducting combat operations with the 1st of the 75th Ranger Regiment. After nine years, in 2005 he was selected for and assigned to a Special Operations unit at Fort Belvoir Virginia. There he spent sixteen years and finished his military career, retiring as a Sergeant Major. He received several awards and decorations throughout his career to include three Bronze Stars.

He currently works as a policy analyst for the Department of the Army in the Pentagon. His wife Misty is an Executive Officer at the National Geospatial-Intelligence Agency; oldest daughter Samantha is an administrative staffer for the House of Representatives in Washington DC; and youngest daughter Delaney is a criminal justice major at James Madison University set to graduate in May 2024.

His love for writing began in the cold mountains of Afghanistan, the dusty deserts of Iraq, and the plains of Africa. He would write short stories for his daughters, so they knew he was thinking of them while he was far away from home. Over the years, those playful fairytales were complete, and it was time for him to tell a more grown-up story for a wider audience. Sean Hagerty has combined over 25+ years of service in the Special Operations community and deep-rooted research instincts from years of academic pursuits in history to tell this story. A story that was written on the back of a daily Washington D.C. commuter bus heading to the Pentagon, during plane flights, car rides, and even on his pontoon boat drifting along the Potomac River. It all came together during evening edits in the small river town of Occoquan Virginia.